Praise for James Hanna's Short Stories . . .

Second, Less Capable Head—a satire that skewers the political left, right, and everything in between. If you are in need of a good laugh, look no further, this is the story you are looking for.
—Adam Dubbin, Editor, *Empty Sink Publishing*

James Hanna's writing penetrates the darkness inside our species, and comes out the other side offering enlightenment, pathos, and hard laughter.
— Christopher Wachlin
Editor, *The Stoneslide Corrective*

We can only call this an instant classic... You have to read these stories slowly, with some breathing room in between, to fully appreciate the genius of James Hanna.
—Grady Harp
Hall of Fame Top 100 Reviewer, *Vine Voice*

The mark of an author at the peak of his literary powers, there are scant few tales that won't linger beyond the page. Without a doubt, *A Second, Less Capable Head* delivers one of the most powerful and cutting collection of short stories you will ever read.
—*Book Viral*

As one reads through each of the stories in *A Second, Less-Capable Head*, one gets the impression that one is reading from a master of the short story and it is very exciting to see how, in a few paragraphs, Hanna reveals a lot about his compelling characters, builds a tension that grabs the readers' attention completely, and guides the reader to satisfying denouements.

—*Manhattan Book Review*

A sinister sense of irony pervades the stories in this perverse, darkly fantastic anthology. Author James Hanna has a unique insight into the most bizarrely curious aspects of the human condition and does not shy from exploring these to their shockingly logical conclusion. *A Second, Less Capable Head* is exceptionally memorable from beginning to end.

—*Midwest Book Review*

A Second, Less Capable, Head

And Other Rogue Stories

By James Hanna

Published by Sand Hill Review Press

www.sandhillreviewpress.com
P.O. Box 1275, San Mateo, CA 94401
(415) 297-3571

Library of Congress Control Number: 2015932221
Fiction/Satire
Fiction/Absurdist
Anthology

ISBN: 978-1-937818-39-5 Perfect Bound released 2017

Cover art by Daniel Gale
Graphics by Backspace Ink

SHRP

Sand Hill Review Press

The following stories have previously appeared in these literary magazines and anthologies.

A Second, Less Capable Head, Empty Sink Publishing, 2015
The Guest, Zymbol, 2014
The Stalker, Eclipse, 2012
Fruits, Fear of Monkeys, 2016
Exposed, Crack the Spine, 2016;
    Literally Stories, 2016
The Outback, FaultZone, 2015
The Sicilian, Literally Stories, 2016
Breaking Vials, Empty Sink Publishing, 2015;
    Literally Stories, 2016
Honey Bunny, The Literary Review, 2013
Jimmy Likes Mermaids, The Artist Unleashed, 2016
Dress, The Sand Hill Review, 2007
Hunting Bear, The Sand Hill Review 2012
Cheating the Jail Out of Time, Literally stories, 2016
The Break, Old Crow Review, 1994
The Wall, Edge City Review, 1999
Hunter's Moon, Red Savina Review, 2015
Another Will Take Your Place, Red Savina Review, 2013
The Body in the Bay, Red Savina Review, 2016;
    Literally Stories, 2016

To Mary

CONTENTS

Introduction   vii
A Second, Less Capable Head   3
The Guest   21
Exposed   39
The Stalker   45
Fruits   57
The Outback   79
The Sicilian   85
Breaking Vials   93
Honey Bunny   97
Jimmy Likes Mermaids   119
The Dress   125
Hunting Bear   135
Cheating the Jail Out of Time   153
The Break   161
The World Baseball League   177
The Wall   183
Hunter's Moon   199
Another Will Take Your Place   219
The Body In The Bay   239
Acknowledgements   244
About James Hanna   245
About the Cover Art...   246
Other Books By James Hanna   247

Introduction

I am of the school that writing should speak for itself. Readers do not require commentators to interpret stories for them; at least that wasn't the case in the past. Just as Queequeg's coffin in *Moby Dick* means different things at different times, stories can be interpreted differently by readers of various backgrounds and education. Does this mean all interpretations are correct? No. In fact, some are flat out wrong while some are much weaker than others. There are, then, superior interpretations, but there is no one interpretation. Authentic interpretation, in my mind, is an individual act, a necessary doing that takes a position on a work of literature, akin to the German philosopher Heidegger's demand that authentic humans must take a stand on Being. So, we are all on our own on that count, alone, aided only by the scope of our awareness of the world and the depth of our experience with literature.

James Hanna, I believe, would agree with me on this point. When asked to write a brief introduction to his collection of short stories entitled *A Second, Less Capable, Head*, I was, of course, honored. After all, I have selected three of his stories for publication in *Red Savina Review*, and I was big fan of his novel *The Siege*. As I reviewed the collection, it occurred to me that an introduction need not include excerpts of stories with which to entice a reader into the text, nor should it simply serve as a map to the book as a whole. Instead, in my conception, an introduction should briefly offer up the spirit of the collection (or one interpretation thereof), in order to connect to the reader as a reader.

As a veteran college professor who teaches literature and creative writing, I do have a depth of experience in both the process and product of writing. As a philosophy professor, I also have a good deal of experience with the theory of interpretation. With that in mind, I would like to offer what I think is the spirt of Hanna's writing in a historical context. I promise to be brief, and, if possible, not too boring.

In his novel *The Siege*, Hanna has written a convincing thriller. It reminded me at some level of Cormac McCarthy meets Freud, and so I enthusiastically wrote a blurb for the novel:

> The Siege *is a Freudian descent into the moral ambiguity inherent in modern institutions. When it comes, as it must, the violence is as tangible and absurd as certain scenes in Cormac McCarthy's* Blood Meridian.

I think that these words hold true for the spirit of Hanna's writing as a whole. The short stories contained in *A Second, Less Capable, Head*, are chock-full of humor, horror, and absurdity as well as violence. In this, I find Hanna's spirit akin to Kafka and, in some strange way, E. E. Cummings. The absurdity of contemporary living, too, has the same spirit as these writers, and one is left, oftentimes and in the spirit of Camus, paralyzed, not knowing whether laughing or crying is the appropriate response to a given situation. A six-inch tall female, a demonic farmer, a two-headed man, can be seen as a kind of dark magical realism such as found in Gabriel Garcia Marquez' "A Very Old Man with Enormous Wings." Was the old man with the wings an angel, a demon, an alien? It is, as it must be, left for the reader to decide. Is Queequeg's box a coffin or a life preserver?

With this in mind, I leave you to read and involve yourself with the strange world of James Hanna. Be careful. It is a dangerous place, a hilariously horrifying realm that bespeaks the truth of our times, a Freudian descent to be sure. Prepare to dive.

John M. Gist
Editor-in-Chief and Publisher
Red Savina Review

A Second, Less Capable, Head

And Other Rogue Stories

By James Hanna

A Second, Less Capable Head

VIRGIL PLOUGHRIGHT—plumber, football fan, Tea Party activist—awoke one morning with a lump on his neck. The lump was soft, red, and fuzzy—like a plum that had been left too long in the refrigerator. Panicked, Virgil phoned his doctor and arranged for an immediate visit.

An hour later, Virgil—dressed in a white cotton gown—was sitting on a table in the consultation room. "Is it malignant?" he asked.

The doctor hesitated, a long pregnant pause that made Virgil's heart pound. "No," he said finally. "It isn't malignant."

"Can you remove it?"

The doctor stood silently, as though he were waiting to catch a bus. When he spoke, it was like a judge pronouncing sentence. "No, I cannot remove it."

"Why not?!!"

The doctor handed Virgil a mirror. "Look closely, Mr. Ploughright. You are growing another head."

Virgil studied the lump on his neck. Although the mirror kept shaking in his hands, he could make out a tiny mouth, a pair of eye slits, a nose no bigger than a button. "It looks like a *shrunken* head."

"For now, Mr. Ploughright—only for now. It will grow. In a week, it will be as large as an orange. In a month, it will be the size of a cantaloupe. Soon after that, it will show signs of human intelligence."

"What's wrong with the head I have?"

"You have a *fine* head, Mr. Ploughright. It fills out your Raiders cap nicely."

3

"Then cut that thing off."

"I can't, Mr. Ploughright. That would be murder."

"Who's going to know?"

The doctor sighed and folded his arms. "I'm going to let you in on the secret. This is not an isolated case. It's happening in other parts of the country."

"Like some A-rab plot?!"

The doctor scratched his chin. His voice dropped an octave. "We don't know what's causing it."

Virgil studied the little head in the mirror. He tilted the mirror back and forth, appraising it from different angles. "It don't look intelligent to me. Cut it off."

"I can't cut it off."

"I got *insurance.*"

"Insurance does not cover murder."

"I got *rights.*"

"You don't have the right to take life."

"What about the gooks I shot in Nam? And those towelheads we're killing in Iraq?"

"This is *innocent* life, Mr. Ploughright. It is practically newborn."

"It don't look innocent to me. It looks like a goddamn A-rab."

"Maybe so, Mr. Ploughright. But I cannot remove it—not without a court's permission, I can't."

Virgil slammed the table with his fist. His fear was turning into rage. "Who says so—the government?"

"Read the Constitution, Mr. Ploughright."

"What about *my* constitution?"

"You're in good enough health. You're just a little thick around the stomach."

"If I was dying, would you cut it off?"

"But you're not."

"So 'cause I'm healthy, I gotta wear this *monkey's* head?"

"If you want to put it that way—yes. I'm sorry."

Virgil could take it no longer. His stomach was churning and he felt a huge belch coming on. The doctor's smugness, his breezy self-righteousness, his probable allegiance with that foreigner in the Oval Office—all required the loudest of rebuttals.

Virgil slammed the table again. "Sarah Palin's gonna hear about *this*."

Virgil's heart was still pounding when he entered his home—a red brick duplex with a foreclosure notice on the door. He was sweating so profusely that he barely felt the cool caress of the air conditioner in his living room. His girlfriend, Trixie—a tall fading blonde—was sitting on the coach watching *Jeopardy* and painting her perfect toenails.

"What are mummies?" she said.

"That's not funny," snapped Virgil.

"But it answers the question, Virgie."

"It doesn't answer *my* question."

Trixie put the cap back on the nail polish bottle. "So what did the doctor tell you?"

"He said I'm growing another head."

"That's so odd, Virgie. What's wrong with the head you got?"

"*Nothing*. The doctor said it's a *fine* head."

Trixie rose from the couch and hobbled towards him, careful of the cotton between her toes. Sweeping her platinum bangs from her eyes, she examined the little head. "It is kinda cute. It looks like a gummy bear—only bigger."

"Don't get attached to it, Trix."

"It's you who's attached to it, Virgie."

"I won't be for much longer. Not after I hire a lawyer." His voice turned into a growl. "I swear, Trix. Give up an inch these days and you're gonna lose a yard."

Trixie tittered seductively. "Atta boy, Virgie. You need every inch you've got." She stroked the little head. "But it *is* kinda cute. I'm gonna name it Alf."

"I'm *serious* about this, Trix."

"I know you are, Virgie. But you're serious about a lot of things. You're even serious about *football*."

"Football matters."

"If it matters, maybe you oughtn't be a Raiders fan."

Virgil puffed out his chest and glowered. He suddenly wished that he loved her less. "Watch your mouth, woman, or I'll ring your chimes good."

Trixie laughed throatily. "Promises, promises. Careful there, hombre, or I'm gonna hold you to it."

Virgil felt his temples start to pound. Across the room, in the center of the living room mirror, the little head seemed to watch him. "The doctor says it's human. I say it's a *monkey's* head."

Trixie arched her eyebrows. "You oughta know the difference, Virgie—you of all people. You picketed that abortion clinic just last week."

"I *shoulda* burned it down."

"They got *sprinklers* in there."

"So what?"

"So you installed them yourself."

"In these hard times, Trix, I gotta take work where I *find* it."

"Well, you ain't that good a plumber, Virgie. If those sprinklers don't work, you could get yourself sued."

She pecked him on the cheek and returned to the couch. Virgil felt his ulcer start to dig. What entitled her to her attitude? She stayed home all day, she drank his good beer, and she didn't even cook. And yet he loved her—loved her ever since he had first noticed her in that sports bar two years ago.

"*What is Lake Erie?*" came a voice from the television. Virgil glanced at the screen. It was "Final Jeopardy!" and a contestant had just lost big.

Virgil slumped his shoulders. If he lost the house, would he lose his girlfriend too? And would that be a *bad* thing? "So why do you stay with me, Trix?"

She laughed. "I don't know, Virgie. You're little and I don't like little men. And you're old and I don't like old men. I guess you're just my little ol' puddin'."

Virgil sighed. Her remarks always caught him off guard. But now was not the time for hesitation. Now was the time to take action.

"I'm gonna write Sarah Palin," he snapped.

A week later, Virgil received an official-looking letter in the mail. His new head, which was now the size of a baseball, smacked its lips sloppily as he tore the envelope open. Virgil trembled as he read.

April 1, 2011
Dear Mr. Ploughright:

Thank you for supporting Palin Productions. These are indeed troubled times. Our country is under attack, not only from foreign zealots, but also from a domestic conspiracy—a conspiracy that has laid siege to our jobs, our institutions of government, and our most cherished values. America—the America we know and love—is being stolen right before our eyes.

If your voice is no longer being heard, if your bankroll is rapidly shrinking, if you cannot keep up with your bills, take hope. Our products are guaranteed, one hundred percent, to resurrect your assets and put the zest back into your life.

This is the lay of the land, my friend. Rise up and take notice.

The letter included a 3" by 5" photo of Sarah Palin—or a remarkable lookalike—clad in a red-white-and-blue bikini and waving a semiautomatic rifle above her head. An enlargement of the photo was available to him for a mere $39.95. Also available were a dozen other likenesses of Sarah.

Furious, Virgil tossed the letter into the trash. "It's a *fake*," he cried. "The carpetbaggers are *everywhere*."

Trixie muted the television. "Didn't Sarah answer your letter?" she asked.

"This isn't from Sarah at all. It's from a *porn* site. The Internet gave me the wrong address."

"You sent your letter to a *porn* site?"

"Yes."

Trixie stretched lazily and giggled. "Maybe that's just as well. I don't think Sarah believes in abortion."

"I told you this is a monkey's head."

"Then why does it look like Robert Downey, Jr.?"

Virgil lifted the pocket mirror, which he now kept permanently in his pants. For the tenth time that day, he captured the reflection of the head. Its greasy skin, unkempt hair, and glazed unintelligent eyes did not remind him in the least of Robert Downey, Jr. It was more like a plant than a human: all it did was stare blankly into space and drool—drool so incessantly that he now carried a towel everywhere he went.

"It's coming off, Trix—I promise you that. I've seen *turnips* with better sense."

"But it snores so cutely when it sleeps."

"Its snoring keeps waking me up. That's just another reason to cut it off."

"Won't it hurt?"

"*Let it hurt.*"

"Not you, Virgie. Won't it hurt *Alf*?"

"*Fuck* Alf. I don't give a damn about Alf."

Virgil put away the mirror and picked up his toolbox. Since the appearance of the head, his business had improved significantly. This was not due to his skill as a plumber, but to the presence of Alf on his shoulder. A lot of housewives in Oakland wanted to pat the little head.

He glared at Trixie. "I'll be back at six. Make sure there's something on the table."

When Virgil returned from work, the television was on full blast. A reporter from Fox News was interviewing a bespectacled scientist from the Centers for Disease Control and Prevention. A thousand cases of Supernumerary Cranial Syndrome, otherwise known as Second Headitis, had been reported—so many cases that that the government could no longer keep the story under wraps.

"*We believe it's being caused by our water,*" the scientist said.

"*Our water?*" the reporter exclaimed.

"*Too much mercury in our oceans. Too many pesticides in our tablelands. Too much leakage from our nuclear waste dumps. These chemicals have been in our water so long that they're having a mutational effect on some of our populace. This was bound to happen sooner or later."*

"Is there anything we can do about it?"

"The first thing to do is not to panic. Remember, this is only happening to a tiny portion of our population. Less than a thousandth of one percent. Simply be alert as to what's going on. And it wouldn't hurt to start drinking bottled water. That comes from mountain springs, so it cannot hurt you."

"It's in our *water*," cried Virgil.

Trixie turned the program off. "That don't affect you, Virgie. All you drink is Budweiser."

"But it's *still* an epidemic. Now they gotta cut it off."

"The president is gonna make a statement tonight."

"Why? So he can raise our water inspection rates?"

Trixie smiled. "Why don't you sell water filters, Virgie? You could take them along with you when you're on a job."

"*Water filters?* Water filters are not gonna stop a *plague*. I'd feel like a *scumbag* doing that."

"You'd soon be a *rich* scumbag."

Virgil shook his head. His stomach was empty, his ulcer was kicking, and—contrary to the order he had given her—there was nothing to eat on the table. "Where's my dinner, woman?"

"All we got is frozen pizza. That and six cases of Bud. Now if you sold water filters, you could afford to take me out."

Virgil suppressed a belch. He hated the betrayal in her voice, her all-too-common assumption that honest labor was for suckers. What would the plumbers' union think if he profited from a government ploy—a sham to keep on bleeding the workingman? Worse yet, what would Sarah Palin think?

Virgil banged his fist off the wall. "Woman, that *ain't* my cup of tea."

Later that evening, the president addressed the nation. Sitting in the Oval Office, dressed in a dark blue suit, he looked personably into the teleprompter as he spoke.

"My fellow Americans. An oath of office is a precarious thing. When taken during prosperous times, it can sanctify all that is good. When taken during troubled times, it can incense

9

and divide. And today a cloud hangs over our nation—a cloud that threatens to drive us apart. And this cloud has been made all the darker by this malady we call Supernumerary Cranial Syndrome.

"Because today, for no apparent reason, thousands of Americans are growing auxiliary heads. But this is not the work of saboteurs and it is not an experiment gone awry. Simply put, it is a phenomenon for which we have yet to find an explanation.

"But there is reason to take heart. My scientists have assured me these heads mean us no harm. On the contrary, they are simple-hearted creatures with a fondness for cheese. So let us not look at them through the veils of rumor and innuendo. Instead, let us extend to them the protection of our Constitution and our tradition of benevolence to the woebegone. With a little nurturing, I am confident these creatures will mature into fine and upstanding citizens.

"My fellow Americans, good night. And may God bless America."

Virgil belched like a cannon. "Does that mean they won't cut it off?"

Trixie nodded. "I think that's what he means, Virgie."

Virgil grabbed the remote and began surfing channels. "I still wanna hear what Sarah Palin's got to say."

Virgil's heart sank as he combed through the networks. There was no public response from Sarah Palin. But there were responses. On CNN, a wild-eyed member of The American Gospel Party was shaking his fist at the cameraman. *"Our chickens have come home to roost,"* he blurted. *"Oh yes. Oh yes. Our chickens have come home to roost. The slaughtered—the multitudes upon whose blood we have built this nation—are returning from their graves. They sit upon our shoulders now—a God-sent reminder of our crimes."*

On NBC, a somber member of The Minutemen—a homespun militia from backwoods Wisconsin—was reading a prepared speech. *"Don't trust them,"* he mumbled. *"Maybe they like cheese and all, but don't trust them. Look at their dark skin, their black bushy hair, their watchful eyes. They gotta be foreign nationals sent to spy upon us. If we don't exterminate them immediately, the Arabs are gonna know every move we make."*

And on Fox News, a gang of Tea Partiers was gathered near the Lincoln Memorial. *"Isn't it enough,"* their spokesman shouted, *"that we are being taxed into extinction—that we are forced to support spongers when we can't afford children of our own? Now, they are attaching the parasites directly to our necks. Are we gonna stand for this? NO."*

The head tensed up and then sneezed. Virgil grabbed it, giving it a jerk. When he removed his hand, his fingers were smeared with orange paste.

"I *told* you to quit feeding it, Trixie," he snapped. "You're making it drool even more."

Trixie closed the bag of Cheetos. "But it's *hungry*, Virgie."

"It's hungry because *I'm* hungry. Isn't it time you got my dinner?"

"Alf doesn't like pizza. I gave him some last night when you were asleep. He made a face and spat it out."

"But it's *my* stomach. Why are you feeding *Alf?*"

"'Cause I'm bored and he's cute. Virgie, I need a change. I want to go somewhere I've never been. I want do something I've never done."

"Why don't you try the kitchen?"

"Why don't you take me out now and then? Or at least you could get me that poodle I been asking for."

Vergil put his hands on his hips. Wasn't it enough that freeloaders were bleeding him dry? Did he have to take the queen of the layabouts out on the town? It was time—high time—that he put her in her place.

"'Cause you don't *deserve* it, woman. And 'cause heads are about to roll."

A month went by, and no statement came from Sarah. The head, perhaps emboldened by Sarah's silence, had now grown to the size of a cantaloupe. And then a remarkable thing happened. The head perked up one morning and began singing in a deep and abiding baritone. *"Everybody looooves somebody sometiiime..."*

Virgil leaped to his feet. *"It's possessed.* Now they *gotta* cut it off."

Trixie put down her nail file. "Golly, Virgie. It sounded just like Dean Martin. I've been listening to him while you're sleeping."

"Dean Martin's in *hell.* He led a wicked sinful life and now he's paying the price."

"Dino? He oughta be in God's choir. I just love Dino." Trixie hopped from the couch and began to sing. "When the moon hits the sky like a big pizza piiiie..."

"Tha's amoreee..." sang the head.

"Enough!" shouted Virgil. Clearly, the head was not taking the situation seriously. And why should it with all the scumbags in its corner?—The Green Team, The Coalition for the Homeless, The American Civil Liberties Union, *even that squatter in the White House.* And Trixie was only making matters worse.

"Enough!" Virgil repeated. "What's next, woman? Sinatra and Crosby?"

"It's singing 'cause it's lonely, Virgie. You oughta make friends with it."

"It's got *enough* friends."

"But it's *you* it's attached to."

"Not for much longer—I'm gettin' it axed. How many times do I have to tell you that?"

"You don't have to tell me that at all—*it's horrible.* Anyhow, what makes you so sure of that?"

"Because, Ms. Jezebel, there's gonna come a reckoning. I'm *familiar* with the lay of the land."

Trixie laughed. "What do you want with the lay of the land? You can't even satisfy me."

Virgil slouched his shoulders—humiliated yet again by the familiar dig. The ease with which she deflated him was outrageous. Wasn't he supporting her, after all? If not for him, wouldn't she be a welfare slug—yet another leach on the back of the workingman?

"Why do you stay with me?" he asked.

"Why do you love me?" she said.

"Ba ba ba booooo," sang the head.

The demonstrations began two months later on the Fourth of July. In Washington DC, several hundred protesters swarmed the Capitol, their battle cry—*Socialism No*—like a snarling wave that would soon shake the building to its foundation. In Wisconsin, members of the American Dairy Association denounced the misuse of their product. The notion that cheese— or even Cheetos—might nurture an alien race was simply un- American. And in Alaska, Sarah Palin finally broke her silence. Her pet phrase—*On a clear day you can see Russia*—was a reminder of the Red Menace about to engulf the nation.

By Labor Day, the White House itself was under siege. A hundred thousand demonstrators—most of them wearing union buttons and Tea Party logos—clogged Pennsylvania Avenue from one end to the other. So imposing was the crowd that the president—standing on the White House lawn and shielded by bulletproof glass—looked like a caterpillar trapped in a jar. Even so, his speech—a sermon on the sanctity of all life—was delivered so condescendingly that he would have been better off remaining silent. *Head lover, cheese burglar, and Commander- in-Thief* were among the milder of the epithets that spilled from the crowd. And so, on the second week of the siege, mounted police were turned loose to disperse the mob—a difficult task as the head busting was somewhat complicated. Since many of the demonstrators were sporting second heads, it was often an auxiliary cranium that was laid open by a baton. But the bloodiest deeds were reserved for the demonstrators. Ultimately, a large group of them scaled the bomb barriers and threw fifty severed heads onto the White House lawn. The amputated heads, their eyes more vacant than usual, were broadcast on Fox News—a sight so grisly that Trixie quickly changed channels.

"Don't look at them," she cried. *"It's horrible."*

"Well, no one invited 'em here," snapped Virgil. His own second head had continued to grow and was now more irritating

13

than ever. It was as large as a soccer ball, and it smelled like garlic and had a wicked-looking cleft on its chin. And it purred like a cat as Trixie ran a brush through its thick oily hair. Trixie spoke consolingly as she worked. "Don't worry, Alfie. That ain't gonna happen to you."

Soothed by her tone, the head began to croon. *"Mooon river wider than miiile."*

Trixie dropped her brush and began to sing along. "I'm courting you in style some daaay."

"Woman, enough," shouted Virgil. He could barely hear the news flash that had interrupted *One Life to Live*. A band of counter demonstrators—college students and priests—had gathered in front of the San Francisco Hall of Justice. They were waving placards that said *Cheese for All* and *God Hates Abortionists.*

Virgil turned off the television. "God hates *meddlers*," he spat. "That's what He hates. There's far too many of 'em sticking their snouts in where they don't belong."

Trixie nodded profoundly. Slowly, soothingly, she continued to groom the head. "No one likes a meddler," she said.

"Meddlers and Muslims—they're pretty much all the same. And this here head is a *Muslim*."

Trixie arched her eyebrows. "Don't Muslims have four wives?"

"Now that ain't the point, Trix."

"No, Virgie, I guess it ain't." She examined the brush and picked off the stray hairs, chuckling as she worked. "That would make you a rascal, Alf."

The head burbled contentedly as she continued brushing it. After a while, she said, "Virgie?"

"What, kitten?"

"Let's have no more talk about killing Alf. You know I'll leave you if you ever do."

"Leave me then."

"This time I mean it, Virgie."

Virgil swallowed his panic. If only he loved her less, things would be so very simple. "All right," he said. "I won't speak of it again."

"And talk to him gentle—even if you don't mean it. It will make things so much easier for me."

"All right, kitten. I will."

The head perked up and smacked its full lips. *"Much cheesier,"* it said.

The demonstrations continued for two more months. Fires scorched cities, troops fought back rioters, and federal buildings were pelted with Limburger. And a battalion of National Guardsmen was stationed permanently around the White House. But by Thanksgiving Day, the troops were reduced and the White House offered a compromise. The president announced that amputations would be permitted on one condition: that the heads would be attached anonymously to the shoulders of people who wanted them.

The announcement rocked Virgil to his heels. "Who would want those greasy fuckers?"

"Someone's bound to want them," said Trixie. "People who are lonely, people who are blind, people in need of money. The government's paying out a hundred thousand dollars to anyone who will accept a head."

"That's bullshit," said Virgil. "Those heads are still gonna spy on people. They're still gonna eat up our cheese. And they're gonna keep singing those corny old songs."

"Hush now, Virgie. You're gonna wake up Alf."

The head, which still stank of garlic, was licking its lips while snoring like a truck driver. The sheer bulk of it was displacing Virgil's own head—so much so that his body now resembled the letter Y.

Virgil lowered his voice. "Trixie," he said. "What if we reattached Alf to someone? We could give him to one of those losers you're talking about."

Trixie put down the brush. She seemed not to hear him. After a minute, she spoke. "That's so *cold,* Virgil."

"Well, at least he won't be spying on a workingman."

15

"But you've got no secrets worth spying on, Virgil. Jeepers, you ain't even working right now."

"How can I work with Alf on my back? He's heavier than a watermelon."

"You never worked that much before Alf was born."

"There's not that much business anymore, Trix. Not for a plumber, anyhow."

"If you get rid of Alf, there's gonna be even less. Women love Alf—that's why you've been getting all those calls."

"So let's give him to one of those women."

Trixie was now staring at him—staring so coldly that he suddenly envied the parasite on his shoulder. "But, Virgil, the transplantations are *anonymous*. Didn't you hear the president?"

"I'm sure Alf will go to a loving home."

"Or maybe he'll go to a pervert."

Virgil clenched his teeth. The conversation had become insane. "Now Trix,"" he said patiently. "What would a pervert want with *Alf?* Alf is a head."

"But he's such a beautiful head."

Virgil hands were now shaking, a spasm so violent that it made his hair stand on end. But his hands always shook when it was time to make a stand. And he was about to make the stand of his life.

"He's coming off, Trix. I'm gonna call the hospital and arrange it."

"But you promised, Virgil."

"I promised not to kill him. I didn't promise not to give him a new home."

"You ain't giving him nothing, Virgil."

"Don't give me that, Trix. I got a damn good reason for what I'm doing."

Trixie folded her arms. Her expression was so fixed that she seemed to be carved from stone. "You've always got a damn good reason, Virgil."

The head stirred as Trixie patted it. The hair on its chin, which now prickled her palm, reminded her that it needed a shave. She started to sob. "Did you hear that, Alfie? Virgil's got himself a damn good reason."

Virgil lowered his eyes. He could only hope now that an item or two might be salvaged from the ship he was about to run aground. "Will you be there when it's over, Trix?"

"You think this is gonna be over?"

"Will you be there? That's what I want to know."

"If you're asking, 'Am I gonna leave you?'— no. You ain't getting off that easy."

Virgil looked at her tenderly, grateful for the pique. If her love for him had ended, her anger would have to do. "At least you were fond of me once," he replied.

"Once upon a time is how I'd put it. And I ain't fond of you no more."

Awake now, the head began to slobber. *"Fondue,"* it said.

Two months later, Virgil lay resting on a hospital gurney awaiting the removal of the head. He was lightheaded from the morphine drip—a soothing sensation that mitigated the sight of Trixie sitting stiffly beside him. Were it not for the embrace of the morphine, she would have looked like a wax statue.

It had taken six weeks to locate a recipient for the head and two weeks more to complete the paperwork—a mound of forms acknowledging the risks of invasive surgery and assuring the anonymity of both donor and recipient. The confidentiality of the operation struck Virgil as ridiculous: he did not have any desire to meet the head's new host. And so he chuckled as he lay on the gurney. "Whoever he is," he remarked, "he's gotta be a total jerk."

The head burped, as though affected by Virgil's comment, and looked at Trixie with glassy eyes. The morphine seemed to have stupefied it—or perhaps it was the dab of Camembert she had snuck it as a parting gift. Trixie gazed at the head as though she were hypnotized. She seemed deaf not only to Virgil but to the bustle of the nurses and the rowdy clamor of the ward's television. Despite the president's compromise—despite the successful completion of dozens of transplantations—riots were continuing in cities across America.

17

Virgil spoke again. "Now don't worry, Trix. When this is over I'm gonna buy you that poodle you've been wanting. This operation ain't costing me a dime, you know."

Trixie continued to stare at the head.

"Thank god I still got my insurance," Virgil said. "Beats socialized medicine any day."

Trixie did not stir.

"Trixie," snapped Virgil. "Quit looking at Alf. Now a greaser like him ain't worth a broken heart."

Trixie broke her silence. "He is my heart, Virgil. He tickles my womb. Haven't you noticed that at all?"

"Well he's my head. And I'll do with him as I please."

"Then don't think you ain't gonna *pay* for this."

Virgil squirmed on the gurney. In spite of the morphine, he could feel the needle in his arm, the chronic ache in his shoulders, and the merciless pressure of his ulcer. "Can I pay for it in Vegas?" he said. "We could hit a few slot machines—take in a show. You wanna see the circus there, don't you, Trix?"

"Fine," Trixie said. "We'll go to the circus, Virgil."

When an orderly came to wheel Virgil away, Trixie hopped from her chair. She said, "Please—one minute more." Using her pocket brush, she combed Alf's hair into a thick appealing Mohawk. "You wanna look *good,* Alf," she whispered. "You wanna look good for your new home." She then kissed Virgil hastily on the forehead and walked in the direction of the waiting room.

Six hours passed before the surgeon came to see her—six hours that she barely noticed. She would have almost preferred it if the operation had taken longer: the surgeon's smug smile, his enveloping handshake, his cheery assurance that everything had gone perfectly only added to her bereavement. How could everything have gone perfectly?

"Do you want to see him now?" he asked.

She nodded woodenly.

Following the surgeon down a long corridor—a hallway that smelled strongly of cleaning fluid—she felt as though she were under assault. The antiseptic stench of the hallway stung her nostrils, the fluorescent lighting burned her eyes, and her high heels seemed to explode upon the slick uncarpeted floor. As she approached the recovery ward, it was all she could do not to bolt from the building.

"He's awake," said the surgeon. "Just a little goofy."

Repressing a dry chuckle, she followed the surgeon into the ward. She walked slowly among the curtained partitions, searching for Virgil's bed. And when she spotted it, she gasped.

The surgeon touched her elbow. "You all right, Miss?"

She sank into the chair beside the bed. *"Go,"* she hissed. *"Just go."*

The irony of what she saw, its dark predictability, in no way diminished its impact—a sight so freakish that she could barely stop herself from screaming. But it was true: Virgil's head— Virgil's splendid head—was no longer attached to his body. Only Alf still remained upon Virgil's stout shoulders—Alf, who was staring back at her with a bland but infectious smile. The hospital had fucked-up big.

Covering her face with her hands, she wept bitterly for twenty minutes. And then she began to laugh.

•

The Guest

ONLY FEMALES HAD ESCAPED the disaster—a hundred tiny creatures known as Aphrodites although the press dubbed them *Thumbelinas*. Their survival was not due to the imprecision of the meteor that had destroyed their little world, but because males had no apparent ranking on the planet Aphrodite. And so a miniature spacecraft, containing only women, had been plucked from the asteroid belt by the mining shuttle returning to earth. So enchanting was the diminutive cargo of the spacecraft that every one of the Thumbelinas had been safely delivered to the NASA laboratories.

Henry Hokum first learned of the creatures from his daughter, Deborah. "Can we adopt one, Daddy?" she asked. "Can we? *Please*? They're only *six inches tall*." He studied the newspaper article that his daughter had thrust into his hands— an article confirming that the government would not be segregating the Thumbelinas at the laboratories. Instead, the women would be placed with a hundred carefully chosen families across the country. This seemed partly due to the fiery temperament of the little creatures, the consistency with which they irritated one another, often coming to blows or stabbing each other with wee hairpins. If left to its own devices, the race seemed determined to self-destruct, and so it seemed wise to assimilate the women individually into their new world.

"A *planet*?" he said. "In the *asteroid belt*?"

His daughter laughed. "It's magic, Daddy—magic."

He shrugged and shook his head. Since the situation defied both science and speculation, it seemed best to submit to a child's interpretation of the matter.

"All right," he murmured, not in the spirit of charity but because he owed his daughter a concession. His daughter had scarcely benefitted when his divorce had been finalized last month, when his ex-wife had reminded him that ten years of marriage were enough. "We were good together, Henry," she had told him. "Just like a pair of old shoes. But who wants to live with an *old shoe*?" He had nodded profoundly and had felt vitalized for the first time in years. A towering man with wandering eyes, he was more like a spring bull than an old shoe. And so he had been trolling the singles bars while his daughter remained with a sitter.

"Can we, Daddy? Can we? Their hair is so *golden*."

He looked at his daughter and smiled indulgently. He was glad to have her for the summer, but she *had* grown clingy since the divorce and her clinginess too often kept him from the bars. Perhaps a diversion, something to compensate for her mother's absence, would help him take better advantage of his freedom.

"All right," he repeated. "If that's what you want. Let's adopt a Thumbelina."

A letter from NASA arrived in the mail. He opened it and read.

May 3, 2040
Dear Henry Hokum & Daughter:

Congratulations. You have been selected as a host family for one of our Thumbelinas. Her name is Clarissa and she will provide you with hours of intrigue and entertainment. You will particularly enjoy it when she sings since her voice is sweet, full, and purer than that of any nightingale. Sometimes, she can be a little temperamental, but this can be moderated with steady attention and a select diet. Please stock up on honey, cantaloupes, and sunflower seeds. These are her favorite foods. She also needs lots of milk, not to drink but to bathe in because her skin is very delicate. We will deliver Clarissa to your home in one week. Should things work out, the arrangement may be made permanent.

Thank you for opening your heart to a little refugee.

The letter was signed by Jean Hargrove, a public relations official with NASA. Startled by the news, Henry called her office immediately. She answered her phone on the first ring, as though she had been expecting his call.

"Ms. Hargrove?!"

"Yes."

"Henry Hokum. You wrote me about a Thumbelina. About my providing a home for one of them."

"We know that, Mr. Hokum."

"There must have been a mistake.

"No, Mr. Hokum. There's been no mistake."

"I'm a barfly, a jerk—a pop music promoter. My wife left me a month ago."

"We know all that, sir. You were carefully investigated."

"Well isn't there a problem?"

"No, Mr. Hokum. There would only be a problem if you were a married *barfly. Thumbelinas are very jealous. They cannot abide the presence of wives, mistresses, or lovers—not for very long."*

"What about my daughter."

"She'll make an allowance for your daughter. Children of ten, they like. Perhaps because they share the same emotional level."

"So how did they build a *spacecraft?*"

"We really don't know, Mr. Hokum. Theories abound but we really don't know. Perhaps it was a gift from an interplanetary civilization. One that takes pity on tiny creatures in distress."

"And how did they survive in the *asteroid belt?*"

"We don't know that either, Mr. Hokum. We don't understand their language—not yet"

"Then why are you placing them with *families?*"

"We believe it will speed up communications. Collectively, they're disinclined to talk to us. Mostly, they just jabber among one another and get into fights."

"I'm *terrible* with women. Just ask my ex-wife. I'm a *bore.*"

"Don't worry, Mr. Hokum. Thumbelinas are not impressed by men. We want her to feel at home, don't we?"

Henry sighed and scratched his head. He was totally out of objections.

"One week," he said.

"One week, Mr. Hokum. And please buy some sunflower seeds."

The following morning, a delivery van pulled into his driveway. A few minutes later, the doorbell rang. Henry cringed as he answered the door.

"A delivery, Mr. Hokum"

Henry looked with astonishment at the miniature house that a pair of deliverymen were carting on a dolly. Moments later, the men were gone and the house lay parked in a sunny corner of his living room.

Henry studied the house. It was a marvelous construction—six feet high, solar powered, and lined with tiny green shutters that complemented its white siding. He slipped loose a panel, examined the interior, and was even more amazed. The house had an elaborately decorated living room, a bathroom with shiny faucets, a spacious bedroom with a telephone—even a gymnasium. Obviously, no expense had been spared to make his small visitor feel at home.

When his daughter came home from day camp, she squealed.

"Is that for *me*, Daddy?"

He shrugged guiltily. "No, Deborah. That's a *real* house."

"It's *wonderful*. How does it work?"

"It's powered by the sun."

Holding her breath, Deborah peaked into the house. She ran her hand over the stunted staircase, a bed no larger than a book, and the little treadmill in the gymnasium. She touched a tiny light switch and gasped when the living room came aglow.

"I can't *wait* till she's here, Daddy. We're going to be such *friends*—her and me."

Henry patted his daughter on the shoulder.

"Even the *plumbing* works," he said.

Six days later, a tall saturnine woman was standing in his doorway. She frowned when he asked her in, as though he were inviting her to bed. She was holding a briefcase and what appeared to be a shoebox with holes.

"Mr. Hokum?"

"Yes?"

"I'm Jean Hargrove. We made an appointment."

"A week ago," he admitted.

"And the week is *over*, Mr. Hokum. I would like to introduce you to your guest. And then I would like to go."

"Why the rush?"

"There's no rush, Mr. Hokum. I would simply like to go."

She followed him into the living room where she dropped the briefcase and then set the box upon the coffee table. She then stared at him critically, as though he were an intruder in his own home.

"Let's wake her gently, shall we? She's napping."

She lifted the lid off the box and he gaped. Asleep on a velvet cushion was a perfect miniature of a woman. She was beautiful, incredibly beautiful—her skin so white and shiny that she appeared to be made of porcelain. Only when she stirred, brushing her long blonde hair from her eyes, did he realize that she was a living being. She looked at him with a mixture of curiosity and reserve.

"You might *introduce* yourself," Jean said.

He continued to stare, too dumbfounded to speak. "*Henry*," he finally stammered, slapping his chest as he spoke. The slap brought a hiccup to his voice.

The tiny woman smiled and he felt himself blushing. Although the smile did not seem spontaneous, it was entirely disarming. Even her dimples had dimples.

Feeling wholly embarrassed, he looked back at Jean, but her presence did not reassure him. Next to the dazzling creature in the box, she looked like a big awkward horse. His eyes, as though drawn by a magnet, returned to the tiny woman.

"Hey there, Dolly," he said.

25

Jean scowled. "Her name is *Clarissa,* Mr. Hokum. Please have the courtesy to address her by her *name.* Now show her the house we delivered you."

Henry pointed towards the little white home with the green shutters. Noticing it, Clarissa yawned. She did not seem surprised or unduly impressed. Obviously, her startling beauty had endowed her with a king-sized sense of entitlement.

"I said, s*how* her, Mr. Hokum. Carry her over to it."

"*Pick her up?*"

"Yes, Mr. Hokum. She *expects* to be carried."

Self-consciously, he extended his hand towards the tiny woman. He felt like a panhandler and was surprised when she hopped instantly into his palm. She was warmer—far warmer—than he expected her to be.

Although his palm itched, he carried her to the house and deposited her in front of the doorway. His embarrassment increased when she looked up at him, placing her hand on her hip, teapot-style. She seemed to be in a hurry.

"Open the *door* for her, Mr. Hokum."

Slowly, as though performing surgery, he pushed the door open with his fingers. As she vanished into the house, he sighed with satisfaction. He felt as though he had passed a test.

"So what happens now?"

Jean opened the briefcase. "*Now* you will sign our agreement, sir. The agreement gives you custody of Clarissa for one month. During that month, you will interact with her, make her feel welcome, and try to teach her some of our language. Just a few words will do—we're not expecting rapid progress."

"I'm a *bad* conversationalist—ask my ex-wife. She says I'm a *Neanderthal.*"

"It's just as well that you *are,* Mr. Hokum. We don't want to *overstimulate* Clarissa, do we?"

She placed the paperwork on the coffee table and handed him a pen. Shrugging, he accepted the pen and signed the contract with an exaggerated flourish. With his visitor now out-of-sight, he began to doubt that she truly existed.

Jean took back the contract and stuffed it into her briefcase. "Thank you, Mr. Hokum. If you have no more questions, I'll leave you alone with her."

His skin prickled as he followed her to the doorway. He felt ill at ease, as though she might suddenly arrest him for fraud. His heart missed a beat when her hand hesitated upon the door handle.

"We'll check back with you in a month," she said.

He nodded.

"And, Mr. Hokum."

"Yes?"

"Good luck with her."

Clarissa did not speak to him for the rest of the day. Instead, she remained in her house—there he could hear her puttering in the bathroom, running on the treadmill, and chatting on the tiny phone in her bedroom. Her voice had a rich lilting quality, but she spoke a language completely unrecognizable to him. Apparently, she was talking to another little refugee somewhere in America.

When Deborah returned home from day camp, she squealed: Clarissa was peeping at her from the doorway of her house. "We're going to be such *friends*," Deborah cried, a prediction that was instantly fulfilled. Within minutes, the two girls were in Deborah's bedroom, laughing, shrieking, and banging about like old friends at play. *They don't even need a language,* Henry thought, and the realization made him envious.

What was going on in there? Aching with curiosity, Henry slipped down the hallway and peaked into the bedroom. The two were playing Whack-a-Mole, a game involving an electronic rodent attempting to dodge a rubber mallet. Deborah was wielding the mallet; Clarissa, skipping about on the game board, was teasing the critter from its hole. She showed no compassion when the mallet struck the rodent, causing it to squeal like a pig.

Noticing him at the doorway, Deborah froze the mallet in mid-air. "*Leave*, Daddy," she said.

"How come?"

27

"Clarissa thinks you're *weird*."

He looked at Clarissa, hoping for some support, and was struck once more by the irrelevance of language. The pout of her little mouth, the thrust of her tiny chin, the iciness of her stare all spoke a clear message: *Get Out*. But even in defiance, she was beautiful—so much so that she appeared to glow. For all true purposes, she might have been a fairy.

Feeling justly chastised, Henry stepped away from the door and slunk back down the hallway. Once he was seated in his den, laughter again spilled from his daughter's bedroom.

The next day, he awoke to a beautiful song—a song so enchanting, so lively and full, that it reminded him of water tripping along a brook. It was the purest sound he had ever heard—so utterly engrossing that, had he been a sailor, he would have run himself aground rather than drift away from it. Spellbound, he arose from his bed and walked in the direction of the song. He walked slowly, carefully—contemptuous of the sound of his feet. Reaching the living room, he paused: Clarissa was indeed singing in her little home—singing so bewitchingly that she might have been an angel of the morning. He stood there for an hour, listening to her sing, and when she was finished he felt an irrepressible sadness.

It wasn't until he heard Deborah cheer that he noticed his daughter beside him. "Wasn't that *lovely*, Daddy?" she said.

"Incredible," he replied. "I never *heard* such a tune."

"Yes you have, Daddy. It's 'Hang on Sloopy.' I taught it to her last night."

He shook his head disbelievingly. The song, on some ethereal level, did bear a slight resemblance to "Hang on Sloopy"—that trivial classic of the sixties. But the thought of this in no way dampened his spirits; he continued to feel such joy—such pure and utter elation—that he could not contain it. He dialed Jean Hargrove on her cell phone.

"*Yes, Mr. Hokum?*" Her voice was like sandpaper.

"She *sang*."

"I know that, Mr. Hokum. Thumbelinas sing every morning—at sunrise. They're singing all across America right now."

"Every *morning?*"

"Yes, Mr. Hokum—every morning. I think it's some kind of ritual."

"It was 'Hang on Sloopy'."

Her chuckle was like the raw cackle of a crow. *"That doesn't surprise me, Mr. Hokum. They've also sung car commercials."*

"It was incredible."

"Maybe so, Mr. Hokum. But singing makes her ravenous. Please don't delay her breakfast."

"Will that make her cranky?"

"Very cranky, Mr. Hokum."

He put down the phone and stumbled towards the kitchen. There, he fixed scrambled eggs and placed a small portion into a bottle cap. He also filled a thimble with coffee. Returning to the living room, breakfast in hand, he tapped softly on the door to the little house.

She was wearing a bathrobe when she opened the door, a loose-fitting garment that puddled around her feet. Clearly, he had interrupted her bath and, clearly, she was not happy. She looked at him so coldly that he almost dropped her breakfast.

"Daddy," Deborah cried. "The *sunflower seeds.*"

Leaving the breakfast at her doorway, he dashed back to the kitchen. *The sunflower seeds.* He located a package of them and poured a small handful into a saucer.

"She likes them *steamy,* Daddy. I gave her some last night."

Panicked, he thrust the saucer into the microwave and hit the timer. When the seeds were hot, he sighed with relief. The plate burned his fingers when he retrieved it from the microwave, but he clutched it stoically and hurried on back to the living room. Clarissa was still standing at the doorway to her house.

"Be careful," he warned her. "They're hot."

She made no reply when he placed the saucer at her feet. Instead, she bent over, gripped the rim on either side, and lifted it like an enormous tray. Without a backwards glance, she squeezed the saucer through the little doorway.

Deborah clapped her hands. "Thank you, Daddy. She'll need a big breakfast."

"What have you two got planned?"

"Songs, *of course*. And maybe a game."

"More Whack-a Mole?"

Deborah giggled. "Don't be silly, Daddy. I'm teaching her Monopoly."

His envy of the girls—their quick and easy rapport—grew with each passing day. But it also annoyed him that Clarissa— although only a fiftieth of Deborah's size—was clearly the dominant of the two. This was never clearer than when Deborah was tardy in fetching Clarissa her hairbrush, fixing her a snack, or heating up milk for her bath. At such times, Clarissa would fly into rages—furies so epic that her voice would become as shrill as chalk scraping a blackboard. Meanwhile, Deborah would scamper about in a breathless effort to placate her little ally.

One day, Henry had had enough. "Why," he asked his daughter, "do you let her push you around like that?"

"She's so *beautiful*, Daddy. I just hate to see her upset."

"She'll be a lot *more* upset when I flush her down the toilet."

Deborah gasped. "*Daddy*. That would be *mur-der*."

He shook his head—undeterred. The thought of an inquisition—even a prison term—was secondary to the joy he would feel in getting rid of the little bitch. But it *did* seem fair to warn her before flushing her down the toilet. He rapped sharply upon the door to her little house.

She was wearing a jogging suit when she opened the door and her skin, normally lily-white, was flushed and glistening. He pointed a finger at her midriff.

"No more *tantrums*," he said.

She looked at him stonily, as though he were something an animal had dropped at her doorstep. Her face was now redder than a cherry tomato.

"NO MORE *TANTRUMS*," he repeated, emphasizing each word with a thrust of his finger.

She continued to glare at him, her arms folded haughtily across her chest. Her eyes were so piercing, her stare so contemptuous, that he suddenly felt like a schoolyard bully. When she slammed the door in his face, he flinched: he could hear her yammering behind the door—a tirade that was only intensified by his inability to comprehend a word of it.

Utterly frustrated, he called up Jean Hargrove. "Please come and get her," he begged.

"*Why?*"

"Just *listen* to her." He held up the telephone then returned it to his ear. "She's scolding me like a shrew."

"*Maybe you deserve it, Mr. Hokum. You are a bit of a hound, you know.*"

"I don't deserve *this much* scolding."

"*Well, you did sign a contract, sir.*"

"Not to be abused in this manner, I didn't."

"*In what manner would you like to be abused? Tell her— perhaps she'll oblige.*"

"What gives *her* the right? I've been a perfect host."

"*Not from what I hear. I hear you were watching her take a bath.*"

"That was an accident. And how did *you* find out?"

"*She complained about you to one of her little friends. A few Thumbelinas have learned a bit of English, sir.*"

"Maybe they could talk to her—tell her to respect her host."

"*Maybe you could tell her. Remember your mission, Mr. Hokum—to communicate with an alien race. Let's not lose sight of it, sir.*"

"I'm doing my best."

"*Are you? Then why don't I sense any progress?*"

"She won't even *speak* to me. She'd rather play games with Deborah."

"*Then it's time you took charge of matters.*"

"How?"

"*Figure it out. Aren't you the mature one?*"

"You called me a *hound*. That's not *saying* much."

"Much *is not required* here, *sir. Just teach her a few words of English. We'll be checking up on you at the end of the month.*"

When the phone line went dead, he felt totally lost. The room was now quieter than a morgue. *What was she up to behind that little door?*

He looked at his daughter. "So what do I do?"

"Stay away from her *house*, Daddy. She thinks you're a *burglar.*"

In the evenings, the three of them would watch television together. At such moments, Clarissa would perch herself upon his shoulder—not in the spirit of intimacy but to get a better view of the programs. She was captivated by *American Idol* and would watch the re-runs for hours, memorizing tunes she would sing the following morning. Complemented by her voice, the tunes would instantly blossom, acquiring a fullness so stunning and rare that the songs, in their original versions, seemed like rank parodies. She also liked movies—old DVDs—and would grow irritable if he failed to replay them constantly. Her favorite was *Pulp Fiction.*

Feeling increasingly trapped in his house, Henry spent more time at the singles bars—a futile pursuit since, whenever he brought a woman home, she would have to deal with Clarissa. Standing at the doorway to her house, her hands upon her hips, she would look at his guest as though she were urinating on the rug. He hoped the women would dismiss Clarissa as a chimera—the product of too much booze—but instead, they would dash out the door while Clarissa hurled gibberish at them.

He changed his tactics, allowing the women to take him to their homes, but the results were pretty much the same. Clarissa would be awaiting him when he returned the following morning—her gaze so intimidating, so utterly self-righteous, that he felt as though he had slighted a queen. And so, feeling like a trespasser in his own life, he would creep to the solitude of his den.

But communications were still an issue—at least to Jean Hargrove who came to see him at the end of the month. After spending an hour with Clarissa, she looked at him sternly.

"*Explain* yourself," she demanded.

"She's taken over."

"I'm talking about language. She hasn't learned a *thing*."

"She'd rather scold my dates."

"Can't she do that in *English*, Mr. Hokum? She's way behind the *rest* of the Thumbelinas. Some are reciting *Hallmark* cards." She sighed, opened her cell phone, and made a notation on her calendar. "One week, Mr. Hokum. You have one week more. If she hasn't learned something—even if it's just *one word*—I'll place her with another family."

"I'll try," he replied—a promise he intended to keep. In the company of his little mistress—her relentless sense of proprietorship—he felt like an unworthy servant. And so he resigned himself to teaching Clarissa English.

The following morning, she was gone. He sensed this instantly, not because the house was silent—not even because the living room window was ajar—but because the little woman was so often incensed with him. But he did not panic until he had checked the little house, looked under the living room sofa, and peered into his daughter's room—and his panic was very brief. Clarissa's absence did create an uncommon sense of dread in him, but then again so had her presence. And so it was not until Deborah spoke up that he realized the seriousness of Clarissa's departure.

"You left the *window* open, Daddy."

"We needed the *air*."

"Now Clarissa's *gone*."

"Maybe she just went for a walk."

Deborah started sobbing. "We have to *find* her, Daddy. A cat's gonna *grab* her."

He tried to joke her out of it—"Feel sorry for the *cat*"—but Deborah was inconsolable. "It's *your* fault, Daddy. I'll hate you *forever*."

While Deborah sobbed, he continued his search. He checked the birdbath in the driveway; he spread the hedges next to the house; he shined a flashlight into the gopher holes in the backyard. Finding no sign of her, he jumped into his car—a shiny red Porsche—and drove up and down the neighborhood streets. Deborah, sitting beside him, grabbed his arm whenever she spotted a robin, a sparrow, or a chipmunk. "There she *is*, Daddy." But the tiny woman was nowhere to be seen—not even after he had been cruising the streets for several hours. Desperate, he began knocking on doors, but none of the neighbors were helpful. One of them, an irate woman with massive forearms, even glared at him. "Waddayawant with a Thumbalina?" she spat. "I hear they suck your breath while you're sleepin'—like *cats*."

At the end of the day, completely exhausted, he phoned Jean Hargrove. "We've lost her," he said.

"Lost *her, Mr. Hokum? Just what do you mean by* lost her?"

"She slipped out the living room window."

"After *you left it open, I assume.*"

"I only wanted air."

"*And did you* get *some air, sir?*"

"Plenty. I've been searching the whole neighborhood for her."

"*That* won't *get you out of the woods, Mr. Hokum. She* was *your responsibility, you know.*"

"What *more* do you want me to do?"

He heard her sigh deeply. "*Nothing. She'll only come back if she chooses to. It's not uncommon for Thumbelinas to leave a home—usually it happens when they're displeased with their host. Was she* displeased *with you, Mr. Hokum?*"

"I guess I was too much *hound* for her."

"*Don't flatter yourself, Mr. Hokum. Probably, you weren't* enough *of a hound. Thumbelinas are only satisfied with blind devotion.*"

"So where will she go?"

"*She'll probably adopt another family. There are plenty of people who would* love *to have a Thumbelina in their home.*"

"What if she doesn't like them either?"

"If she doesn't like them, she might give you another chance."

"When is that likely to happen?"

"Maybe in a week or two—if she doesn't like them. That will give you an opportunity to make amends."

"Become her *slave*, you mean."

"If you *want to put it that way—*yes."

"I *do* want to put it that way."

"I'll make a note of it, Mr. Hokum. Let us know if she shows up."

Three weeks passed and Clarissa did not return. Deborah, true to her promise to forever hate him, went to live with her mother full time. She left while he was out on one of his prowls. Returning home, he saw a note upon the coffee table—a note with his ex-wife's scrawl.

He picked up the note and read.

Henry,

When I left you, I had hoped you might grow up a little. But it seems I've overestimated you once again. So now it's a living Barbie doll. How <u>did</u> you get involved in something so sick? And don't try to say it was Debbie's idea—she calls you an oinker behind your back.

Weren't your other toys enough for you?—the speed boat, the sports car, that damn swinger's network you made me join. Did you have to get involved with a fickle little alien? And did you have to let Debbie fall in love with her?—you know how attached she gets to stray things. But stray things wander off, Henry—you of all people should know that. Really, I've never been more disappointed in you.

The damndest thing is you will have to fetch her back. Debbie is heartbroken—she cries every day—and I'm left to pick up the pieces once again.

I'm furious with you, Henry, so please don't try and phone me. Your daughter will be staying with me until further notice—or at least until that ridiculous pixie is found.

He put down the letter and started making plans. Since further searching seemed useless, it was time to seek distractions—ways to ease the time until Clarissa might deign to return. *Thank Heaven for his toys.*

He continued to cruise the nightspots, picking up women at random. In defiance of Clarissa, her rare and uncompromising beauty, he grew less selective: it was now easier to overlook platinum blonde hair, starched face-lifts, and sagging boobs. Solace, not beauty, was the point after all: the warmth of a cocktail, the glow of muted lights, and the thrill of anticipation before he moved in for the kill. And his pickups, recognizing him for the hound he was, did not grow cross when his conversation lapsed and his eyes wandered fleetingly around the bar. "You're a one-nighter, Slick," one of them remarked before he took her home. "But one-nighters are the best of all."

And so, in the absence of his little mistress, he had himself a ball.

She came back on a Sunday morning, awakening him with the musical lilt of her voice. The song was coming from the living room, where he had left the window open. And the song was so captivating, so stunningly rich, that he barely recognized it as "Baby One More Time"—a Britney Spears number. She must have learned it wherever she had been staying—there had probably been a teenager in the house and they had not gotten along.

He crept into the living room, careful not to make the slightest sound. He could hear the water running in her bathroom: a lyrical tinkle that mingled so perfectly with her voice that she might have been a siren perched upon a river bank. But not even a siren could have sung a song so beautifully. It therefore seemed a sacrilege when he picked up his telephone and dialed Jean Hargrove.

Jean answered him on the first ring. "*Yes, Mr. Hokum?*"

"She's back."

"*I know that, sir. I can hear her.*"

"Am I out of the woods?"

36

"*Has she learned any English?*"

"I don't think so."

"*Then you're not out of the woods, sir.*"

"Give me a break. She's been gone for three weeks."

"*You've* had *your break, sir. I'll be over in one hour. If she's not speaking some of our language—even if it's just a word—I'll be taking her with me.*"

He hung up the phone, grateful for the delay—grateful that he would have another hour to hear her sing. And her last trilling note had just faded away when he heard the knock on the door. A moment later, Jean Hargrove was standing in his living room.

"Well, Mr., Hokum?" He face was expressionless, like that of an executioner, and she was carrying the shoebox with holes. Her eyes followed him as he rapped tentatively upon the door to Clarissa's house.

She answered the door in her bathrobe. She looked weary and ruffled, like a housewife recovering from a hard day—but the curlers in her hair and the cream upon her face in no way diminished her startling beauty. She watched him coquettishly as he patted himself upon his chest.

"*Henry,*" he declared.

She smiled, a smile more dismissive than spontaneous—obviously, she was in a hurry to return to her bathroom. Shaking her head, she drew a deep breath.

"*Oinker,*"" she piped.

The water kept tinkling.

He looked at Jean Hargrove and smiled. "There you are."

•

Exposed

HE WAS A TALL SHEEPISH GENTLEMAN in his late fifties. His eyes were gentle, his chin was weak, his shoulders were starting to stoop. His legs were thin and wobbly, his hair was thinning and gray. And he walked with the hesitant stride of a crane, his head bobbing forward with every step. Watching him amble along the street, one would never guess him to be an artist. A servant, perhaps, a beggar more likely, but not an artist: a soul unencumbered by earthly snares and committed to only the Muse. But an artist he was, and no mere artist at that. He was an artist in the most gallant of mediums: the daring realm of street performance.

He did not suffer dullards well, and so he performed in the Mission District. The Mission was always full of tourists: inquisitive sorts who could better appreciate his craft than flint-eyed drug dealers or self-absorbed commuters. It was the tourists who gasped breathlessly, riveted their eyes upon him, and laughed with something other than derision. It was the tourists who lifted their cameras, snapped his photo, and hailed his display as a charming motif of San Francisco. And so he honed his skill for the tourists, determined to reward such generosity of spirit. He wore only the best of London Fog raincoats, the most stylish of Panama hats. He timed to perfection the nuances of his pitch: the wiggle of his eyebrows, the teasing flicker of his tongue, the preliminary flaps of his raincoat. And his Monty could best be described as heroic: a godly embrace of liberty and life. An eagle soaring above the Grand Canyon was no more stately in its wingspread.

Considering the quality of his work, it was regrettable that he preferred select audiences. But it is nobler to touch a few profoundly than to court the vulgarities of the masses. And with this charitable philosophy, the good man plied his trade, exposing himself to just one or two spectators before making a discreet exit. He was adept at exits, having committed to memory every alley in the Mission, and so he was rarely accosted. But on those occasions when the police did nab him, the consequences were pedestrian. Otherwise, he might have become a martyr to his gift, a trailblazer whom adversity had lifted to fame. But, sadly, this was not to be. "Ah," scoffed the jailers whenever the cops marched him into booking. "It's Sylvester again. How's it hanging, Sylvest?" He would spend one night in jail, no more, and receive a sheriff's release the next morning. Never was he afforded the spectacle of courtroom drama—the opportunity to suffer for his cause.

Despite the fickleness of fortune, he remained a purist. He loathed those thespians who bastardized their scripts: the rapists, the pedophiles—those who gave flashing a bad name. He did achieve an erection on occasion, but never for the sake of seduction. His erections were merely to complete the aesthetic, much like the painter's signature scrawled at the bottom of a portrait. And being a perfectionist, he worked meticulously on style, bringing to each performance a new measure of affect. He learned new ways to flutter his raincoat, new ways to tilt his hat, new ways to smile seductively as he allowed the flaps to drift. Who could doubt that he might one day produce a masterpiece?

But time had stolen his confidence and his dream was starting to fade. And so he worked harder to catch it, willing to risk it all for an indelible blaze of glory. And should he fall like Icarus, his wings torched by the sun, this would not be too great a price to pay for the culmination of a vision. He believed implicitly in the stoutest of clichés: the age-old truism that one who never gives up is one who will never be conquered. And so, with each passing year, he struggled for the perfect pose.

He achieved a masterstroke on his sixtieth birthday—a late flowering, perhaps, but a bloom nonetheless. It was a practice performance, a casual warm-up, that provided him with the impetus of genius. The catalyst, Mabel Albright, was a coltish young lady from Iowa enjoying her first day in the city. As he watched her stroll along Folsom Street, he knew she would be an ideal foil. Her skin was parlor pale, her gait was halting, and she glanced about with the doe-eyed wonder of a debutante attending her first ball. *Was she too easy a target?* he wondered, a thought he was quick to dismiss. Compassion should never destroy inspiration—not when a dream is at stake. That is the anarchy of art.

He nodded politely as she approached him. Conversation was unnecessary, but good manners were still important. And so he waited until she returned his gaze, until her eyes lit shyly upon his, before giving the Muse her rein. Ever so slowly, he fluttered his raincoat; ever so teasingly, he smiled. Botticelli's Venus, awakening from a nap, could not have moved more sensuously. And when he let the flaps of his raincoat part, his boner was lively and full, like a plump and mischievous puppy that romped with the joy of life.

Her shriek was piercing but vital. Her eyes were terrified yet awed. And when she swooned, it was not from terror but an overabundance of excitement. Such is the nature of sheltered souls: they can stand just a glimpse of the sun.

As he made his retreat, he could feel his heart pound. What a reception! What a performance! And yet her response seemed excessive: a validation he had not truly earned. He knew he could do even better; he knew he could rise to much more. Today would surely be the day of his masterpiece.

He waited an hour at the corner of Folsom and 23d Street. The area was filled with druggies, and so he did not feel conspicuous. They were sure to alert him with cries of *"Five-o"* if a cop car should appear. But the sidewalks lacked worthy spectators: he saw only crackheads, day laborers, and insular youths with gang tattoos on their arms. It was almost by consolation that he chose his next target: a hefty woman of fifty by the name of Wanda Polanski. She worked in a local sausage factory and smelled of beer and sweat. Little did she know she was about to witness an opus. And little did she care.

Retrieving an iPhone from his raincoat pocket, he harvested a tune. What else but the opening of *Also Sprach Zarathustra*—that epic movement from Stanley Kubrick's *2001 A Space Odyssey*? As he stepped in front of her, smiling pleasantly, the orchestra droned to its crescendo. *Uummm, uummm, UUMMMM, AH-AAH!!! Boom, boom, boom, boom, boom, boom.* When he spread his raincoat, his eyes were aglow, his grin was as bright as a headlight. And his Willie was straighter than a baton as it nodded in perfect time with the drum beats. This was his moment. This was his statement. This was his stroll with the gods.

She stared without expression. It was the gaze of a cretin—a creature more animal than human. A beast that feasted on carrion and never pondered the stars. Never had a face looked more churlish. Never had eyes looked more dead.

"Buster," she slurred in a voice coarse as sand. "Yer mama know watcha doin'?"

Sadly, an eagle needs wind drafts to soar; a rose needs water to blush. And a cheeky cock robin cannot hold its trill if the sun does not peek through the clouds.

He slapped his chest theatrically, but his spark had already been doused. "Madam, surely you jest," he joked.

Snorting, she folded her ham hock arms. "It *looks* like a prick only smaller, mister."

"Madam, you truly jest," he repeated. He was not adept at repartee; body language was his gift. So in the face of this cold, imperious attack, it was all he could think of to say.

She snorted again. "*Perve,*" she muttered. It was just one word, one trite little word, but a word that for her said it all. It takes only one's pinkie, held close to the eye, to blot out the brightest of dawns.

She left him hanging alone on the street; she would think of him no more. She had errands to run, beer to belch, and sausages to stuff.

Is the Muse as dismissive as Wanda, an incurious, beery frump? Visit any bar and you will find scads of local prodigies. They will talk of their projects to any who listen: books they will never write, portraits they will never paint, songs they will never compose. For what can these dabblers accomplish without sturdy, hermitic souls? Without blinders to see their tasks through to completion though all else may tumble to ruin? Geniuses lacking this coldness of mind will wither away on the vine. And journeymen will thrive in their place, their works praised as stark and brilliant by hordes of reviewing hacks.

And so the Muse is a slattern, no more, a callous, teasing witch. Her eye wanders too quickly, her favors don't last, her heart is fickle and mean. She knows from bitter experience that few will pick up her chant, that for every brave soul that might march to her hymn, a thousand will die in the dust. To only the brashest of suitors, to only the boldest of swains, will she sing her full-throated song.

Was Sylvester too fine for his mission? Was his soul too inclusive, his spirit too noble, his heart too tender and large? How else to explain the power of chance: that a rude and despicable creature, a woman more common than dirt, had broken his mighty spirit. "Ay, 'tis a scratch," cried Mercutio, but he perished from Romeo's blade. And so fell Sylvester, his heart slashed to pulp by that shallow, illiterate tongue. Oh courage, courage, why did you flee him? Why did you yield to a sow?

He returned to the Mission a few more times, his raincoat yet cocked, his eyes yet alert, his iPhone yet blasting a tune. But his dramas were meek, uninspired affairs, mere parodies of art. His arms were so stiff, his face so bland, that he better resembled a scarecrow than conduit to the gods. So what was left for this talented man but hang up his raincoat for good?

He took to travel to bury his sorrow, but travel could not free his soul. What traveler does not carry with him the things he is destined to find? So like Byron in *Childe Harold's Pilgrimage*, he only pondered ruins: the Parthenon, the Coliseum, the temples of ancient Rome. Only these glorious relics could stir his failing heart.

And when travel proved too exhausting for him, he found quicker escape in booze. In booze he could blur his debasement, in booze he could soften his shame, in booze he could glimpse the specter of what he might have become.

He died in Athens, his liver worn out, his spirit a windblown husk. He was buried in a pauper's grave.

•

The Stalker

OLLIE IS A STALKER. I say this to define him not delimit him; his receding brow, poached-egg eyes, and sunken chin inspire to no nobler assessment—nor does his voyeuristic stare imply that he is anything other than a seeker of second-hand spoils. I do not know him from Adam—I do not even know that his name is Ollie—but I have to call him something if I am to purge myself of a rather loathsome series of events: a sequence that started six weeks ago when I first saw him sitting at my kitchen table. "Already?" I said when I spotted him in my kitchen; I had at first mistaken him for a tradesman, the gardener who came monthly to my bungalow home, but when he looked in my direction I realized that he hadn't been invited. His gaze was too humble, too unintelligent, and conveyed little more than impotent longing—as though he would have liked to engage in conversation but lacked the facility of response. Were it not for his clothing, a neatly-pressed woolen suit, I would have considered him to be a tramp who had wandered into my house. I sat across from him at the table and curiously returned his stare.

He would have to leave, of course, but I saw no good reason to call the police. In spite of the intrusion, he seemed too chubby—too soft in body and soul—to survive very long in a jail. Anyway, I did not want the help of the police: as a retired probation officer, a veteran with thirty years street experience, I was not intimidated by this short creature and could easily have cuffed him up myself. I wondered if I had done so at some point in my career—if he was among the many miscreants who had threatened me in open court after I had put them in jail. But he aroused no affinity: his face was that of a total stranger and his presence in my kitchen conveyed not a hint of Karma. It seemed, in fact, that it was *he* who expected retribution: he was trembling as he watched me, as though he were expecting me to punch his face.

I decided to fix breakfast—not because I was particularly hungry but because I did not want to give him credit for interrupting my daily ritual. I prepared toast, coffee, and scrambled eggs for two, watching him from the corner of my eye as I worked. He did not stir in the chair, not even after the breakfast was ready and I had placed a small helping in front of him. Ignoring the plate, he watched me as I ate, his face so solemn that it became inhibiting for me to chew. Finally, as though doing me a favor, he picked up a single piece of toast, took a few bites from the center, and discarded the crusts onto his plate. The timeliness of the gesture suggested that he did have a modicum of intelligence—enough to realize that he had overstayed his welcome and it was time for him to go. I rose from the table, took him by the elbow, and gently walked him to my front door.

Opening the front door, I hesitated: a heavy cloudscape blanketed much of the city, so obscuring the view from my Russian Hill home that I could barely see the bay. Even Alcatraz, that formidable rock, seemed irrelevant in the fog—a landmark less than a floating companion to the garbage scows that were heading out to sea. "Do you want an umbrella?" I asked him. He did not reply—nor did I expect him to. It did not console me that he was probably a mute; a month of retirement had made me too nostalgic for clamor: the din of the streets, the clanging of jail cells, even the occasional pop-pop-popping of a Glock seemed preferable to the sacrament of silence. I had almost considered returning to work, but a bullet still lodged in my hip, a souvenir of a gun battle I'd been in a month ago, had given me an overdue hint of my mortality. I had almost become grateful for my post traumatic stress: my exaggerated reflexes and hyper vigilance were useful in the tennis matches I now played daily at the club.

"Do you want an umbrella?" I asked him again. He smiled faintly but made no reply, and so I escorted him to my front gate. Frowning and shaking my head, I unlatched the gate and pushed him out onto the sidewalk. "*Now* you can go," I said; he smiled once again. He then straightened his tie and walked in the direction of Polk Street.

He was sitting at my kitchen table the following morning. His eyes were still hungry, like those of an orphan, and he was still wearing his neat woolen suit. A bump on his forehead, larger than an egg, suggested that he had fared poorly on the street and I wondered if I should have given him money for safe lodging in a hotel room. But he did not really strike me as destitute; probably he had enough cash for a room and his plush but humble appearance had contributed to his getting mugged.

Watching him closely, I put on the coffee and opened the refrigerator door. He showed no interest as I fixed breakfast—another indication that he did not lack for funds—nor did he move a muscle when I placed his helping in front of him. He just sat as I ate, his eyes roaming the room in the manner of a stockroom clerk taking inventory. Eventually—I'm sure it was out of courtesy—he picked up a single piece of toast, nibbled at the center, and dropped the crusts onto his plate.

"Are you ready?" I asked him. I had decided to deposit him at a shelter in the Tenderloin District—an imposing chore since I would have to forgo the doubles match I was scheduled to play in an hour. This was not an easy sacrifice; I had honed my approach shot to the point that I was now assured of a quick put-away at the net—a feat that distracted me from the seductions of memory and the constant throbbing in my hip. Still, I did need to get rid of him—an accomplishment that did not seem likely if I allowed him to hang around my neighborhood. And a shelter in the Tenderloin would not endanger him quite as much as jail; he did not seem totally without resources—not if his intrusions into my home were any indication. At the very least, he was adept at picking locks.

When I had finished my breakfast, I rose from the table and took him by the elbow once again. He hung his head as I led him to my front door, his manner so passive that I felt the urge to bully him. Instead, I guided him through the gate and out onto the street where my car, a newly purchased Ford Hybrid, was parked. After fastening him into the passenger seat, I slipped behind the steering wheel, turned on the motor, and began the downhill descent towards the Tenderloin.

He lifted his head as we turned onto Van Ness Avenue and then looked intently through the passenger window. The shops, civic centers, and city parks seemed like novelties to him—sights so compelling and rare that I began to feel like a tour guide. But the city had grown unconvincing to me, as though it were an estranged girlfriend whom I no longer wanted to take to bed. And so, as I turned onto Ellis Street and headed towards Glide Memorial Church, I began to pity him.

As I pulled into the church parking lot, I hesitated: the church, a magnificent relic, did not seem a promising sanctuary but an edifice that was itself in need of charity. Still, a large group of homeless people were queued up outside it, waiting to be let in for the noon meal. Later in the day, when the doors again opened, many of them would be back in the hope of acquiring a cot for the night. But the sight of the church did not dampen my sense of mission; instead, I felt a perverse thrill of accomplishment. Since Ollie was an intruder in my home, he did not deserve a comfortable deliverance. He was in fact lucky that I hadn't taken him to the police.

I pulled into a parking space, turned off the engine, and looked at him sternly. "Are you ready?" I asked him again. His lack of response seemed appropriate; the deteriorating church with its marginal bounties was not at all conducive to anticipation.

Shrugging, he unfastened his seat belt and opened the car door. He then stepped from the car to the parking lot where he stood stock still, as though tied to a stake. I watched him for a second or two, afraid that he would change his mind, but his face was so impassive that he reminded me of a statue. I hit the accelerator, backed up the car, and eased back into the city traffic.

He was back in my kitchen the following morning. The sight of him again sitting at my kitchen table was practically a relief since it spared me the irritation of further suspense. He had already made himself toast, perhaps to save me the trouble of feeding him, and the crusts were deposited neatly on a saucer in front of him.

He looked at me and smiled, and his smile bore a hint of condescension as though he were convinced that he had done me a favor. I shook my head sternly, not letting on that his presence now challenged me. Getting rid of him was going to be a bigger task than I had anticipated—a project rather than a chore, and I was somewhat in need of a project. I studied him carefully and began formulating my plan.

I decided on Vegas. I usually went there once or twice a year so the trip would not be an inconvenience for me. I did not go there for the shows or the gambling, but for the sensual vacuum it provided me: a sense of unreality not dissimilar to the sight of Ollie in my kitchen. And so Vegas seemed a good place to unload him; given his doggedness, his obvious talent for obsession, it would be easy enough to hypnotize him with a slot machine while I made my escape. With any luck, he would then wander into a hotel room, startle a tourist, and get himself thrown into jail on a trespassing charge.

This time I handcuffed him. He stood obediently as I placed his hands behind his back, slipped the bracelets over his wrists, and set the safety locks. He even turned his palms outward, an indication that he had been handcuffed before. "We're taking a holiday," I said. He smiled—an expression of irony rather than gratitude; his obvious contempt for boundaries suggested that his entire life had been a holiday of sorts. "Vegas," I added and he nodded pleasantly.

He was humming as I led him to my car—a jaunty tune belonging to an old truck commercial ("You *asked* for it, you *got* it—Toyota."). I doubt that he meant anything by it—probably it was the last thing he remembered seeing on television—but I felt somewhat vindicated as I fastened him once more into the front seat of my car. Under the circumstances, a Hybrid would have to do him.

We drove all day and half way through the night, hitting the Vegas strip a few minutes after midnight. But although it was late, the strip was jammed with tourists: a transient sight that justified my contempt for excess baggage. I parked in front of the Sands Hotel then carefully removed the handcuffs. When his hands were free, he patted me on my shoulder, a gesture that alleviated my sense of discord—the vague but uncomfortable notion that I could be reported for kidnapping him. He rubbed his wrists as I led him to the hotel restaurant and he straightened his tie while we waited for a booth. We snacked on hamburgers (he again ate very little) then I led him into the casino where I bought him a stack of silver dollars. "Go for broke," I said, a statement that struck me as somehow redundant.

I sat him in front of a dollar slot machine and ordered him to insert a coin. He complied gingerly, probably because his wrists were still sore, and I pulled the lever for him. The tumblers, as though wise to my plan, produced three lemons as they pop-pop-popped to halt. A landslide of coins tumbled into his lap. "Go for broke," I repeated. He glanced at me, startled by his luck, but picked up another dollar and slipped it into the slot. This time, he pulled the lever himself: the tumblers again whirled, stuttered to a halt, and three more lemons fell into a row. Again, a flood of coins poured into his lap, a flow so abundant that it looked as though the machine were trying to bury him. He clapped his hands eagerly and began feeding coins back into the machine. He was humming as he worked—that same stale commercial—but his attention was so fixed upon the tumblers that I was able to stroll lazily from the casino and return to my car.

I drove for several hours before stopping to rest at a motel near Fresno. I slept until noon then got back into my car and finished the remainder of the drive to San Francisco. The street lights were on when I arrived at my home, but the house looked rather dark and so I checked the windows and locks before entering. In my eagerness to validate my deed—a neat but unsavory triumph—it rather disappointed me that there were no signs of entry.

A SECOND, LESS CAPABLE, HEAD

Once inside the house, I continued my inspection, walking from room to room and opening the closets and cabinets. The search was unnecessary but engaging, a reminder of the many houses I had searched for weapons and drugs, and so it did not bother me that my efforts now seemed lame—a triumph of compulsion over practicality.

When I had finished my inspection, I locked the front door and turned on the TV. Since retiring, I had resumed my addiction to television—news and sports mostly although I was not immune to the reality shows. I did not watch the reality shows out of interest so much as a sense of obligation, the ethical notion that a foray, once begun, had to be seen through to its conclusion.

I sat in my recliner, still stiff from the drive, and grimaced as the screen came alive. I was immediately irritated by the fruity glow of the Tivo screen: its extensive display of unwatched programs hung before me like a list of chores. I picked up the remote from the side table, warily lowered the volume, and turned on *Survivor*.

The following morning, he was back. He was sitting at my kitchen table and stroking a towering stack of coins. Perhaps he intended to pay me for our short vacation—a notion I did not dismiss as excessive. He had profited from our excursion, after all, while I was still stuck with the task of getting rid of him.

I decided to take a small break from him. Retrieving the *Chronicle* from the front porch, I sat on the opposite side of the table and began reading the news. I read only the crime reports—another habit I had fallen into since leaving the probation department. The muggings and drug busts seemed surreal to me now and so I could enjoy them as though watching a sport. After all, I was no longer responsible for controlling the behavior of criminals.

When Ollie started humming again, I put down the paper. He was humming the theme tune of *Leave It to Beaver*—that iconic classic from the sixties about a kid who always fucked up. Since I had repeatedly failed in my attempts to dispose of him, the implications of the ditty seemed timely and wholly deserved.

But this time I would be successful. I had thought it over while reading the paper and had decided to fight banality with banality: I would implement a scheme so artless, so stunningly trite, that even an aspiring haunt would be stymied by it. I would maroon him on an island.

I decided to take him to Kauai. I had visited the island several years ago and had been struck by its many anachronisms: sunken shipwrecks, prehistoric trees, and jaunty wild roosters that strutted about like plantation lords. Since Ollie was clearly a man out-of-place, I had little doubt that he would find his element among the fossils. If not, let him rot in a tropical jail.

I turned on my computer, went on-line, and booked two airline tickets to Kauai: one of them round-trip and the other one-way. I then cuffed up Ollie and marched him out to my car. I popped the trunk out of pragmatism—not spite: the sudden realization that I had made stalking too attractive to him. When I shut him in the trunk, he bawled like a calf and began to kick furiously at the locked lid. Ignoring the racket, I dashed back into the house, stuffed some clothes into an overnight bag, and quickly returned to my car. The thumps became fainter as I drove to the airport, muffled by the heavy base from my CD player.

Arriving at the airport, I parked the car in Long Term Parking and let Ollie out of the trunk. His suit was torn and he was bleeding slightly from the scalp, a superficial graze that I was able to clean up with a handkerchief. "You *do* have a choice," I said to him sternly. "Don't think that you don't have a choice." He looked at me solemnly, his eyes wide open with fear. "Don't flatter yourself that I'm kidnapping you. You *do* have a choice. You can come with me *now* on another vacation or you can accompany me to the city jail." He winced at the mention of jail, his eyes still wider than doorknobs. "Now I *know* you've been to the jail," I said. "Have you been to Kauai?" He shivered and shook his head. "Come on then." He began to relax as we headed towards the terminal and soon he was ambling beside me like a faithful dog.

A SECOND, LESS CAPABLE, HEAD

I flashed my police badge as we passed through security. The security officer nodded, intuitively aware that I had a renegade in tow, and allowed me to herd Ollie through the metal detector. I displayed my badge again as we boarded the plane—a pertinent reflex since I suspected I would have to break out my handcuffs once again. My suspicions were confirmed only half way through the flight when an ear-splitting cry from a female passenger woke me from a nap. Turning my head, I noticed that the seat beside me was empty, that the beverage cart lay capsized, and that the stewardesses has cornered Ollie at the back of the airplane. When the woman screamed again, I knew that the worst had happened—that she had forgotten to lock the bathroom door and Ollie had pushed his way in. I sprang from my seat, shouldered my way past the stewardesses, and grabbed him firmly by the shirt collar. He did not struggle as I hauled him back to his seat nor did he flinch when I pulled out my handcuffs, encircled his wrist, and then fastened his arm to my belt. He in fact looked relieved, as though it were he who needed rescue, and he spent the rest of the flight leafing through an airline magazine with his free hand.

I released him from the handcuffs when we landed in Kauai. I had hoped to lose him at the airport, but he gripped my hand tightly as I walked through the concourse and followed behind me like a child. He was clearly overwhelmed by the bustle of airports and seemed hopeful that I would protect him from these new surroundings. "Tuck in your shirt," I said to him finally. He complied eagerly as though the gesture would convince me not to ditch him.

I rented a car, a white Ford Fiesta, and we headed towards the Na Pali Coastline: a rugged expanse of rain forests, waterfalls, and steep cliffs. I drove quickly, stopping only to visit a scuba shop where I bought him some goggles and a spear gun—not to provide him with tools of survival but to maximize the dangers to which he would be exposed. Perhaps he sensed my intentions because he hesitated before accepting the gifts and held them tentatively in his lap as we drove along.

After an hour, I turned off the highway and followed a narrow dirt road towards the coast. The rainforest embraced us like a church, caressing our eyes with a warm filtered light that appeared to sanctify my scheme. Even a wild rooster, perched cheekily by the roadside, shared in the pregnancy of the moment. *Son*, he seemed to say, *I screwed three hens before breakfast. Top that!!* Since the rascal was protected by state law, I rather hoped that Ollie would track him down and eat him—an infraction that would earn him several months in jail.

I pulled off the road when I spotted a steep hiking trail leading down the mountainside. "Let's go," I said, getting out of the car. I immediately began my descent towards the coast, not bothering to wait for him since I knew he would follow after me. I walked for an hour before stopping to rest on a low bluff overlooking a stretch of sand: a beach so isolated that it reminded me of *Fantasy Island*, a popular TV show from the eighties. I rested until Ollie caught up with me and noticed with satisfaction that he looked exhausted. "Hungry?" I said. He nodded and I handed him the spear gun and goggles. I pointed towards the ocean. "Fetch dinner," I said. "I'll start us up a fire."

I suspected that Ollie was not a good swimmer, but I knew also that he would not hesitate to go into the ocean. The desperation in his face, the perpetual plea in his eyes, convinced me that he was less afraid of drowning than the thought of displeasing me. We hiked the remaining half mile to the beach and I watched him critically as he dropped his clothes onto the sand. His body was slumped and anemically pale—so pale that he looked like an alien when he put on the goggles and walked stiffly towards the ocean. I watched him flounder among the waves and waited until I could see only the tip of his snorkel peaking above the water. I then dashed back to the forest and began my ascent towards the car.

A rooster crowed as I finished my climb: a piercing *Halleluiah* that seemed to trumpet my liberation. But the rascal was probably mocking me instead and so I left little to chance. After driving to the opposite side of the island, I registered at the Holiday Inn under an assumed name. I then began a more modest celebration: body surfing, deep sea fishing, and touring the local gardens. I stayed on the island for almost a week, changing my hotel each day—a tactic that disenthralled me after

I found myself involved in a rather cloying affair with a divorcée from Sacramento. Tiring of the woman's incessant chatter, I found it convenient not to tell her of my whereabouts when I made one of my daily hotel switches. On the seventh day of my vacation, when I had relaxed to the point of boredom, I took an early flight back to San Francisco.

The next morning, when I entered my kitchen, he was there. He was sitting at my kitchen table and buttering a piece of toast, and he did not seem to notice me when I walked into the room. His detachment was not dissimilar to my own: he was brown as a berry and smelled vaguely of fish so it took me a moment to recognize him. I stood there watching him for a minute or two and then sat down at the opposite side of the table.

"*Leave*," I said firmly.

He raised his head, smiled, and then put down the toast. Nodding pleasantly, he folded his hands in front of him and gazed compliantly in my direction. For a moment, I was afraid he would honor my request—a concession that would have only put off the problem. Since he would be certain to return, it was essential that I take full responsibility for his disappearance. And there were still many places I could dump him: the Australian outback, the Alaskan tundra—perhaps I could even sneak him aboard the NASA shuttle.

I retrieved the newspaper from the porch, returned to the table, and began reading through the travel section. While I read, he continued to butter the toast—an effort so prolonged that he looked like an artist touching up a painting. I was grateful for his predictability, his total simplicity of soul—qualities that assured me that his luck could not possibility endure. But his transparency in no way affected my resolve—my steely determination to get rid of him entirely.

He coughed and I looked at him, shaking my head while suppressing an inevitable pang of pity. This time, I knew what success would require and this time his frolic would end. I studied the paper and planned my campaign while he puttered around with the toast.

He has come to see me each day for the past month. He shows up in my kitchen every morning at 7:30 sharp and then makes his departure around noon. He seems oblivious to the intricacies of my plotting—a masterful plan that will relegate him once and for all to the graveyard of unwanted guests. And he continues to eat little: half a piece of toast with an occasional pat of butter is usually enough for him. On Sundays, he takes jam.

•

Fruits

And so there grew great tracks of wilderness,
Wherein the beast was ever more and more,
But man was less and less...
                                    —Alfred, Lord Tennyson

AFTER TIPPING THE CAB DRIVER, dabbing some lipstick onto her mouth, and taking a firm grip on her Samsonite boarding bag, Molly Groot waddled towards the Hoosier Park Casino. As she approached the casino, she saw her cab reflected in the glass doorway. It hadn't moved. Had she tipped the driver enough?—five dollars seemed plenty. Or had she made a mistake in mentioning the name of Jeb Judson, the man who had answered her on-line matrimonial ad? The man who had bought her plane ticket from Iowa to this modest community of Anderson, Indiana. The man she soon might marry. He had told her to meet him in the casino, where he liked to place bets on the horses. He had promised to be there by noon.

Molly did not know that much about Jeb—only that he was a Yale graduate, ruggedly handsome, and had once been a member of Skull and Bones, a very elite fraternity. He also had a PhD in organic chemistry and grew experimental crops for the government on his farm outside of Anderson. But at the mention of his name, the cab driver, a mealy-mouthed little man, had turned into a positive brute. "Jeb Judson," he had sneered. "We don't mention that person in these parts, ma'am. *Nobody does.*"

Surely, that cab driver was nothing but a crank. Jeb Judson seemed the perfect gentleman, having courted her for three months by e-mail before sending her the plane ticket. And he was better looking than Clint Eastwood if his photo could be believed. But it was the last of his e-mails that had made her swoon: he had promised her a fancy luncheon on his homestead veranda then a tour of his twenty thousand acre farm. And, should they tie the matrimonial knot, a life befitting a manor queen. And what a wicked sense of humor he had. Yesterday, she had asked him the title of his favorite book—a question she posed to all her on-line acquaintances. His answer, *Frankenstein*, had made her laugh out loud. But there was nothing droll about their rendezvous: he was clearly a very lonely man, tiring of bachelorhood and wanting a wife. And he was interested in her, Molly Groot, an overweight librarian pushing forty—a spinster with nothing to fuel her passion but picketing her local Wal-Mart. It was truly ironic that they were meeting in a casino. With a roll of the proverbial dice, her future could well be decided for the better.

Molly paused at the casino door. Looking over her shoulder, she heaved a sigh of relief. The cab had vanished. She was no longer being watched by that ill-tempered man.

What a depressed little town she had come to. On the cab ride from the airport, she had seen weedy sidewalks, barren storefronts, and gangs of hoodlums lurking on almost every corner. But the saddest sight of all was the abandoned General Motors plant and the boarded up headquarters of the United Auto Workers. The town seemed to exist as a relic—a ghost to better times. But wasn't she a bit of a wreck herself? Her push-up bra and wobbly pumps made her feel like a truck driver in drag. Thank God for Jeb Judson. He would carry her off like a bandit on a steed and bring out the real woman in her. Perhaps they could even have a child together.

Molly looked at her wristwatch and felt her face flush. Her heart began hammering like a rent collector at the door. It was fifteen minutes to noon.

Entering the casino, Molly suppressed a gasp. The glitter of wall-to-wall slot machines was truly a symphony of color and light—an utter contrast to the decaying town. And yet the casino was no less depressing: the hypnotic stares with which patrons watched the tumblers, as though the single pull of a lever might rescue them from food stamps and unemployment checks, hit a little too close to home. Holding her breath, Molly stood near the doorway and watched nervously for Jeb.

He strode through the door at 12:00 o'clock sharp. And her heart nearly stopped when she saw him. He looked exactly like his picture: a lean handsome man in his sixties with a shock of silver white hair. And his tight squint was positively presidential—in a George Bush sort of way.

How easy was his stride as he ambled towards her—how snug the fit of his Wrangler jeans. His sun-browned face and sharp blue eyes— his aura of rugged individualism—all suggested a marshal in a spaghetti western. And the political button on his shirt—*Keep our troops in Afghanistan*—only added to his gunfighter image. There were so many horrible bombings these days. Whatever was the world coming to?

He spotted her immediately. "Molly," he drawled. "*Molly Groot.*" When his hand squeezed her fingers, she felt her knees tremble. His palm was warm, dry, and surprisingly smooth for a farmer. His smile was broad but measured, as though he had been saving it only for her. As he patted her hand, she felt a stab of long dormant sexuality.

"J-Jeb," she stammered. "How funny you were. Of all books—*Frankenstein.*"

His laugh was deep but controlled, as though it were something he had borrowed. He did not strike her as a man who laughed often, and yet he was laughing for her. "You came anyhow, darlin'," he murmured. "I must have done something right."

"Against my better judgment," she teased. "Really, Jeb. *Frankenstein*?! That book is positively baroque."

He swallowed then looked at his boots. "I shouldn't have tried to impress a librarian. Not with the trash *I* read. "

She folded her arms, as though cross with him. But she was trying hard not to smile. How long had it been since she had flirted with a man? "Well, you have impressed me, Jeb Judson," she chirped. "But *not* with your choice of books. And *not*," she looked critically around the casino, "with your choice of pastimes."

He chuckled deeply and gazed across the room. On a giant television screen above the bar, a cluster of harness racers were jockeying for position along the backside of a track. "Suppose I let you reform me," he said. "Suppose I don't bet on the nags today?" He hooked his thumbs in his pockets and smirked. "There's nothing but losers in this place anyhow."

She looked at him coyly then laughed. "I'm not sure I want you reformed, Jeb Judson."

He arched his eyebrows. "You sure of that? Give a woman long enough, she's bound to find fault with a man."

"Oh really?" she teased. "It seems the *whole town* has found fault with you, Jeb. Just what are you up to on that farm of yours? A second campaign for Mitt Romney?"

He grinned and shook his head. "Let's just say it's a much bigger hustle. Let's just say it'll make me a rich man."

"And me a manor queen," she joked. "Or will you make me Frankenstein's bride instead?"

Was he blushing beneath that deep tan? she wondered. How easy it was to flirt with him. And how delicious that they now had their own private joke. But why were his eyes avoiding hers? And why did his smile seem so out of place? *He must not be used to courtship*, she thought. *He must want me to put him at ease.*

She rolled her eyes coquettishly and planted her hands on her hips. "Just why are you stalling, Jeb Judson?" she asked. "Didn't you invite me to lunch?"

He smiled and held out an elbow. "A lunch befitting a queen," he drawled. "Let's take a little drive, honey. Whaddya say?"

She hooked her hand on the crook of his arm. "I'd say you're a mighty big talker, Jeb. But I am rather famished—it's been a long trip. I hope you've prepared a big meal."

An hour later, she was sitting on the veranda of a rustic Italian-style farmhouse. Looking out on Jeb's estate, Molly felt deeply content. But her surroundings did not seem to merit her mood. Just how lonely was she to be moved by a place like this?

The estate, if one could call it that, consisted of half a dozen enormous silver barns—the kind that existed on factory farms where swine were force-fed in tight crowded pens, never to see the light of day. Close to the barns were several massive waste lagoons, gulches so discolored and septic that they looked like huge open wounds. And what was that smell that tugged at her lungs like an infant demanding attention? It smelled like a ripe diaper.

But at least they were sitting upwind from the scent. And the lunch, a thick stew that tasted like veal, was positively delicious. She was starting to feel tipsy from her third glass of wine and Jeb, dear dear Jeb, was gazing at her with his clear blue eyes—eyes the color of robin eggs. What a magnificent hunk he was. And didn't he say he was going to be rich? But how?

"Jeb," she whispered, her voice thick with wine. "What *is* going on out here?"

Slowly, as though performing surgery, Jeb topped off her glass. "If I told you," he joked, "I could never let you leave. But that might be best for us both."

A man with a mystery, Molly thought. *What more could a woman ask for?* She took a deep sip of wine. "Jeb, you're such a tease," she said. "I feel like a heroine in a Charlotte Bronte novel."

Jeb shrugged and burped. "I don't read that women's stuff much," he said. "*Brave New World*—that's more to my liking. And *1984*."

"Oh really?" she scoffed. "Such political tastes. No wonder you're working for the government."

He frowned and topped off his own glass of wine. "A lot of folks work for the government, darlin'. Gardeners, chemists, animal trainers. Some of 'em work right here." He gestured towards the barns where a handful of Mexican laborers were

61

ambling around, toting shovels and hoes. To Molly, they looked as charming as Snow White's seven dwarves.

"Let me guess," Molly teased. "You're growing an army of mutants. You'll use them to take over the country next year. Is that what you're up to, Jeb Judson?"

"No, darlin'," Jeb murmured, his voice rich with mirth. "Next month."

Is he serious? Molly wondered, a thought she could not totally dismiss. She remembered the words of the cab driver— "We don't mention that person in these parts, ma'am"—and a tremor invaded her spine. Had she come to the home of an eccentric? Had she thrown too much caution to the wind? Was the Internet really the best of places to seek the love of her life? But what did she have waiting for her back in Iowa? A studio apartment, a couple of cats, and a job that barely paid her rent. And how she ached for the touch of a man—her nipples were harder than bullets.

As she looked at Jeb's strong handsome face, a warmth crept into her heart. *He needs me to nurture him,* she thought. *He needs me to take his hand.*

But what was that curious sound she now heard? It was coming from one of the barns—a series of shrieks that sounded like a woman making love.

"J-Jeb," she stammered. "What's happening in there? Is somebody butchering a pig for our dinner?"

Jeb answered her firmly. "We don't kill creatures here," he said. "Not if we can help it. We think of them like family."

Creatures? Family? Her foolish panic awoke once again. Was he cloning animals? Was he tinkering about with genetics? Was he working with a hunchback named Igor who dug up graves at night? She put down her wine glass and drew a deep breath. *What nonsense I'm thinking. What crazy thoughts. Thank God I can blame them on the wine.*

Jeb smiled at her and her palms began to sweat. His eyes were so clear—so wise and embracing. How boorish of her to have doubted him.

"Darlin'," he said, "You came out here for a reason. Let's not lose sight of that."

"What reason might that be, Jeb Judson?"

"Your biological clock is ticking. An' it's almost out of time."

"Do I really seem so desperate?" she snapped. She pretended to frown, but the effort was useless. Her eyes were now glittery with tears.

Jeb looked at her reassuringly then cupped her chin with his fingers and thumb. "Yes, darlin', you do," he said matter-of-factly. "Why do you think I sent for you? Desperate women don't judge their men."

"Oh, really?" she said. She turned her head away from him. "With you one might make an exception, Jeb Judson. Did you bring me all this way because you thought I might be *desperate*?"

"Times are tough—folks are upset. A man needs to take comfort where he can find it."

"Even from desperate librarians?" she muttered. "You must have a rather dark side to you, Jeb, if frumps are the best you can do."

He shook his head sadly and patted her cheek. "Do I scare you that much, honey?"

"You scare me a little bit, Jeb. But you intrigue me even more." She placed the palm of her hand on his wrist. "And I have been alone such a very long time."

Jeb laughed and rose slowly from his chair. "Let's have a little adventure. It's time you met the family."

As she followed Jeb to the nearest barn, Molly felt as though she were crossing an ocean. She remembered a line from *Julius Caesar*, her favorite Shakespearian play. *And we must take the current where it serves...* But how would this current serve her? Would it lead her to love and good fortune or to something she'd rather not see? Even Jeb seemed to sense the pregnancy of the moment. His face had lost its ironic smirk and had hardened into a soldierly resolve.

When they reached the barn, Jeb nodded to a Mexican laborer. Slowly, as though cracking a safe, the man unlocked the door. Molly smelled the interior of the barn before she saw it—a smell so strong that it made her nose itch. Her eyes began to water, her head began to swim, and she felt as though she were walking in quicksand. And so it seemed strange, when she entered the barn, that she saw little reason to panic. Inside the barn was a large shallow field beneath rows of low-hanging grow lights. And peeking through the ruts in the soil were a few dozen orange balls the size of cantaloupes. Men in white lab coats were ducking beneath the grow lights, adjusting sprinklers and carefully inspecting the balls. *Is this what had me so worried?* she wondered. *A silly pumpkin patch?* She was not at all impressed.

"Jeb," she said when she was able to draw a breath. "You call this an adventure?"

"We call it our nursery," Jeb replied. "Here is where we plant the mutants. Where we let 'em ripen like fruit on the vine."

He took her by the elbow and guided her onto the field. The damp earth pulled stubbornly at her pumps, and it was all she could do not to trip. Releasing her elbow, Jeb paused for a moment then knelt beside one of the larger balls. He squeezed it tenderly, as though fondling a breast, then began to dig gently with his fingers. "Prepare yourself, darlin'," he said. "This is all the adventure you're ever gonna need."

Jeb's fingers blackened from the soil and the ball began to loosen. As he started to pull it from the ground, Molly suppressed a gasp. It was not a pumpkin—it was a little head, complete with bulging eyes, a scrunched up nose, and a wide rather slobbery-looking mouth. A pear-shaped body followed the head as Jeb continued to tug—a body with a ropey umbilical cord and tiny hands and feet. It was the size of a newborn baby.

"This one's ready for harvesting," Jeb announced. He pulled a box cutter from his pants pocket, pushing out the blade as he did so, then he cut the umbilical cord in two. A substance that looked like green custard dribbled onto the ground. After rinsing the creature under a sprinkler, Jeb mopped it dry with a handkerchief and handed it to Molly.

"The smell will soon go away," he said. "But don't be holdin' it too long. We don't want it thinking you're its mother."

Molly clutched the thing with shaking hands, too startled to let it drop. The creature was cute, in a French Bulldog sort of way, but how ridiculous to think she might pose as its mother. Its body was cold, its skin was rough, its fingers were wiggling like worms. And its wide gaping mouth was emitting a sound that set her teeth on edge. "*Eeek, eeek, eeeek,*" it went, a noise just like chalk being scraped along a blackboard. And it smelled so strongly of fertilizer that it was all she could do not to sneeze.

Molly held the creature away from her. "Take it!" she said. "Take it away! It needs a cage, not a mother, Jeb."

As Jeb took the thing back, tucking it beneath his elbow, she remembered a Biblical quote. *Ye shall know them by their fruits.* She was not at all religious—she rarely went to church—and so she now realized the full impact of her shock. If runts like that thing were the fruits of Jeb's labor—cold little cretins that smelled like an outhouse—he might not be the nicest of men.

She started to sob. "J-Jeb, how could you? It looks like a freak. It smells like a toilet."

Jeb grinned sheepishly then shrugged. "The whole country's in the crapper, darlin'. That's why we need desperate measures. And desperate women too."

"You sound like you just made a deal with the devil."

Jeb flushed like a scolded schoolboy, a sight so touching that she knew she was going to forgive him. He seemed so lonely, so in need of companionship, that she wanted to pull him tightly to her breast. But when he spoke to her again, her stomach knotted. "You sound like an exorcist, darlin'," he said. "Don't turn away the devil until you've heard his offer."

"W-what do you even feed it?" she asked; it was all she could think of to say.

Holding the podling under his arm, Jeb began stroking its head. "We raise 'em on dog food," he said with a smirk. "It'll reach its full growth in six short weeks. That's when we start training them."

"Training them?" Molly muttered. "Training them to do what?" As she watched the thing squirm in Jeb's hands, her mind began to rebel. *Was he actually fond of that little gremlin? Did he think she would find it endearing as well?* But her heart was starting to bleed for him, and she knew she was falling in love. What a sad and lonely man he must be to regard such a thing as a pet. How badly he needed a good woman's love to save him from himself.

"Darlin'," he said, "let's get on with our tour. I've told you the answer already."

Smiling thinly, Jeb scratched the creatures belly. *"Eeek, eeeek, EEEEK,"* it went, like a mouse in a trap.

As he walked her to another barn, Jeb took her hand in his. A chorus of squawks was coming from the barn, as though circular saws were biting into timber. The squawks were so raw, so primitive and sharp, that they stung the fillings in her teeth.

Jeb unlocked the door to the barn. "We're breaking these in for the auto plant," he said. "They get a bit feisty at first, but they go with the program soon enough."

Jeb's voice had lost its gentleness and now sounded smug and pedantic. *Has he actually bested the devil?* thought Molly. *How could that possibly be? He's so clearly a man cut off from the world—a broken, discarded soul.* As Jeb pushed open the door to the barn, generous tears filled her eyes.

Her tenderness for Jeb vanished the moment she stepped into the barn. Never had she seen anything remotely like this. A mob of the freaks, each six and a half feet tall, was standing alongside a long conveyer belt. Their eyes were glassy, their shoulders were sagging, their bodies were pitted with large crusty sores. Behind them stood more men in lab coats—men clutching hypodermic syringes and cattle prods. The men watched closely as the creatures lifted chassis, engine blocks, and tires from the conveyor belt and lugged them to nearby tables. When one of them deposited its load on a table, it was rewarded with an injection. *Miracle-Gro,* Molly guessed, *or maybe some kind of sedative.* If one dropped its burden, a cattle prod stung it. *"Rawk, rawk, RAWK,"* cried the things when given electrical shocks. They sounded like angry crows.

Jeb squeezed her hand and beamed. "Next month," he said, "the GM plant will reopen. We'll be fitting these fellas with memory chips—they'll be working the robot arms. If things work out as planned, the entire auto industry will return to America."

Molly felt as though someone had punched her and run away with her purse. How alarming to know she'd been charmed by a man who merited only contempt. *What an elitist. What a swine. I must have been crazy to want him. I must have been out of my mind.* "Those poor, poor creatures..." she mumbled, her tongue so dry she could barely form the words. It was only a perverse fascination that kept her from leaving Jeb's side.

Oblivious to her heartbreak, Jeb continued to lecture. "Low maintenance would better describe them," he said. "No more health care to pay, no more strikes to settle, no more pensions to drain away the budget. These go-getters work eighteen hours a day and make good fertilizer when they die. The stockholders will be overjoyed."

"No more jobs for the people in town," Molly blurted, a remark so reflexive that she instantly regretted it. Jeb's attitude had grown so superior, his manner so professorial, that she felt like a child who had scattered her toys and neglected to put them away. She wanted to cry on his chest, but she felt too stunned to move.

Jeb sucked a tooth and shrugged. "The people," he muttered, "are cattle as well. This isn't that big a transition."

Before Molly could reply, a commotion arose at the other end of the barn. A few of the freaks—all blazing with sores—were standing in a row. They were bound to one another with waist chains and watching a cluster of tackling dummies. They were squawking excitedly among themselves.

"Watch this," Jeb instructed. He removed a whistle from his back pocket, put it to his lips, and blew. At the chirp of the whistle, the things lowered their heads and assembled into a flying wedge. Jeb blew the whistle a second time and they lumbered towards the dummies. The sound of their skulls bashing foam thudded throughout the barn.

"There's bound to be demonstrators," Jeb said. "Those UAW shirkers who drove the industry abroad. This'll send them packing."

"And so you're a strike breaker too?!" Molly cried. Her mind was reeling, her senses were numb, but she could not tear her eyes from the sight.

Jeb grinned. "There will be no more strikes—no one's getting his job back. Scab labor is going to take over."

Molly held her face between her hands. What a revolting man he was. What a self-entitled boar. If he had been born in the eighteenth century, he'd have surely been a slave owner. "Jeb, take me from here," she sobbed—it was all she could manage to utter.

Jeb smiled kindly and cleared his throat. His face had lost all self-consciousness now and he seemed to be looking at her from a very great distance. *What a child you still are*, his eyes seemed to say. *How much you still have to learn.* "Let's go back to the house, my darlin'," he said. "You haven't had dessert."

"Devils food cake!" Molly cried. "You're serving me devil's food cake?!" Jeb finished cutting the rich chocolate cake and handed her a piece. There was not a trace of irony in his face.

They were sitting at a coffee table inside an enormous study. The walls were lined with dozens of bookcases, all of them crammed full of books. There were science logs, history books, manuals on animal husbandry. There were texts on organic farming, molecular biology, and plant pathology. There were rows and rows of philosophy books: Spinoza, Kant, Spencer, Nietzsche filled up two whole shelves. There were endless volumes of literature: Shakespeare, Homer, Chaucer, Goethe—the titles went on and on. There was even a sagging bookcase devoted entirely to erotica. Molly's head began to ache.

Jeb smiled at her reassuringly and took a bite of cake. "Yes, darlin'," he said. "I've read every one of them. Some I've read several times." He looked at her thoughtfully, took a slow breath, then he spoke as though reading out loud. "'Football, films, and beer filled the horizons of their minds.' That's from George Orwell, *1984*. I think it describes the goddamn people you feel such sympathy for."

Molly shook her head and tried to scowl, but could not hide the shock in her face. "So what does that make *you*, Jeb?" she snapped. "An *educated* monster?"

"Maybe," Jeb chuckled, his mouth full of cake. "But at least I've impressed a librarian."

"Have you?" she spat. "Have you really?" She did not wish to make that concession to him, and yet she was deeply in awe. Clearly this man, this very strange man, was far better read than she would ever be. Perhaps, he was even smarter. Perhaps, he was a genius.

Determined to puncture his maddening pride, she sniped at him again. "What good have all these books done you, Jeb, if you treat those poor things like slaves?"

"Darlin'," Jeb said, "there's a far bigger picture." He burped, rose from his chair, and wandered over to one of the bookcases. He fingered the books as though tuning a piano then recited some titles out loud. "*Commodore: The Life of Cornelius Vanderbilt. Last Man Standing: The Ascent of J.P. Morgan. Today and Tomorrow: The Autobiography of Henry Ford*." He looked at her kindly and folded his arms; his eyes were twinkling like stars. "These men were monsters—all of them. But they rose above the horde. And they took the country to places nobody could have imagined."

My God, Molly thought. *What an ego he has.* How could I ever have though of reforming this dreadful, impossible man? "Jeb, there's cake on your chin," she murmured. "Besides that, you sound like Satan."

"Devils are all around us," Jeb shrugged—he rubbed the cake from his chin. "Not all of them can be bargained with. Not all will bother to court you. Better we should out-monster them than allow them to eat us alive."

Oh no! Molly thought. *He's a Nietzsche nut too.* She had always hated that little German prude. His rants about apes, man, and the superman to come were so pompous, so smug, so

69

utterly contemptuous. *Why—out of all the books in his study— did Jeb have to quote from Nietzsche?!*

"So you're the ascender of man," she joked. "I always wondered what he would look like."

Jeb laughed and shook his head. "I'm not that ambitious, darlin'," he said. "I wish only to be a monster."

Molly felt her skin crawl. The man was insane, totally insane—no wonder he was alone. And yet his eyes, his clear blue eyes, were as tranquil as a lake. It was the accommodation in his eyes—the gentleness with which he now looked at her— that gave her the courage to lecture him. "The townspeople are all against you, Jeb. They think you're a monster already."

He chuckled proudly and smirked. "I would only be worried if they were my friends."

More Nietzsche, she thought; her fists tightened into balls. "Must you keep quoting that crass little German? What are your thoughts, Jeb. What is inside that head of yours?"

He returned to his chair, slowly sat down, and picked up the remainder of his cake. He poked at the cake as though touching up a sculpture then put it back on the coffee table. It was a minute before he spoke. "I'm a jaded man, darlin'," he said. "I am drunk with power, poisoned with knowledge, callous to all that I touch. But the people, without even trying, are far greater monsters than me."

Look into the abyss, Molly remembered, *and the abyss will look into you.* Was that vain little Kraut actually right about something? Was the nihilism in Jeb Judson's eyes about to seep into her soul? The thought only made her angrier. "Oh really?" she muttered. "Just what is their sin?"

"Ignorance," replied Jeb—the word struck her like a hammer. "Willful, church-bred ignorance. They breed, they doze, they die—that is all. Like cattle on a plain."

Molly could hardly believe her own thoughts. Did this arrogant man, this self-centered pig, believe he was some kind of savior? "You tether innocent creatures," she stammered. "You bury their babies in dirt."

Jeb looked at her sharply and glared. How quickly his moods changed. "Knowledge can kill you," he said with a shrug.

"Nietzsche probably died of it. But it also can make you a brute."

"Just what do you mean by that?" Molly snapped.

"I plan to tether the people as well. Lead 'em around by the nose. Their kind of monster we cannot empower—the world is too dangerous a place."

He rose from his chair, cracked his knuckles, then turned on a small television. "Nietzsche had it wrong," he said. "Mankind will never ascend. Not..." An NFL playoff game was on—a contest between the Titans and the Patriots. The stadium was packed with fifty thousand people, all of them on their feet screaming. He looked at the game disgustedly then turned the television off. "Not," he repeated, "'til they can get that excited over things that really matter."

Despite the condescension in Jeb Judson's face, Molly felt a stirring in her heart. Was she, an unstable female, being swayed by this alpha brute? *Your damn bitch is having puppies in my brain.* This line from *East of Eden*, a novel she adored, flashed like a warning sign through her head. Utterly ashamed of herself, she buried her face in her hands.

She felt Jeb's hand on her shoulder, a gentle protective touch. "Finish your cake, my darlin," he said. "There's much I still have to show you."

He led her to a third barn. The door was sealed shut by a heavy iron bar and a padlock the size of her fist. Jeb opened the lock with a thick key and they entered a small sally port. Beyond the inner door, Molly heard ravenous sounds: chomping, gulping, slurping noises that chilled her to the marrow. Her fear only increased when Jeb unlocked a gun cabinet and removed a semiautomatic pistol. He slapped a magazine into the grip.

"Stay close beside me," he ordered. "*Whatever happens.*"

He tucked the handgun behind his belt then unlocked the inner door. As they walked into the barn, Molly clutched his elbow and gasped. In front of them was a deeply ploughed field—a field also fitted with grow lights and incidental hoses. But poking through the topsoil were hundreds and hundreds of fierce-looking orange heads. The heads were aligned in rows,

71

like troops awaiting inspection, and some of them were devouring the craniums in front of them.

Jeb shook his head; he seemed to be embarrassed. "A crop of adolescents," he said. "Guess we planted 'em too closely together."

Molly could only shudder and stare. What on earth had possessed her to follow Jeb into this barn?

"We've injected these with steroids," Jeb went on. "They're going to fight our wars. Once they've reached their full growth, that is, and we've put memory chips in their heads."

"Are they really?" Molly asked. She wanted to cover her eyes. She wanted to vomit her cake. "I find the very sight of them revolting."

"Soldiers *should* be revolting," Jeb said. "One look at these chaps and our enemies will be sweating in their turbans. It'll make 'em think twice about taking back their oilfields."

Molly released Jeb's elbow and gasped. She was ready to bolt from the barn, but her legs felt rubbery and spent. "And so you're a warmonger too," she stammered. "Or is that a war profiteer?"

Jeb shrugged and winked. "I'm more of a war economist," he said. "There's not much profit in war anymore, but at least we can trim the tab. These suckers will fight for nothing and they like to get down in the dirt." He chuckled at his own joke and gazed serenely at the heads. "No more hospital expenses for the wounded," he said. "No more military pensions. No more lawsuits from veterans who have outlived their usefulness."

Molly could feel her nails stabbing her palms. She wanted to claw out Jeb's eyes. "So you're going to replace them with *cannibals*," she cried. "Jeb, I find you disgusting."

"Do you, darlin'?" Jeb buried a chuckle. "We're already fighting our wars by proxy—this isn't that big a step. And once we lower the goddamn cost, we can fight our wars to win."

Molly clenched her teeth. *He's a murderer,* she thought. *A cold blooded calculating murderer.* "Those beastly, beastly wars!" she cried. "I never ever believed in them!"

"No one believes in our wars," Jeb shrugged. "Not enough to fight 'em anyhow. But our enemies are growing stronger—

they want their oilfields back." He cleared his throat and spat contemptuously. "If you don't want us killing off Arabs, darlin', give up your goddamn car. You can't have it both ways."

"You're disgusting," cried Molly. "You're evil and cold. Somebody needs to stop you, Jeb Judson."

"And *who* is going to stop me?" Jeb laughed. "Your spoiled and precious people?"

"*Somebody* has to stop you. This is a crime against God!"

"God's not as proactive as me," Jeb shrugged. "And the people won't give a hoot. If we give 'em their gas guzzling cars, if we give them their baseball and beer, if we give 'em their sitcoms and TiVo, they'll stay happy as pigs in shit. Hell," Jeb blew his nose and laughed. "Once we've lowered the price of gas, we won't even have to beat up demonstrators..."

A predatory squawk interrupted Jeb's speech. He yanked the gun from his pants.

"Get behind me!" he ordered. He quickly racked the slide then went into a shooter's crouch. "Behind me!" he repeated. "Plug up your ears!"

Only then did Molly realize that one of those vile little gluttons was loose. Somehow, while she was scolding Jeb, it had managed to uproot itself from the ground. It's eyes were blazing, its jaws were snapping, and it was tottering towards them on newly discovered legs. "*Raaawk!*" it cried, a soulless sound like a nail being ripped from a coffin.

POW.

The podling kept lumbering towards them.

POW.

The beastly thing barely flinched.

POW POW.

Molly jammed her fingers into her ears. "*Kill it,*" she screamed. "*Kill it, Jeb.*" The little brute seemed unstoppable.

Pow Pow... Pow.

As the seventh shot echoed, the thing stopped walking. Its legs began to liquefy, then it thudded to the ground. Even so, its jaws, pasty with pulp, continued to gnaw and snap.

Molly removed her fingers from her ears. She felt stunned, as though she had just walked away from a car crash. But her blood still boiled when she looked at Jeb. "For a war economist," she accused, "you're really not much of a shot."

Jeb grinned. "They have seven nerve centers," he said. "Two are in their ankles, two are in their knees, three more are in their head. You gotta hit each one if you want to take them out." Setting the safety catch, he tucked the pistol back into his pants. "Once we've programmed them properly, they'll attack only towelheads. They'll blow 'em to bits with grenades then gobble up their brains. Put the fear of Allah in 'em."

Please God, make him stop talking, Molly thought. *Can't he see I'm about to be sick?*

With morbid pride, Jeb kept lecturing. "They make great suicide bombers too. We'll wire them up with TNT then detonate 'em by remote control."

"J-Jeb," Molly stammered, her knees were shaking. "If you care for me at *all*, you will *stop* this conversation."

Jeb's eyes began to soften and he took her by the arm. "Very well, darlin'. I'll say nothing more. But the tour's not over *yet*."

Slowly, as though walking through smoke, Molly followed Jeb to yet another barn. Her horror had morphed into an eerie enthrallment—the same captivation she'd felt when she'd first read Dante's *Inferno*. What else did this man have to show her—what new and unprecedented horrors? She felt as though she were hypnotized.

Jeb unlocked a fourth barn and they walked inside. There were fifty or so creatures in the barn, all of them fully grown, and they looked like a failed experiment. Their craniums were uncommonly small and long drooling tongues were hanging from their mouths. "*Quack,*" they kept crying. "*Quack, quack, quack.*" They looked as though they were trying to utter words.

"These will be our politicians," Jeb said. "They're on a break now, but speech therapists are working with them ten hours a day. That's why their tongues are so big."

"Politicians?!" Molly cried. She could not believe her ears. "Jeb, is this some kind of joke?"

"Mayors, congressmen, senators, you name it. The politicians in office now pretty much stay in line, but one of 'em gets a wild hair now and then. Obama's a perfect example—what with his blocking the Keystone pipeline. And his goddamn socialized medicine. He's forgotten he's bought and paid for."

Molly felt laughter welling up inside her—sunless, hysterical mirth. The creatures looked so comical, she could hardly hold it in. "Jeb, do you hear what you're saying?" she giggled. "Who would ever vote for these clownish things?"

"As long as they're preaching the politics of fear, it won't matter a damn what they look like." Jeb placed his whistle between his lips. "Listen," he said.

At the blast of the whistle, the mob began to babble. "*You are under attack,*" they cried out in unison. "*Quack, quack, quack. You are under attack.*"

One of them, apparently better schooled than the rest, parroted several sentences. "*The government will protect you. The government will make things right. Just give it all your money. And give it all your rights.*"

Jeb put away the whistle and smirked. "Not a wayward thought among 'em," he said. "How about that?"

Molly covered her ears with her hands. The Pavlovian clamor—the horrid *quack quack quacks*—were making her head buzz. But her palms were unable to shut out the sounds—she could hear yet another voice: a monotonous riveting croak that reminded her of a frog. "*Stop all handouts,*" it droned. "*Don't control businesses.*" One of the freaks, a yard shorter than the rest, was speaking directly to her. It's eyes were wide, its nostrils were flaring, its face was a mask of self-righteous composure. "What on earth is *that*?" she screamed.

Jeb stuck out his chest and grinned. "*That* is a special project," he said. "A Clarence Thomas replica." He pushed the dwarf away from her then patted it on the head. "*Clarence Thomas*—think of it. The most conservative, program averse, pull-yourself-up-by-your-bootstraps jurist ever to pass the bar. If we get eight more like him on the bench, the people—as a class—will be completely disenfranchised."

75

Oh judgment, Molly thought, *you have fled to brutish beasts!* Was there no limit to this man's madness—no bounds to his swinish ambitions? And would the people—the stupid, lotus eating people—really allow him to succeed? As she looked at Jeb's face, his crafty intelligent face, she feared that the answer was yes. *The people are cattle,* his eyes reminded her. *And cattle should stay in herds.*

"Jeb," she cried. "Jeb, this is total insanity."

"Well and good," Jeb replied. "That'll push things along. You can't stop a madness whose hour has come."

He put his whistle to his lips and blew it once again. The voices grew even louder.

"YOU ARE UNDER ATTACK!"

"WE'VE GOT YOUR BACK!"

"THERE'S NOTHING YOU'LL LACK!"

"QUACK, QUACK, QUACK!"

As she started to faint, Molly heard random laughter—laughter that seemed to arise from a void. And so she did not recognize it as her own.

She recovered on a bench outside of the barn. Jeb Judson was patting her cheek. "Darlin'," he said, "The tour is almost done. But maybe you've reached your limit."

As she stared at his hawkish attractive face, her eyes hardened with resolve. "Show me the rest!" she commanded. Why she said that she did not know. Perhaps it was the fastidiousness in her soul, her librarian's need to delimit and define. Or maybe she needed a complete inventory of the man to totally cast him out of her life. After all, he was still one hell of a hunk.

"Show me the rest!" she repeated. Just one more outrage ought to do it. Just one more horror ought to kill her affection for him entirely.

"Very well," Jeb replied. He helped her to her feet. Taking her by the hand, he guided her to a fifth barn. She waited impatiently while he unlocked the door.

As they entered the barn, Molly felt her jaw drop. The freaks in this barn were hourglass-shaped and their skin was pale and smooth. With their heroic busts and swelling hips, with their hair tumbling down to their tiny waists, they looked like lewd parodies of women. They were watching Jeb as he closed the barn door, appraising him like dogs smelling meat.

"These," Jeb explained, "are our sex toys."

This has to be the final straw, Molly thought. *He's obviously a pervert, to boot.*

Reading her thoughts, Jeb stifled a chuckle. "They're for the goddamn people—not me," he said. "A gift to make sure they keep out of our hair."

"A gift for pigs just *like* you," Molly said. "What will the wives say?"

"They'll be too busy competing for their men. Watch."

Jeb put the whistle to his lips and blew. Immediately, the things fell onto their backs and began thrusting their hips into the air. *"Baby, baby, baby!"* they shrieked. *"Nobody does it like you!!"*

Molly could stand it no more. The vulgarity of the display— it's utter depravity—blew away the last of her reserve. "You sexist!" she cried. "You Stepford pig. Is *that* what you think of women?! Is *that* what you want me to do?!"

"No, darlin'," said Jeb. He took her hand gently in his. "You I will treat like a queen."

Snatching her hand from Jeb's grasp, Molly slapped him across the face. The creatures, aroused by the sound of the blow, began thrusting their hips even harder. *"SPANK ME, SPANK ME, DADDY!"* they cried. *"NOBODY DOES IT LIKE YOU!"*

"Why?!" Molly sputtered, her eyes bright with tears. "Why *this*, Jeb?!"

Jeb shrugged. "A little insurance to keep folks distracted. Beer, films, and sports may not always be enough. But sex," he rubbed his cheek and winked conspiratorially. "Nothing'll make people dumber than sex."

"But this is so insulting..."

Jeb laughed. "The country's already obsessed with sex. Films, clothes, commercials—you name it, it's there. This will help us secure our power and save our beloved land."

77

He clapped his hands twice. "That'll do!" he instructed. The creatures shuddered orgastically then collapsed in exhausted heaps. But they continued to plead and babble as he walked Molly out of the barn. *"Daddy, daddy, daddy,"* they cooed. *"Nobody does it like you."*

She sat silently on Jeb's veranda, clutching another glass of wine. The sun had set but an afterglow lingered and the horizon looked like a bruise. Molly stared hypnotically at the barns, ignoring the bowl of mangos and pears that Jeb had set beside her.

"Don't think the worst of me, darlin'," Jeb said. "Have a piece of fruit."

Molly put down her wine glass and dabbed her eyes with a Kleenex. "Just what do you want with me, Jeb?"

Jeb cupped her hand lovingly in his. "I want you to be my wife," he said. "I want you to give me a son."

"Those loathsome, loathsome creatures you're raising."

He squeezed her hand gently and smiled. "A towering, godless, unblinking son who will one day manage all this." Releasing her hand as though freeing a bird, he pointed towards the barns. "A son to make Nietzsche proud."

Jeb fumbled in his pocket, retrieving a small leather case. He opened it slowly and showed her the ring. The diamond was as big as her knuckle and it winked in the cold evening light. "Marry me, dear, and I'll make you my queen."

As she looked at his face, his strong paternal face, her anger melted like snow. His gaze was so warm and protective, his eyes so clear and blue.

She slipped the ring onto her finger and sighed.

"Shall we set a date?" she said.

•

The Outback

TWO DROVERS WERE CAMPED in a dense grove of fig trees. While the shorthorns grazed on a swath of Mitchell grass, the men rested on their swags. A dingo watched them from the edge of the grove.

Jim Cooper, a rangy stockman with a squint, poked a stick at the billycan as though urging it to come to a boil. But the crackle of the scrubwood was faint and unpromising. A livelier sound came from the flying foxes high overhead—a thick cloud of rat-sized rodents, which, at a distance, looked almost like birds.

Tom Hemmings brushed at the flies dotting his face and gazed at the dingo. The animal unnerved him, he had to admit. Although comely and small, with permanently cocked ears, it exhibited none of the sociability he associated with dogs. Its gaze was opportunistic, not fawning, and it appeared to have taken measure of the rifle in Jim's hand, a .30-06 Remington he had pulled from the scabbard on his saddle.

"They're little yellow bah-sterds," Jim muttered, removing a slim cartridge from his hip pocket and coaxing it into the breach. "Only bugger I know of who will ravage without good cause. In Queensland they put up special fences to keep 'em away from the sheep, but it don't do much good. The buggers know how to dig under fences. And they'll wipe out a flock of sheep just for bloody sport."

"Are there bounties on them?" Tom asked. He suspected the question was naïve, but he was determined to learn all he could about the Northern Territory of Australia, his new homeland since dropping out of an Ohio college six months ago. The land was so stark and irrepressible that it would never attain statehood.

"There are in Queensland," Jim said. "A dingo scalp there fetches a hundred quid in some parts. But in the Territory they can run amok for all anyone seems to care."

"That speaks well for the Territory," Tom said. "They put up with mongrels here."

Jim grinned. "They do at that. But a dingo ain't a mongrel. A pure-bred devilment is what he is." He released the safety and sighted the long barrel in the direction of the dingo. The animal, as though charmed, continued to watch them. Dissatisfied with the range, Jim lowered the rifle to his lap

"So what were you doing in Sydney?" he asked. "Catching up on your rooting?"

"I did lose my cherry there," Tom said, a dubious boast for a twenty-one-year-old man. But he hoped the turn in conversation would distract Jim from the dingo. Tom did not want the animal shot.

"Good on ya," Jim said. "You'll have Buckley's chance of it in the Territory—not with twenty blokes for every blooming sheila here. Course, you could get a bit on the reservations—if you don't mind jockeying a darkie, that is. The lubras will do you there for a swig of plock, they will."

"Have you spent much on plock?"

"Haven't lately," Jim chuckled. "But I have jockeyed me share of 'em. Can't say it did me any harm either. There's not much that separates strumpets, you know. They're about all the same in the dark."

Tom sighed deeply. He envied Jim's devil-may-care attitude—a perverse inner harmony to which he could only aspire. His companion in Sydney, a prostitute named Jenny, had not been so easy for him to dismiss. He regretted missing her as much as he did, yet he found her memory more sustaining than her company had been. With the practical gaze of a hustler, she had looked without sentiment into his soul.

"You're wild, Thomas," she had told him one day. "And that's really all that can be said about it. Not that you seem that way, mind you. You're as skinny as a bloody boong and I doubt that you know how to make love at all. But that really doesn't change matters, does it? A law unto yourself, you are, and as wild as the blooming sea."

He had parted company with her on a rainy morning several weeks before arriving in the Territory, as abruptly as he had once burned his draft card. He had left her asleep in a King's Cross boarding house, not wishing to wake her. They had argued the day before and he did not wish to renew the argument. But he had sent her his address at Birdstone Cattle Station and, in spite of himself, looked forward to the arrival of the weekly mailbag from Darwin. She had told him once that she wrote to Servicemen in Vietnam, so he hoped she would be as charitable to him.

The dingo yawned as the billycan steamed. Jim put down the rifle. Moving awkwardly, he dangled the billy from a twig and carried it to his tucker-bag. After smothering the steam with a fistful of tea leaves, Jim stirred the concoction with a swirl of his finger and set it aside to brew.

"I don't do well with women," Tom blurted. "They're too damn clingy."

"Women," Jim spat. "They're more trouble than they're worth, if ya ask me. The palm of your hand will do you no worse a job and you won't end up catching the clap from it." He yanked two tin cups from the tucker-bag and set them upright on the ground. The billy he handled more carefully, pinching the base with a rag to avoid being singed by the scalding metal. He filled only one of the cups before setting the billy back on the ground. Squatting back down, he sipped cautiously at the hot tea.

"It's a fair dinkum life here without 'em," he said. "If you can handle the heat and the flies. Good place for a draft dodger, anyhow. The authorities won't hunt a bloke down in the Never Never. Wouldn't be much point to it, would there?"

"Have you given them a reason?" Tom asked. Watching the ambivalence with which Jim sipped the tea, he decided he did not want any.

Jim nodded. "I have at that," he said. "Had a bit of a donnybrook in a Darwin pub last month and they hauled me in front of the magistrate. But he cut me loose the same day, he did. Said I coulda gone to Fannie Bay Jail, but they needed it for the boongs."

"Was it over a woman?"

"No fear," Jim replied. "What I done was punch a little Englishman who let his mouth override his arse. 'Stead of standing me a beer when it was over, like any gentleman woulda done, the pommy bah-sterd went to the cop shop and pressed charges. Cost me a pretty quid, he did, but I'm not saying it wasn't worth it." He shrugged like a martyr and shook his head stoically. He took another sip of the tea. "But I did get locked up in Brisbane. Spent two years in the Boggo Road Jail. That seems as far back as the Dreamtime, it does."

"That's a lot for a brawl," Tom muttered. He spoke angrily, perhaps because the Outback, with its endless expanse of mudflats, bull dust, and crocodile-infested swamps, had forged an uncommon bond between them—a willingness, on behalf of either, to honor the misadventures of the other.

"Guess I showed 'em me arse." Jim laughed. "Rape of a minor, they called it, but a fair go is what it was—a little Tasmanian tart who lied about her age. She did five other blokes the same night she fucked me, then tried to charge me a tenner for stirring sloppy seconds. Ran straight to the cop shop when I wouldn't cough it up."

Tom nodded with genuine sympathy, not doubting for a moment the merit of Jim's story and the shortsightedness of the judge who had taken his liberty. That Jim's liberty was a shoddy affair—a continuum of whoring, drunkenness, and cattle rustling—did not devalue it in the slightest.

Jim finished the tea with a heavy gulp and tossed the wet dregs on the ground. "My oath," he remarked, "it's a fair dinkum life out here. If a bloke don't go troppo, that is."

Shaking his head, Jim picked the rifle back up. He blew sharply upon the muzzle, clearing the dust from the sight—an extravagant gesture since the dingo was no longer visible.

Removing a soiled handkerchief from his pocket, he began to wipe the barrel clean.

"It appears he lucked out."

"Would you want to wager on it?" Jim said. "I'm bettin' a quid I get a shot off yet. They're persistent little buggers when they get a notion into their heads."

Soon the barrel was gleaming, spitting off sunlight. Jim cradled it lovingly. His attention to the weapon seemed almost licentious—a reminder to Tom that Outback dwellers were all a little crazy. What troubled Tom, however, was not Jim's eccentricity so much as his own desire to emulate him.

Watching Jim stroke the rifle, caressing it as though it were a lover, Tom was reminded of the extent of his own displacement. He remembered an old couple with grandchildren in New South Wales who had picked him up on the Pacific Highway after the Land Rover he bought in Sydney broke down. They had taken him to their home, a large bungalow in Lismore, where he had stayed for less than a day. They had wanted him to stay longer, but the strain of making conversation had been too high a price to pay for clean sheets and warm food. He had left the next day before sunrise and hitchhiked to Brisbane, where he had hired on with the Birdstone Cattle Corporation. He remembered the utter relief of returning to the open road. The paradox of his departure—that he found less to be missed in empty spaces—had not escaped him.

The shot, when it came, seemed as impotent as a firecracker, so Tom was surprised by the sudden revelry of the flying foxes. A distant sprout of dust marked the course the bullet had taken. Well beyond the dust, he could see the disappearing hindquarters of the dingo. It consoled him—the wide margin by which the animal had eluded the slug—and he wondered for a moment if Jim had pulled his aim.

Jim was prying the shell from the gun's stubborn breach, mumbling under his breath. He broke into an embarrassed laugh when the shell dropped finally to the ground. "The cheeky little bugger," he said. "You were right about one thing. He's lucky as sin. In Queensland he'd have been a corpse long ago."

•

The Sicilian

ASK ANY SHRINK or probation officer, "What is the most troubling kind of client?" You will hear the same answer every time: stalkers. Not the run-of-the-mill stalker—the jilted boyfriend type—but the schizo who obeys no authority save the voice inside his head. Lecture him, he will not listen. Warn him, he will not be impressed. Put him in jail and when he gets out he is likely to stalk you.

The e-mails started the week I retired from the San Francisco Probation Department. The threats had a wholesale quality about them, a banality that prevented me from making a personal connection with the sender. *Watch yur back. I'll see u real soon. You r not God*. What could I do with remarks like these but put them in my junk file? I did not even recognize my stalker's name—at least not at first. Who was Nathan Scudder? A hacker, a spammer, a religious nut? And what had inspired him to visit my blog and latch onto my e-mail address? It was only as the threats continued to pop up, that I remembered him.

I had arrested him several months earlier while I was still a probation officer. A runty kid with long grungy hair, he was on probation for a trespass charge. I remembered him as a celebrity stalker, the kind who might shoot a VIP for the sake of notoriety. And so I was somewhat surprised that he had bothered to come after me. Still, I had put him in jail so he had reason to harbor a grudge. Since his rap sheet listed countless arrests for intimidation, grudges probably came easy to him.

I had locked him up for violating his probation. For sending death threats to a well-known movie actress, accusing her of becoming a Hollywood whore. He had not even looked at me

85

when I booked him; instead, he kept cocking his head to one side as though listening to an unseen presence. But now it appeared he was back on the street and I was on his radar.

I filed the requisite police report, arranged for police drive-bys of my home on Nob Hill, and loaded my Glock 40. I also reported the matter to Jerry Ferrari, the probation officer who now had Scudder's case. Jerry told me a judge had released Nathan from jail and put him back on probation. The Hollywood actress, busy on a movie shoot, had not appeared in court to testify. A warrant was now out on Nathan because he had not checked-in at the probation department after getting out of jail. And the Sheriff's fugitive recovery team was trying to hunt him down.

How could I have failed to anticipate the actress not coming to court? Most stalking victims, after filing complaints, did not show up to testify. And so their complaints were dismissed, their predators released.

I chastised myself for my thoroughness, my fastidious sense of duty. Once again, I had tried to protect a victim who did not want to take the stand. Once again, a court, top heavy with cases, had set a criminal free. And now the revolving door of justice had made me a victim too.

God's angel will git u. I'll see u in hell. U r going to dissapear. The e-mail threats continued to pour in—up to a dozen a day. As a matter of habit, I closed my eyes and recited my peace officer's mantra: *Show up, do your job, let go of the results.* But how could I let go of results like these? I wanted to break his fingers. I wanted to shut him down. And since a court had set me up for this, I was glad to have retired my badge.

I went to the records department at the Hall of Justice, filed a request for information, and reviewed the report I had written when I booked him for threatening the actress. Nathan's profile was similar to that of John Bardo, the nut who had gunned down TV star Rebecca Schaeffer at her doorstep in Los Angeles. Like Bardo, Nathan fixated on female actresses. Like Bardo, he had showed up outside a studio lot carrying a teddy bear. Nathan had even served a year in Orange County for pulling a knife on a studio lot security guard. *It is only a matter of time*, I had stated in my report. *Given the opportunity, I believe Mr. Scudder will consummate one of his threats.* Sounding the alarm seemed quixotic to me now—a smug and superfluous risk. For want of a willing witness, Nathan Scudder was back on the street.

I had lectured victims on safety plans when I was a probation officer. *Be aware of your surroundings. Change your route to work. Alter your appearance.* How empty these words sounded now: a veritable blueprint on how to remain a victim. The fact that stalkers had more rights than victims was becoming an intolerable bore.

A wolfish anger was rising up inside me, the surly whelp of judicial reticence and long term public apathy. And the melancholy mantle of reason was lifting from my soul. It was time to forsake an authority that had blindly forsaken me. It was time to renounce the yoke of due process and become a law unto myself.

When fighting monsters, Nietzsche warned, *be careful you do not become one.* But who but a fallen angel can fathom the criminal mind. If you choose to conquer what lurks in the void, you had best be a monster yourself.

I decided to cyberstalk him and put him in fear for his life. The courts would not hold me accountable—I knew that from long experience. Who would bear witness against me? That crazy sociopath? For once, I was grateful for the selectivity of the law.

Prudence, my girlfriend, looked at me curiously when I told her about my plan. Her gaze was cold and critical, an all too familiar reminder that our relationship was waning. But when a woman is close to leaving you, she loses the privilege of judgment. "Who do you think ya are?" she snapped. "Michael Corleone? You take things waaay too personally and you're turning into a fruitcake."

"Why *shouldn't* I take this personally? He's threatened to see me in hell."

She folded her arms tightly across her chest. "Well, you don't have to be such an asshole about it."

"Should I allow him to knock me off first?" I asked. "Should I wait until he comes to my doorstep?"

"What you *might* do is stop your ranting, Tom Hemmings. He's just some sad little creep."

"A creep who knows how to find me," I muttered. "You can thank the goddamn Internet for that."

"Really, Tom." She sighed like a furnace. "You're such an avenger, you know."

She was looking at me so dismissively that I felt like a stranger to myself. But it was a stranger I chose to welcome. A stranger who was long overdue. The kind of stranger who rides a pale horse and shoots up all the bad guys.

I waited until Prudence was out of the house before firing up my computer. Nathan's e-mails were still queuing up in my mailbox, but this time I did not read them. I was ready—damn ready—to write my own script.

I went to gmail.com and created a dummy account. And I looked no further than the Godfather movies to find my pseudonym. My handle, vito@silician.com, did seem a little transparent. But how much was needed to fuck with the mind of a paranoid schizophrenic?

Flushed with rebellion, I bent over my keyboard and typed a caustic message. But my first foray into monsterdom was pitifully clichéd. *Little man*, I wrote in emboldened font, *you are being noticed, you know.*

I hit the "send" button then bowed my head as though waiting for lightning to strike. But the prose police did not bust me for writing such stilted tripe. It was like throwing a stone into a pond and watching the ripples spread.

His answer came back almost instantly, which was kind of a surprise. In my shame, I had actually endowed him with a literary eye. But the message that found my inbox had the style of a comic book reader.

Who the fuk r u, man? his misspelled memo read.

I imagined him alone in some roach hotel, his iPad in his lap. Was he glancing out the window? Was he fearing a knock at the door? Was my campy imagination enough to impregnate his scrambled brain? Since his mind seemed rather patented, I kept my response short and succinct.

Some call me the Avenger, I wrote. *Others, the Sicilian.*

I pressed "send" and held my breath. I chuckled when he replied.

Big fuking deal, man. Git yurself out of my face.

How inebriating it felt to be in control. How empowering to make him squirm. I waited ten minutes to let tension build then authored another gem.

Take care, little man. I do not like your tone. No one addresses the Sicilian without showing proper respect.

I felt like a ghost had possessed me as I slowly re-read the message. Who was this Sicilian? I wondered. A hammy ghoul who made his home in the swamplands of my mind? Or Yeats' rough beast whose preordained hour had come around at last? For all his intemperate blather, the Sicilian had captured my soul.

I tapped the "send" button. Nathan answered at once.

What r u going do about it, man? And what r u, some kind of fag?

A sinister laugh interrupted my plotting. A sunless shivery chortle that I did not recognize as mine. But since my better angels had let me down, how much could sanity matter? I composed another reply.

You are going to be punished for that, little man. I am trying to decide just how. Hmmm. Let me see. Shall I skin you alive or shall I just slice off your prick?

I sent him the message and waited. He did not reply right away. Had I come on too strong? Had I scared him off? Had I failed to set the hook? It was not until nearly an hour had passed that he sent me another response.

U better not, Sicilian. I can make guys like u disapear.

I relaxed. He was hooked. I grinned like Count Dracula then wrote another bon mot.

How boastful you are, little man. How fun you will be to impale. It is always the braggarts who scream the loudest when I hang them onto hooks.

An annoying reluctance gripped me as I let the message fly. Had Prudence been right? Was he someone to pity? I took stock of my situation as I studied his retort.

Do you think u r bigger than Moses, man? Do you think u r bigger than god?

Fuck it, I decided; I was going to play on. I was now a noble assassin, like Brutus in *Julius Caesar*. I was riding a full foreboding tide to be taken at the flood. I composed a message so dark and delinquent it startled even me.

I am the godfather. I am the punisher. I am the boogeyman under your bed.

This was getting too easy; I wanted more challenge. I felt like the gods had cheated me when I read his feeble reply.

The FBI is going to git u, man. The CIA is going to git u.

But the game still demanded a morbid commitment; I had no other choice but to strike.

The CIA does not make a move without asking the Sicilian.

The contest continued throughout the day, a battle of mismatched wills. As his taunts grew increasingly desperate, my attacks grew more skillfully barbed. It was like the struggle between the old man and the marlin, and I was the one with the gaff.

What have I don to u, man? he wrote finally.

I gloated like Marley's ghost. How refreshing to know that, as low as I'd sunk, I could still take the moral high ground. I composed my retort with such lofty scorn that I felt like an Old Testament prophet.

You're a pox on God's green earth, I wrote. *A boil on the butt of humanity. A piece of maggoty flotsam that needs to be flushed down a sewer.*

I struck the "send" button, releasing the message as though it were a falcon.

I'll kik in your teeth, he responded.

I'll cut off your balls, I sent back. *But not until I skewer you onto my cock and roast you like a pig. That is the fate of any and all who anger the Sicilian.*

Long minutes passed. I hoped he would rally; I hoped he would fight off the ropes. Our battle had grown so compelling that I could not bear the thought of its ending. But when his next message came, the shadow of closure spread over my fevered mind.

Yul have to kill me first, Sicilian. I don't bend over fer fags.

How utterly lame. How totally gauche. What a pitiful foil he'd become. He did not deserve my rapier wit, but heroically I pressed on.

Death will not put you out of my reach, you miserable little shit. When you writhe in that sea of eternal flame, my minions will piss in your mouth. Not even in Hades does a pissant escape the wrath of the Sicilian.

His answer was so regressive that I knew the game was over. Only a child—a terrified child—could make such a callow remark.

I'm telling my father on u. He's going come kik yer ass.

Time now to finish him off, I sighed. Time to reduce him to pulp. Time to release every goblin and ghost that lay hid in his haunted brain.

Your father? I wrote. *Little man, little man. Your father is one of my henchmen. I have ordered him to cut out your heart like Abraham of old.*

He had to be crapping his pants right now; he had to be frantic with fear. An untimely pity touched me as I read his next remark.

U and whuz army, Sicilian? he wrote. *If u keep on laying this shit on me u r going to be in hot water.*

I wanted to show him some mercy. I wanted to blunt my sting. But I also wanted him to run raving through the streets and bump into a cop. I composed another reply and let fly.

You are babbling, little man. For that, I will rip out your tongue. No one mixes metaphors when addressing the Sicilian.

Fuk u, he replied.

That does it, I wrote. *I am coming to get you right now.*

I pressed "send" as though ringing a doorbell. There was nothing to do now but wait.

A half hour later, my cell phone chirped. It was Jerry Ferrari; he sounded excited. Nathan Scudder had turned himself in.

I attended Nathan's arraignment the following day and I pumped my fist in triumph. He was wearing a jail-issued jumpsuit and he looked like a frightened troll.

I would not have to testify anytime soon regarding his threats on my life. The judge took one look at his disheveled state and turned him over to the Department of Mental Health. Nathan would spend sixty days in Napa State Hospital then return to court to be evaluated for a hearing.

His gaze met mine as the bailiff marched him back to the holding tank. He nodded. "Mr. Hemmings. How goes it, man?" He looked like he needed to pee.

I feigned compassion. "Two months in a loony bin. Sorry about that, kid."

His eyes scanned the courtroom. "It sucks," he said. "But at least the Sicilian won't get me."

•

Breaking Vials

WHEN I BECAME a San Francisco probation officer, I hadn't expected to do drug sweeps. Drug sweeps are typically performed by police better trained in the use of force. But one day, a dozen of us were deployed on a two-month sweep. Our task was to pat down our probationers and smash their vials on the sidewalk.

Working in pairs, we cruised the Tenderloin, the Western Addition, and Powell Street—seedy pockets of San Francisco where ten dollars buys a vial of crack. Or maybe a pinch of cornstarch if a customer is not a regular. Some customers, noticing our black probation officer jackets, complained to us after blowing their money on cornstarch. They wanted us to cuff up the dealers that gypped them and drive them to jail. But although selling a lookalike substance is illegal, the crime didn't evoke our sympathy or concern. Instead we focused on breaking the vials, dropping them on the sidewalk and exploding them beneath our boot heels, utterly indifferent as to whether they contained crack cocaine or cornstarch.

My partner, Ron Rosso, a roguish Italian, chided the probationers while searching them. "Spread your legs wider," he quipped as he patted them down from behind. "Pretend it's your lucky day." Since our mission was an inherently dangerous one, I was grateful when the probationer laughed along with him. For my own part, I assumed an expression of total neutrality, as though I were a plumber repairing a leak. *Don't mind me,* my body language said. *I'm only here to fix the pipes.*

We wore Second Chance vests beneath our jackets, which we fortified with steel plates. Heavy police duty belts hugged our waists like orphans. Our consignment of field items—pepper spray, handcuffs, tasers, batons—clung tenaciously to our belts, and the Glock 40s locked into our holsters gave us the aura of urban cowboys.

Much of the time we felt overly equipped. The dealers would spot us from a block away and vanish like startled cats. Our probationers would greet us meekly and allow us to empty their pockets. But it wasn't the conventional criminal that concerned us. It was the freak, the aggressive loner, the nut who, in a psychotic moment, might hurl himself upon us and try to take us out. And there were plenty of them in San Francisco: predatory panhandlers, raving schizophrenics, religious zealots with fierce yet vacant eyes.

We were out there to show that the probation department was getting tough on drugs. Our orders came from an out-of-touch supervisor, someone who had probably never worn a field jacket, worked a caseload, or faced the business end of a gun. A politico hoping to justify his existence by placing ours in jeopardy. But there were compensations to roaming the untamed streets. The city was cool and breezy, the prostitutes curvy and lithe. And Rosso, who loved to eat, knew the best ethnic restaurants in town. And so we performed our shakedowns, content with the knowledge that at least we would be dining well.

After a week of breaking vials, I noticed that we were being followed. We were doing our frisks on Powell Street, a trash-littered neighborhood where tramps squatted in doorways and police cars rarely stopped. That is when I noticed a large cloud of homeless people on the opposite side of the street. Their faces seemed uninhabited; their eyes were sunless and wild. And they tailed us with the tenacity of shadows. When we paused, they paused; when we moved, they moved; when we propped a probationer against a wall, they tarried like crows on a fence. I loosened my taser as I watched them, but their expressions were not hostile. It wasn't us they were interested in; it was the crack smudges on the sidewalk.

I glanced at Rosso and shook my head, underwhelmed by the fruits of our mission. We were hardly ridding the streets of drugs; we had simply created a cost-free supply. The moment we drove off, these vagrants would descend in a pack, elbowing one another aside in a frenzy to lick the residue from the pavement. They did not seem a natural part of the city, more a tribe of lepers. And we had only contributed to their isolation.

As we slipped back into our cruiser, I felt a sense of transgression, as though we were conspirators leaving the scene of the crime. Fascinated, I looked at them one last time. I was hoping we might have spooked them. I was hoping they might move on.

But their eyes stayed upon us as we pulled away from the curb. They looked like pigeons ready to feed.

•

Honey Bunny

I CALL HER HONEY BUNNY—an utter cliché. That's lame, I know, but I value clichés. They *do* set limits. And limits are the bedrock of sanity: without them passions would be too dark, wounds too deep, and fear would never take a holiday. So thank heaven for good stout clichés.

My mother, bless her soul, called everyone honey bunny: even my uncle who began creeping into my bedroom when I was twelve, even my brother who quit school because it was interfering with his porn habit—even my father who only seemed endearing *after* he got shot to death thirty years ago. And my mother died at the ripe old age of 95—died with a Bible in her hand, a twinkle in her eye, and a monkish insistence that God will protect us.

I strive to be more like my mother was, but I have only *one* honey bunny in *my* life. I met her a year ago in San Francisco—at the annual Pink Parade. The parade, as usual, depressed me—perhaps because of the total irrelevance of what it was celebrating. Why on earth would I want to celebrate being a lesbian, and a failed lesbian at that? I may as well celebrate the color of my hair, the length of my fingernails, or the alarming frequency with which I masturbate. And so I hung despondently at the edge of the crowd and listened to the boisterous shouting of the dykes on motorbikes.

It was she—my very own Honey Bunny—who started the conversation. Touching my elbow ever so gently, she asked me if I had a hair clip. A hair clip! You can buy those anywhere so I knew she was reaching out to me. There was something so very pathetic about her: she was thin as a rake, paler than ivory, and her eyes were like the eyes of a beggar. Yet those sorrowful eyes looked straight into my soul—my shoddy, pedestrian soul. Thankfully, her gaze was charitable—it seemed that her own life, an obvious shipwreck, had spared her the conceits of judgment. It also appeared that she needed rescuing.

"Here," I said. Removing a hair clip from my already disheveled mane, I handed it to her. She protested—"Oh no, you still need it"—but when I pressed it into her palm, she took it without hesitation. She pinned back her dark bangs and I was able to look at her more critically. Her forehead was shiny and swarming with freckles, her jaw was entirely too weak, and her ears were clownishly large. Only her eyes, her dark luminescent eyes, rescued her from homeliness.

We drank iced teas at an outdoor café—she paid—and I listened as she rambled on about her life. She was an interior decorator but not a very accomplished one—she had not worked in months. Her love life, like mine, was the ultimate cliché: her husband had left her for a man. And she was an alcoholic now struggling to recover. I listened to her with staccato nods of my head. I wanted to appear cosmopolitan. I wanted to appear chic. I wanted to appear breezy. I wanted to be anything but what I was—a farm girl from Iowa suddenly in love.

She patted my wrist before she left and handed me her business card. It read *Annabelle Chilton, Living Rooms & Kitchens, Visits by appointment.* "In case you drum me up some jobs," she said— another sure signal. With the entire Internet at her disposal, why would she need me to find her jobs? Clearly, we had made a once-in-a-lifetime connection. Or perhaps we had known each other in another life: a life cut short by some cruel circumstance. The plea in her eyes, the sob in her throat, the tremor in her hands all told me that there was unfinished business between us.

I pocketed her card as though it were a check and walked away from the parade.

I phoned her the following morning. She answered on the very first ring—probably she had been waiting for my call. I invited her to lunch and she accepted at once. I told her it was *my* turn to pay.

I dressed conservatively: sandals, a cream-colored blouse, and a dark pair of slacks that minimized my stocky hips. I shortened my hair with a pair of scissors, teased it into a pageboy do, and then stood before the full-length mirror that hung from the door in my studio flat. I barely recognized the woman looking back at me: with every hair in place, I looked more like a CEO than a part-time nurse's aide. But Annabelle *needed* a person of stature—someone to anchor her free-floating spirit.

We met at the same café. She was sitting at a table, bent over a pack of Tarot cards that she was arranging face-up. The way she nibbled her lip as she concentrated on the cards was absolutely touching. "Oh," she said, startled by my sudden appearance. I sat down beside her and she returned her attention to the cards.

"Are you reading my fortune?" I asked.

She put down the deck. "If you *must* know, I'm reading mine. Things are so crazy I have to read it every day."

"Why every day? That Death card looks scary."

"People usually think that," she laughed. "But it's actually a card of transition. It means old things die—new things replace them."

"My father was *young* when he died," I replied. "And *no one* took his place, thank God." I don't know why I told her this—the incident, though traumatic at the time, was now more of an embarrassment to me than anything else. But when something is ordained—when it is plainly in the cards—there is not much point in holding back.

"I'm so very sorry," she said. And she meant it.

"Don't be," I replied. I did *not* want her pity—that would never do. "He was shot to death in a hovel, you know—a goddamn brothel. Some say he needed killing."

She turned over another card—the Queen of Swords.

"Now *that* bitch *is* scary," I said.

99

She laughed. "She *can* be mean. But she's really a card of judgment."

"A dyke with a sword? What kind of judge would *she* make?"

She giggled like a child. "Not a very good one, I'm afraid. She's too conflicted *herself*. She's part *man*, you know."

Her come-on was so banal that I could only smile indulgently. Opposites attract. Opposites repel. And so the game goes on. I scooted my chair closer to her and watched as she lay down more cards.

She told me a bit more about her life and my pity for her grew. She had gotten married straight out of a Catholic women's college. For five years, she had clung to a safe but passionless marriage. When her husband had confessed to an affair with another man, she settled for a no-fault divorce and came to San Francisco to pursue a new dream—that of becoming an interior designer. It was a dream for which she lacked the slightest qualification—a dream as fanciful as her bullshit marriage and her trust in those silly Tarot cards. But her tenacity, even in the pursuit of lost causes, was to be admired. My own bullshit marriage had ended years *before* my ex- husband came out of the closet. It had ended in its very first month—when I heard him brushing his teeth for the two hundredth time. Try as I may, I could not stand the sound of him brushing his goddamn teeth. And so, when I got my divorce papers, I gleefully packed a bag and set off for San Francisco—not to chase a dream but to put as much distance as I could between myself and Iowa.

She plopped down another card. It was the Magician.

"Now what does *he* stand for?"

She laughed and patted my wrist. "He has very striking powers," she said. "He turns gravel into gold."

As it turned out, it was the Queen of Swords who had striking powers. She was not an abstraction—an interplay of Yin and Yang—but an actual person: a towering drag queen who was approaching our table like a ship that had drifted off course. She was vampire pale with Madonna length hair and her eyes were looking daggers straight at me. I recognized her instantly as a hustler, one of those bottom feeders that hung around the Mission District—the kind who preyed on the homeless waifs that poured into the city every day. What did she want with my Honey Bunny? Did she want her to sell drugs, work as her pimp, pose for lewd photos? I could tell by Annabelle's demeanor—the way she stiffened as this bitch approached—that she had already been caught in her snare. What a silly thing to do, but *that's* my Honey Bunny.

The Queen of Swords sat at our table, glowering like a sunset as Annabelle introduced me. She introduced me as Rebecca—the name I had adopted since coming to San Francisco, a name that symbolized my complete and utter relocation from Iowa.

"Eve," she said hesitantly. "Eve this is Rebecca. Eve and I are *roommates*, you know." She spoke the word *roommates* as though she were describing something vile—a mooring of desperation. A port of last resort.

"*Charmed*," the Queen of Swords muttered. She took my hand, squeezing it with a man's grip. I was stunned by the reptilian strength of her fingers. But I was also rather glad to meet her. Now I knew my mission. Now I knew what my Honey Bunny needed to be rescued from. Now I knew what would make me the Magician in her eyes.

An invasive chill settled over the table—a chill as penetrating as that of an Iowa winter. It was Annabelle, dear and vulnerable Annabelle, who broke down first. "Eve was in a movie," she blurted. This was not a disclosure so much as a cry—a frantic attempt to break the silence.

I nodded woodenly. Movie, my ass. It was probably a film clip: the kind you saw in the Mission Street sex shops. So *that* was the Queen of Swords realm—the goddamn basement of the goddamn porno industry. Was she planning to recruit my Honey Bunny—get her into those flicks? I swore I would never let such a thing happen.

Arching my eyebrows, I looked back at Eve. "I don't much like movies. They get on my nerves. But *you* are *very* photogenic." I said this not to flatter her but because I could easily picture her face on a police mug shot.

The bitch lit a cigarette—a Salem—and smiled like a ghoul. She had accepted my comment as a compliment, but this did not stop her from blowing a veil of smoke in my direction. "Take care of your gifts, darlin'," she said. "I'm sure you have gifts of your own."

I shrugged. "Not a one," I confessed. "Not unless *loyalty* counts." That was a lie, of course. I had never been loyal to anything in my life—certainly not to my uncle who tried to bribe me with a kitten, my ex-husband who hid gay porn under our bed, my mother who *never* lost that fucking twinkle in her eyes. But today—*today*—I was ready to make a change.

Eve blew more smoke at me and chuckled. "I *do* hope you're fibbing, darlin'. What good is loyalty in the Mission?"

I looked at her as though I were looking at a piece of shit. What a hypocrite she was to say something like that. As though she, the Queen of Swords, had not demanded total fidelity from my Honey Bunny. "Do I look like I'm fibbing?" I snapped.

She groaned, her tenor voice giving way to a deep baritone. "Maybe to yourself, darlin'," she said. "You look like a woman in search of a cause."

I continued to stare at her. It did not matter that she had read me like a book, that I had broadcast my intentions, that my soul was so barren, so utterly transparent, that even this street shark could take its measure. I had stood up for my Honey Bunny. That was enough.

But now it was time for a strategic retreat—time to go home and plan the first step of my campaign. I rose from the table, feigning indifference when my Honey Bunny frowned at me. *Don't leave me, please* was the plea in her eyes—she looked like a jilted lover. But I would have to leave the silly creature for now.

"I must go," I said firmly.

Her eyes began to water. "Go where?" she blurted. "You were *about* to buy me lunch."

I smiled mysteriously. "To the movies," I said.

I went straight home and lay down on my bed. I hated to abandon my Honey Bunny, but I needed some time to think.

Time had always been my ally; it had served me well after my father was shot to death thirty years ago—after I identified his body, as stiff as a manikin, lying upon a gurney in the county morgue. Only time could have mitigated my memory of his drunken fits. Only time could have given me a few bits of nostalgia: he had taught me how to hunt—how to load and unload a gun. And time would assist me where Honey Bunny was concerned. Since her sanctification was vital to my mission, I needed time to forgive her her folly—time to accentuate the very best in her. Dreams are so very vulnerable, after all.

I started with an e-mail, a few short sentences that I revised several times. When the message was ready, I looked at it with satisfaction.

Annabelle,

Can we meet? Not in a restaurant but a cavern—a place where only the Magician might appear. Remember, it was Eve who forsook Paradise, Eve who perverted Man—Eve who stole the apple from the Tree of Knowledge. I will wait to hear from you.

Your friend,
Rebecca

I pressed the *send* button and waited for a reply. I waited several days, but that did not surprise me. Were my Honey Bunny quick-witted—were she able to think on her feet—she would not be caught up in a hustler's web. Her reply, when it finally came, was short and succinct—a sharp departure from her usual garrulous ramblings.

Dear Rebecca,

Thank you for the invitation. I'm afraid I must decline. A little knowledge can go a long way.

Regrets,
Annabelle

Was my Honey Bunny miffed at me? Probably—I *had* walked out on her at the restaurant. Or were these *Eve's* words?

103

I sincerely hoped they had come from Honey Bunny. Good things protect themselves, after all, and now I could truly hope that my Honey Bunny was not promiscuous—that her precious affections would have to be earned. Be wary of finding your love on a single night. Love that comes too easily is too often counterfeit love.

I composed another message:

Annabelle,
Thank you for your reply. A little knowledge does go a long way. There is no need for you to meet me—I understand why you can't. But drop me a line now and then—just a few words to let me know how you are doing. That will be enough and enough is as good as a feast.
Your friend,
Rebecca

I forwarded her the message along with an invitation to be my Facebook friend. She did not answer right away, thank God: her reticence gave me time to reflect, time to consider my options, time to woo her in small increments. Rapture, after all, is better pursued in degrees—otherwise, the impact could prove overwhelming. And so I sent her one e-mail a day—one and *only* one—just to remind her that I would be there no matter how perilous the journey. After a month, she replied.

Rebecca,
Enough is not a feast. Enough is enough. Do not correspond with me further. Abandon your notion that we're good for lunch. Invite the Magician if you wish, but leave me out of your daydreams. Please.
Annabelle

I re-read her e-mail and gasped. How desperate my Honey Bunny must be to resort to so silly a code. Was it a fear of rapture that prompted her to do this or was it her obedience to the Queen of Swords? In any case, her message—*Do not abandon me, please*—was too disturbing to ignore.

104

Thankfully, I still had her address. It was printed on her business card—how convenient. She lived in a fleabag hotel in the Mission District—at the intersection of 24th Street and Folsom. It was an hour's walk from my flat in the upper Castro, but what did distance matter? It was imperative that I check up on my Honey Bunny right away.

I walked the entire 20 blocks to her hotel. By the time I got there, my feet were so blistered that I could barely hobble. I should *not* have worn flip-flops for such a long walk.

It was a mercy to my feet that I did not have to wait long. In a matter of minutes, she emerged through the doorway to her hotel—as though the Magician had summoned her. Thank God she's psychic. Thank God she came so quickly. But when I saw her, my heart began to bleed. She was hollow-eyed, shoeless, and clad in a cheap summer frock. And—surprise, surprise—she was with that bitch, Eve. What Eve had done to my Honey Bunny, I could only imagine—but gone was her vitality, her lively innocence, the childlike luster in her eyes. She looked like a crack whore.

I waved—hoping to attract her attention. She noticed me at once, and her face began to soften. She then jerked her head in Eve's direction—an urgent effort to warn me away. A few minutes later, the pair of them disappeared into a subway tunnel.

I walked back to my flat—the entire 20 blocks. My feet were like pulp by the time I got home, but what did that matter? For the sake of my Honey Bunny—my dear and precious love—I was prepared to give my life.

It's so strange to be knocking upon heaven's door. What if it were to open too quickly? What if I were unworthy of walking through it? What if heaven were too great a challenge—not only for me but for my Honey Bunny as well? As I thought more about it, I started to choke; it felt like a python was crushing my lungs. Thank God I could turn on some music.

Desperate for YouTube, I went on line. I selected one of my favorites, "Knocking on Heaven's Door"—not the Bob Dylan original but the more dynamic version performed by Guns N

Roses. As I listened to the riffs of the lead guitar and the gravelly drawl of Axel Rose, I began to get out of my skin. And soon I was singing along. "Knock knock knocking on heaven's door—*hey, heeey, yaaay.*"

But it was time I knocked louder. And so, when the song ended, I composed another e-mail to my Honey Bunny.

Dearest Annabelle,

Don't snub the Magician. He is wiser than us both and far more resourceful. And, after seeing you this morning, I fear it is time for a transition. But come to me on your own accord—not like a lamb but a fearless queen. Don't make me play the Death card on you.

Your friend,
Rebecca

I paused before sending the message. What if my Honey Bunny had been turned against me? What if she were less courageous than I imagined her to be? What if Eve were to intercept the message?

But what if I did nothing? What if I abandoned my Honey Bunny to drugs and destitution? Surely, I would be hell-bound—deservedly so—without a prayer of *ever* reuniting with her. And so, there it was. *One* of us would have to be brave.

I took a deep breath and looked fear in the eye. And then I hit the *send* button.

An hour later, I heard a knocking on *my* door. Had heaven come calling so soon?—I rather doubted it. But, having taken the leap, I was prepared for whatever was to come. Be it bliss or be it woe, I was *ready*. Anything was better than this maddening limbo.

Quickly, eagerly, I opened the door. Standing outside were two dykes wearing pantsuits. They were stately, tall, and beautiful, and their faces glowed with the righteousness of angels. Why couldn't my Honey Bunny be so brave? The women were an escort—that was clear—and I was ready to be escorted. And so I said nothing when they slipped the bracelets over my wrists, walked me down the hallway, and eased me into the back seat of a police van. One of them scooted in beside me and began reading the warrant. But I wasn't listening.

"You look like Wonder Woman," I said.

She laughed. "Take it easy on me."

"Were you sent here by a queen?"

"Take it easy."

The one who was driving glanced over her shoulder. "It was a homely looking chick with dirty feet. She seemed kinda batty."

I smiled with relief. "That's my Honey Bunny," I said. "Crazier than bat shit."

"She isn't worth jail time—that's for sure."

I laughed and agreed. But, of course, I was lying. For my Honey Bunny, I would *gladly* go to jail. I loved her with all her flaws. I loved her in all her moods.

I saw her three days later during my arraignment. She was sitting at the back of the courtroom and she looked like a train wreck. Her hair was disheveled and greasy, her dress was badly rumpled, and her eyes were so dark that she looked like a mugging victim. But I was a fright myself: clad in a jail-issued jumpsuit—no makeup on my face at all—I was not at my best for Honey Bunny.

She looked at me and blushed, and I felt my pulse starting to pound. What joy—to know that she was penitent, to know that she yearned for a glimpse of me. But how heartbreaking to see her in such a state.

My public defender, a short owlish man, told me I could probably take a plea. I could cop out to five years probation—the standard term for felony stalking—and agree to a ten-year stay away order. My heart leaped at the possibility. How merciful. How utterly convenient. I could *never* put my Honey Bunny through a trial. I could *never* force her to take the stand—to submit to the whiplash questioning of a lawyer. I could *never* ask her to betray me publicly. Such an experience would crush her bird-like spirit forever.

No, no—a thousand times no. I would stay loyal to my Honey Bunny. I would continue to set the standard. And one day, she would surely come to me.

She wrote me while I was still in jail—unmindful of the restraining order the judge had issued. The letter was brief, a single mottled page that appeared to be dappled with tearstains.

Rebecca,
The DA said not to write you, but write you I must. I never thought the Death card could be scary. But now I see you each night in my dreams. In my dreams, you are the Charioteer—a most unsettling card. In my dreams, you wear a bright red tunic and come to me like a conqueror. I want these dreams to end.
You scare me, Rebecca. You scare me so.
Annabelle

I put down the letter and started to weep. The subtext—*I want you so*—was plain enough, but it was the body of the letter that most affected me. The fact that no good deed goes unpunished was simply unacceptable where my Honey Bunny was concerned. I would have to let her know—*and know right away*—that only the Queen of Swords need be feared.

I composed a quick note.

Dearest Annabelle,
I confess. I want to be your hero. And you need a hero, my darling. Still, I would rather die than frighten you for even an instant. So let us dispense with chariots and tunics. Let us settle, instead, for a single red rose. Tape a rose upon the door of your hotel if you want me to come to you. I will check your hotel every day for a rose. A rose is all I need.
Your friend,
Rebecca

I stuffed the note into an envelope—thank God they don't monitor the correspondence in here—and gave it to the jail chaplain to mail out. I waited a week and then shivered with joy.

Since lightning did not strike me—since the DA did not bust me for violating the restraining order—I knew for sure that my Honey Bunny was having second thoughts. I knew, without a doubt, that our love would win out in the end.

Thirty days later, I went back to court. I stood before the judge, held up my head, and nodded stoically as he recited the terms of my probation. When I had taken my plea bargain, I looked around the courtroom, hoping for another glimpse of my Honey Bunny. She was there, of course, but how sad she looked. Sitting again at the back of the courtroom, her face buried in her hands, she resembled a mourner at a wake. When she finally looked up at me, my heart almost burst. Oh, for a bit of lipstick! Oh, for a dab of rouge! With my pasty complexion—my jailbird pallor—I must surely have looked like a ghost.

The following morning—alone in my flat—I reevaluated my strategy. Since I was now a specter to her—a shadow from heaven's door—I would have to approach her as such. Shattered as she was, my Honey Bunny could only *handle* ghosts, pallid reminders of what still might be. And so I created a Face book phantom—a parody of my masculine self—and I named him Ruhben. The anagram of Ben Hur would be instantly apparent to her: an assurance that the Charioteer was not to be taken seriously.

It seemed almost redundant to send her a friend request. She was with me constantly now, her presence like a warm breeze that caressed me daily—or sometimes like an arctic winter chill. But it wasn't enough that she was psychic—I needed to hear from her as well. And so I sent her a Facebook invitation—one that she instantly accepted. She even posted my "picture"—that of a bronzed surfer dude—on her friends' page. *Ruhben*, she wrote coquettishly. *Are you from India?* What a tease she can be.

The next day, as I walked to the probation department, I felt such joy that I almost floated. How good it was to be out and about, to feel the warmth of sunshine on my skin again, and to know my Honey Bunny was thinking of me. I had lost my job at the hospital—thank God. Now I was free—free at any hour of the day—to dash to her side and kiss away her tears. Who knew when she might need me? Who knew when she might call for me?

I liked my probation officer—a handsome woman who reminded me of Jamie Lee Curtis. After she had referred me to a therapist and given me a chit for food stamps, we talked about movies. You've got to know how to handle these people if you want them to cut you some slack. I even patted her shoulder before leaving her office and promised I would report back to her in a week.

Later that day, after checking my Facebook feed, I went out to feed myself. The taqueria at 24th and Folsom—the one across from my Honey Bunny's hotel—was perfect. There, I could be closer to her. There, I could feel the full strength of her vibes. There, I would be ready if the love she so feared, yet so desperately wanted, delivered her to my arms. And so I went back, every day for a month, and watched for a single red rose.

Betrayal has so many faces. Omission is one, denial another, and *settling* must certainly qualify. But first one must betray oneself. First one must sanctify dark habits. First one must decide that another dead end marriage—another bullshit union—is not salve but salvation. *What is beyond your capacity seek not.* My mother used to quote that from the Bible whenever she wanted to put me in my place. And maybe she was right. But I felt only grief—unfathomable grief—when I read my Honey Bunny's announcement.

To all my Facebook friends:

You are invited to the wedding of Annabelle Chilton and Emmanuel Vasquez—stage star and illusionist. Our hearts are full, our faith in life restored. Love has truly found us.

Services will be Saturday afternoon, 1:00 p.m. at Glide Memorial Church. Refreshments will be served afterwards at the Treasure Island Yacht Club. Come one, come all, and share in this magical moment.

I lowered my head and wept. What a sell out! What a farce! And *who* was Emmanuel Vasquez? I studied the picture she had posted beside her own—that of a tall sweaty man in a T-shirt. I practically retched when I realized it was Eve. How utterly disappointing to see her out of drag—to realize she was not a vampire but a slob. Oh, Annabelle. Dearest, dearest Annabelle. How very frightened of life you must be.

Thankfully, I was still brave enough for the both of us. Thankfully, I was bruised but unbowed. Thankfully, my freedom, my life, *my very soul*, were not too much to risk for my Honey Bunny. I would give them all up for an instant of bliss, a single sweet smile from my beloved's lips.

Dispensing with Ruhben, my own sad illusion, I composed a short e-mail.

My Dearest,

A boat in port is safe. But that isn't what boats are designed for. So please do not rot in a withering harbor. Instead, put your faith in a mutinous sea. For only the lost— only the truly lost—can ever be found.
Rebecca

After sending her the e-mail, I dashed from my flat, flagged down a cab, and gave the driver directions to her hotel. I asked him to hurry, but he all he did was poke along. It was twenty minutes—twenty excruciating minutes—before we pulled up alongside her building. And still I hesitated. What to do now? Should I push my way past the security clerk, pound on her door, throw myself at her feet? Of *course*, I should—even if it meant jail. Since my Honey Bunny was already imprisoned, it was only fitting that I share in her fate. Her pain was my pain, after all.

And so I felt proud, incredibly proud, when I heard the murmur of a siren—when a squad car pulled in front of the cab. And I smiled when my probation officer, accompanied by two uniformed dykes, approached me.

I got out of the cab. "I surrender," I piped. "Don't shoot me."

111

She chuckled. "It didn't take you long to fuck up."

I stood like Joan of Arc as she fitted me with handcuffs and read me my Miranda rights. After I was strapped into the squad car, we chatted a bit more.

"It sure didn't take you long, Rebecca."

I shrugged. "I guess not. But that's kind of a blessing."

"I was staking out the building, you know."

"Did she call you?"

"This morning. She told me she was getting married. So I knew it wouldn't be long until I saw you here."

As we drove to the city jail, my heart felt astoundingly full. So my Honey Bunny, my crafty but timid Honey Bunny, had been testing me—testing the depth of my love. And surely I had passed—passed with the brightest of colors. Together, we would now bear the weight of her cross. Together, we would bind ourselves to exile. And together we would be when this test—this loathsome test—had paved our way to heaven.

My probation revocation hearing was a disappointment, not because of the sentence I received—it was only the two-year minimum—but because my beloved wasn't in the courtroom. I craned my neck, hoping to get a glimpse of her, but she was nowhere to be seen. But that may also have been a blessing: had they put her on the stand—had they made her admit she had trapped me—she might never have forgiven herself. And I wanted her to come to me like a child—like the child she truly was—when I held her to my heart.

A few weeks later, the prison bus took me to the Reception & Diagnostic Center at San Quentin. But even at San Quentin, even in my six-by-eight-foot cell, I could anticipate the joy of my persistence. The rock-solid walls, the perpetual racket, the frozen bars were *nothing* compared to the bliss I would feel when I reunited with my Honey Bunny. And so my happiness endured—even as I completed a battery of tests, even as I stood before the inmate classification board, even as I was transferred to the Valley State Prison for Women in Chowchilla.

A SECOND, LESS CAPABLE, HEAD

The Warden at Chowchilla, impressed by my high IQ score and my meager criminal history, assigned me to work in the prison library—a trustee type job. And there, it was so easy to access the Internet. Using the pseudonym Miranda—a reference my Honey Bunny would quickly grasp—I created a new Facebook account. She accepted my friend invitation at once and our accounts, like our hearts, were intimately joined.

But perhaps I should have left well enough alone. Perhaps I should have left her to the sacrament of my memory. Perhaps I should have vilified her: at least, as a Jezebel, she would have stayed mischievous and lively to me. Because her life—the life intertwined with my own—was not going well. How heartbreaking to learn that, unable to find work, she had moved into a public housing project in the Tenderloin. How devastating to know that she had developed a type of leukemia and was undergoing monthly radiation treatments. And how sad that her marriage had already ended. This was bound to happen—the marriage was a sham—but even a sham can provide someone with a semblance of company. And now my Honey Bunny was utterly alone.

I wish I could say that I rose to the occasion, but I found myself shying away from Facebook. If one must serve time, it is best to serve it as a hermit. And so I let myself fall into a deadening routine: a routine of meals, sleep, and shelving books—a routine that kept my spirit numb and my earned credit time intact. I did not even allow myself a pauper's thrill—the titillation a prison affair might have given me. *That* would have been the ultimate betrayal. *That* would have sealed my unworthiness of her.

I have always been prone to sudden depressions—not the garden-variety blues but gut checking, hand wringing, crippling depression. I go down like a dazed boxer, my senses reeling from the punch. I go down so hard that there *is* no up or down. And so the ultimate checkout—the forfeiture of my remaining senses—can seem like a sort of deliverance. Of course, it would be a sin to hurry death along but, given the utter worthlessness of my life, it could hardly be much of a sin. But how could I leave my Honey Bunny behind? How could I face myself in the afterworld if I allowed her to dwindle in a slum? How could I leave her to flounder and fade when there's room on the chariot for two? Were I to abandon her, not even *purgatory* would parole me.

It took almost a year—a year of forbearance—to get myself on parole: a parole based not upon self-renewal but the deadening of my soul. And so, it was not until I was leaving the prison that I began to feel the full weight of my funk: a funk that only increased as I collected my $300 gate fee and a bus ticket back to San Francisco. And by the time I had gotten off the bus, reported to the district parole office, and checked into a state sponsored halfway house, I felt like a pallbearer at my own funeral. But there was still a bit of the zombie left in me— enough, at least, for me to last a week at the New Beginnings Halfway House. It was an *entire week* before I had had my fill of petty regulations, enforced curfews, and pedantic staff members—themselves former felons. After that, I had to check out.

I still had my gate money—thank God—and so I bought myself a little chum. The gun—a Glock .27—looked almost like a toy. How easy to buy a gun in the Mission. How easy to hide it inside my bra. And how simple it was to find my Honey Bunny. Of course, her address was unlisted but the police *do* know how to find people. I only had to go to the nearest police station, file a false harassment report, and beg them to serve her with an emergency protection order from me. Sure enough, the next day I had her address: it was on the receipt of service. Thank you, thank you, Keystone Cops. But I felt no triumph, no conquest, no thrill—it was all I could do not to bawl like a child. *Never, never* in my wildest dreams, did I imagine I could be so devious. Oh Annabelle, Annabelle, Annabelle. Have you cast a spell on me?

She was still living in the Tenderloin—in a subsidized housing project not far from the strip joints. I had walked past the project once or twice in my rambles so I had no trouble finding it. But it sure wasn't much to look at: a dozen crumbly apartments accessible through a breezeway. The apartments

114

looked like prison dorms; the breezeway smelled of urine. Surely, my Honey Bunny deserved better than this.

I stationed myself at a Cantonese restaurant on the opposite side of her street. I treated myself to sweet and sour pork, a dinner that had all the solemnity of a last meal. And when I could eat no more, I rose from the table, left a fat tip, and went looking for my Honey Bunny's flat. Thank God it was evening: the shadows were dark, impenetrably dark, and the streetlights were glowing like halos.

Her apartment was so very easy to find. The address made me chuckle—69 Hyde Street—an erotic joke, perhaps, but an omen as well. The numbers on her door—so naughtily suggestive—were nothing if not providential. Oh Annabelle— dearest Annabelle. What more of a sign could we want?

A light was on in the window so she *had* to be at home. I waited a minute. I took a deep breath.

I knocked.

When she answered the door, I almost didn't recognize her. She was thinner than I remembered, her hair was bottled blonde, and she was leaning on a cane. But her brow was still freckled, her ears were still large, and her eyes had recovered their luster.

"Rebecca," she breathed. The cane clattered to the floor as she pulled my hands into hers. "Rebecca. How *long* you have been in my thoughts."

She kissed my chin—her breath smelled of wine— then she wrapped her arms around my neck. I crushed her body to mine and wept. How frail she was—how much like a bird. And how I wanted her: my nipples were like bullets. Oh, my darling. My darling. My darling.

A minute passed before I released her. Or did she let go of me?—I'm not really sure what happened. I only knew that she was giggling. I only knew that she was flushed. I only knew her apartment looked dreary: a ten-by-twelve-foot hovel—nothing in it but a bed, a refrigerator, and a tiny television.

"I *knew* you were coming," she whispered.

I gasped. "Was that in the cards?"

"*No*, you silly queen. You had me served with a protection order."

I laughed. I kissed her lips. How warm and soft they felt. "Protection," I said. "What a con that can be. What a sad and silly con."

She looked at me oddly and nibbled her lip. Had foreboding reclaimed her? Had she felt the gun inside my bra? Had the police been coaching her? *Buy yourself time. Tell the stalker what she wants to hear.* But all she did was titter. "I *knew* you were coming, Rebecca. I bought you a present."

As she limped away from me, I noticed Eve's picture on the windowsill—*Eve in drag*. How vapid it looked, how totally dead—like something that belonged in a museum. But inside the refrigerator there was something fresh. She giggled as she took it out. It was a rose, a single red rose, in a slender vase of water. My hands trembled as she handed it to me. The scent was so pure, so tangy and ripe that I almost swooned.

I gazed longingly at the rose. I licked the petals. My lips were damp when I looked back at her. "Thank you," I said. "I have *so* wanted this."

Of course, she was holding a gun on me now—a standard issue Glock the police must have lent her. But that *too* was a gift. What better time to go than now? And what better way than at the hands of my beloved?

She was bracing the gun against her hip, pointing the barrel up at me. Her face was like wax. "I wish," she stammered, "that you didn't want this also."

She was trembling so much that my heart almost burst. I *had* to make it easy on her. I *had* to stop her from thinking about it. Otherwise, she would fail me once again. I stumbled towards her.

She fired.

I gasped.

How clean was the blow that walloped my chest—a kick from the chariot's most powerful stallion. I rose, I literally rose off the ground, before I felt the floor pressing upon my back. The room was now ringing—a shrill but thrilling sound. I never *knew* an explosion could be so shattering.

It was not until the ringing subsided that I heard her sobs, that I saw her dear face above me—that I noticed that my chest was as red as a robin's. And her floor was wet, so terribly wet that I hoped she would hand me a towel.

She was holding the gun in both of her hands, pulling it against her groin. Her face was remarkably tender, but it was tender in betrayal. Why, oh why, did she hesitate? *Put two in her breastbone then one in her head.* Wasn't that what the police had told her? Yet all she did was sob.

I noticed my gun—it was somehow in the palm of my hand. Surely, my Honey Bunny had seen it first. Surely, this explained her procrastination, her betrayal, the tentative hope with which she looked at me.

Ever so slowly, I lifted the gun. It would be a sin, a cardinal sin, not to oblige her. And so I wept—wept like a child—as its weight pulled my hand to the floor. How very heavy it was.

But, no—no let it be this way. Let me precede her to the afterworld. Let the debt be hers. When her turn arrived—and it would probably not be long—she would fly to me straight as an arrow.

A blow stung my wrist—the gun went spinning from my hand. There were others in the room now: police, paramedics. A sharp voice interrupted my Honey Bunny's sobs. *"Ya shoulda emptied the gun."* It sounded like the voice of my father.

How irritating the paramedics were: loosening my clothing, tightening a compress to my chest, loading me onto a gurney. Why were they trying to rob me of life?—of a few vital moments with my Honey Bunny. How *much* I had paid for those moments. How dearly I had earned them. And yet those few moments were not to be: the voices of the medics—somber and surreal—prevented me from even hearing her. "Just how bad is she hit?" I heard one of them say. "Bad enough," said another. "It's amazing what a hollow point can do."

My body is numb—deliciously numb—as they roll me out of her apartment. The police are now bat-like: they dart to and fro as though locked in some grainy old movie. But although I hate movies, my heart skips a beat. Two naked strangers—hermaphrodites—are standing in the breezeway talking to each other. How handsome they are—how regal and tall. As I roll through the breezeway, they look at me pleasantly and then resume their conversation.

An ambulance awaits me on the street, its bright lights racing, chasing off shadows, bathing me in a rosy red glow. Yet my skin is cold—so sticky and cold that I cannot feel any warmth. Without her dear kisses, what more can I be but a statue made of wax?

And so, on an evening far shorter than any other, I throw away the Death card. I go like a mariner into the night. I go to make a home for her.

•

Jimmy Likes Mermaids

THOSE WHO PREACH HONESTY as the best policy have never been seriously tested. Working as a San Francisco probation officer, I quickly learned the pitfalls of compulsive honesty. Criminals are prickly revisionists, particularly the paranoid schizophrenics, so it is wiser to humor their delusions rather than risk getting hurt. This is not to say honesty does not have its place, but not as an end in itself. When convenient to do so, it is practical to tell the truth. That way, when it makes sense to lie, you are more likely to get away with it.

Each week, I conduct an orientation class for new probationers. I met Jimmy Wong at one of these classes. He was a moon-faced fellow, around sixty, with heavy shoulders and a frozen smile. As I talked to the group about terms of probation—obeying all laws, paying court fees, reporting to one's probation officer—he raised his hand in the manner of a child eager to impress a teacher.

"Mr. Hemmings," he said, "if a father is m-molesting his daughter, can Jimmy break his stay away order?"

"No," I replied. "Leave that matter to the police."

Obviously, a stalker, I thought. *And not a very bright one.* He had been assigned to my caseload a day earlier and I had not yet read his case file. But I already knew what his file would reveal: *Narcissistic disorder with rescue fantasies.* For stalkers with mental health issues, this was the boilerplate profile—a banality that failed to reassure me. Pathological stalkers are hard to supervise: they tend to obey darker laws. And if you tell them what they don't want to hear, they might decide to stalk you.

When I was done with the class, I told Jimmy to wait in the reception area. I then returned to my office and skimmed through his file. He was on felony probation for stalking, having tailed a high school girl who did not know him at all. For a week, he had followed her to school in his car, pestering her with offers of rides then driving off as she punched dialed 911 on her cell phone. He was arrested after the girl spotted his car parked in front of her home. When the police cracked the trunk of his car, they found a Molotov cocktail. The presentence report did not recommend probation, but a judge had given him a five-year grant of probation and a stay away order from the girl.

Finishing with his file, I brought him to my office. He sat mute as I read him his probation contract. When I was done, he looked at me curiously, as though he had just heard the sound of my voice. "W-would you like to come to my wedding?" he asked. "I can still get m-married, can't I."

"Yes, you can still get married."

He clapped his hands and beamed. "Would you be Jimmy's best m-man?"

Was he planning to "liberate" the girl from her father then turn her into his "wife"? Given the bizarreness of his rescue fantasy, that did not really seem far fetched. I tried not to frown. "Jimmy," I repeated. "Let the police handle it."

I wrote him a referral to Center for Special Problems, a cash-strapped city program on Jackson Street that handled mental health cases. A private therapist was out of the question. Private therapists charged steeply for their services and Jimmy was indigent and living in his car. Anyhow, most therapists were scared of stalkers and refused to work with them. But a city program, even an underfunded one, did not have the right of refusal. At worst, the program would put him on a waiting list.

I provided him directions to Center for Special Programs and told him to go there at once. After he left my office, I reviewed his file in more detail. He had a slew of police reports, all with the exact same modus. He targeted teenage girls, usually in shopping malls. After complimenting their looks ("Jimmy thinks you're pretty"), he offered to drive them wherever they wanted to go.

What was this predator doing on probation? Had the overworked District Attorney's Office, desperate to clear its calendar, settled blindly for another plea deal? Since treatment was scarce for his type of disorder, I would probably have to lock him back up.

I phoned the girl's father, coached him on victim safety, and gave him my cell phone number. I asked him to call me immediately if Jimmy Wong turned up on his doorstep. A half hour later, the father called me back.

I was not surprised by how quickly Jimmy had violated the stay away order. But I was rather stunned by his hubris. He had knocked on the door of the residence and cried, "Did you call for a cab?" And then he had hopped back into his car and pealed on down the road. The police, arriving a few minutes later, failed to locate him.

I logged the incident in his case file then quickly devised a plan. As a stalker, he was certainly artless, but that meant he'd be easy to catch. Fortunately, he had a cell phone and I had copied down the number.

He answered my call on the very first ring; probably he had been expecting it. I feigned desperation. "Jimmy," I said. "I need you real bad."

"Y-you want me to rent you a tux?"

"I'm putting that molester in jail." I said. "I just sent a squad car to his house."

"You want a carnation for your c-chest?"

"I want your *statement*, Jimmy. How many times did he fuck his daughter? Unless we have a witness, we can't keep that pervert locked up."

"I-I'll be there in ten minutes, sir."

When he arrived at my office door, I placed him under arrest. "Not again," he sighed as my partner, Ron Rosso, fitted him with the bracelets. He sang a song from *My Fair Lady* as we marched him off to jail. It was *Get Me to the Church on Time.*

Deputy Lockhart, a slim woman in her early twenties, was working the intake bay as we brought Jimmy Wong through the electronic door. She was new to the job, having graduated from the Sheriff's Academy only three months ago. As we unhooked Jimmy, she threw up her hands. "Another nut case, Tom Hemmings?" she said. "You trying to drive *me* crazy?" Her nose was too blunt for beauty, but her eyes were mischievous and bright.

"Gotta keep you honest, " I said.

She leaned on the intake counter, propping her chin on her fists. "I was about to have my morning coffee," she pouted. "Whyja have to spoil that again?"

"Did you finish the book?" I asked. She had told me she was an avid reader so I was in the habit of recommending books to her.

"*The Great Gatsby*—yeah, I finished it. What a doofus! He never even got his dream girl!"

"His dream was already behind him," I quoted.

"That's *not* why he lost her!" she said. "He lost her because he was an asshole. Who in her right mind would marry a dork like *him*?"

"*I'm* getting m-married in the morning," said Jimmy.

"Com're, hon," she replied. Gently, she rolled his fingerprints as I filled out the booking card. Before snapping his mugshot photo, she winked and told him to smile. Jimmy smoothed back his hair and grinned broadly.

I inventoried Jimmy's property—two condoms, a porno book, and an empty wallet. I then walked him to the nurse's station at the opposite end of the counter. While the nurse took down his medical history, I chatted with Deputy Lockhart. "Ya still wanna read my story?" she asked. She was taking a creative writing class at City College and was teasing me about reading her work. She had been offering to show me the story for weeks, but had yet to hand it over.

"When are you going to give it to me?"

She shrugged. "Keep your pants on, Tom. It's all about a mermaid and I gotta get the imagery right."

"A mermaid," I said. "That shouldn't take long. Mermaids are nothing but tail."

She giggled. "Next time you bring in a nut case, I'll let you see my tale."

After the nurse cleared him for intake, I took Jimmy to a holding cell. He continued singing tunes from *My Fair Lady* as I scanned him with the security wand. "See you in court," I said finally and I thanked him for reporting.

He nodded and smiled. "Jimmy likes m-mermaids," he said.

Rosso nudged me with his elbow as we strode towards the sally port gate. "Why do you keep flirting with that blonde?" he asked. "There ain't no doubt she wants it, Tom, but she's young enough to be yer granddaughter."

"I'm giving her food for thought," I replied. "We're going to have coffee together."

"A big Italian sausage is what *that* bimbo needs."

"I saw her eyeball your crotch," I replied. "All she did was yawn."

It was our usual male bonding humor, but I wanted to say something more. "She wants a man with some culture," I said. "Not an Italian brute."

As we stood beneath the security camera, waiting to show our IDs, Rosso thrust his hips back and forth. "She's *still* gonna need an Italian, Tom. You can't handle that much puss."

I fanned myself with the booking receipt. "She *might* need you to cool her off. There's some heat in this old buck yet."

As Rosso stood there, rolling his eyes, I hummed *With a Little Bit of Luck*. I then flashed my ID to the camera and watched the gate slide open.

Two days later, Jimmy appeared in court. He quickly pled guilty to violating his probation and was sentenced to a year in county jail. Later, I visited him on the psych range.

"You still gonna be my best m-man?" he asked as he peeped through the bars of his six-by-eight foot cell. The bars were chipped, the cell was bare, and the range smelled of vomit and piss.

"You should have asked the judge for a transfer." I said. "To the Department of Mental Health."

He grinned like a fox. "Jimmy took a s-sweet deal. I g-get to stay in 'Frisco and be near the one I love."

"Your fair lady," I joked.

"My w-wife," he replied. "The jail chaplain promised to marry us."

A few days later, there was a letter from him in my office mailbox. It was printed on jail stationary in sprawling, infantile handwriting.

Mr. Hemmings,
You don't have to worry about me any more. I'm not going to bother no girls. It's Deputy Lockhart I'm going to marry. That woman is fine, fine, fine.
Jimmy Wong

I dropped by the county jail that evening to tell her she had a stalker. She laughed, "Jimmy Wong is the one who should worry. My boyfriend's a street cop, ya know. He'll knock his goddamn head off." So she had a boyfriend—the thought left me cold. But I stopped despairing when she handed me her story. She winked flirtatiously and said she would meet me for coffee.

As I rode home on Caltrain, I started to feel rather tired. I tried to read her story, but sadly the story sucked. I would need a stronger enchantment than mermaids if I did not want to doze past my stop.

Opening my Kindle reader, I downloaded *The Great Gatsby.*

•

The Dress

TOM WAS STRANDED by the roadside thirty miles north of Ti Tree. His supplies, which had been meager to begin with, had diminished to a few tins of bully beef and half a canteen of water. He had felt no misgivings a week ago when his ride, a Land Rover from a local cattle station, had melted into the desert, but he knew he would soon have to decide whether to continue on to Darwin, still three hundred miles north, or return to Ti Tree for as long as it would take him to replenish his supplies and then hitch another ride north. The thought gave him the first sense of anticipation he had felt in days, a small thrill of novelty that persisted even though he knew the option was false. It had been two days since he had seen a vehicle traveling in either direction.

His situation was precarious but not uncomfortable. He had made his camp in a tiny grove of paperbarks where he could erect his groundsheet as an overhead against the rains. The rains, though unusual for the Red Center, had been hammering down for fifteen minutes every afternoon, a routine he had come to look forward to since it gave him some relief from the flies and the sultry heat. And afterwards, when the clouds again parted, the trees would be suddenly ablaze, not with the splendor of renewal—the bark was too worn and flaky—but with a hint of dispensation, a short reprieve from their aura of obsolescence. The sight was so ghostly and rare that it hinted of otherworldliness.

Three weeks ago he had been in Sydney, but the memory of Sydney did not tax his complacency. This was probably because Sydney had become an even greater monotony to him; he had

125

been roaming the continent for the better part of a decade and it seemed every year or two brought him back to Sydney—a city he enjoyed for its white surfing beaches but which grew tiresome to him when the surfing was poor. Nor did Darwin, his destination of the moment, provide him with a sense of mission. He was still attracted to the far Northern Territory, but the tolls of Outback living—ravenous flies, skin ulcerations, hips stiffened by long days on horseback—had begun to diminish its lure. Darwin now struck him as secondary to the direction he had chosen for his return: a familiar jaunt through the MacDonnell Ranges and the ghost gum country of Alice Springs. The scenery was a little too spectacular since it reminded him of the dilemma of travel—that the process was generally superior to the arrival.

He was a tall American in his late twenties, finely boned, with eyes too distracted for spontaneity though he persisted in thinking of himself as an adventurer. But the seven years he had spent on the continent had been apportioned a bit too neatly among the Outback cattle stations, the townhouses of Sydney, and the fishing boats of the Tasman Coast. It was as though his adventures came with a six-month warranty after which they acquired a redundancy that made them too weighty to endure further. Still, there were worse deceptions than wanderlust and he wondered only rarely what had set him adrift on an island continent. The Vietnam War was a credible excuse—he had participated in a march on Washington before dropping out of college years ago—but he had sacrificed little in dodging the draft and suspected his sojourn could better be attributed to a shortage of imagination. He had realized his banality the last time he was in Darwin; a New Zealander had made him aware of it by alluding too bluntly to three months he had spent as part of the hippie colony of Lamaroo Beach. "A Sodom and Gomorrah they call it here, mate. A den of iniquity if you want to believe the newspaper. But look at who's been here longest of all—a quiet American with a bagful of books." Tom would have forgotten his ineptitude by now had it not been for a band of Aboriginals he had met a week ago in Coober Pedy. He had been perched by the highway for several days, waiting for a ride to take him beyond the Great Victoria Desert, when a group of

126

them approached him. "You *stay* there," they had insisted. "You wait for truck. Don't try to walk it alone." The advice had been so empathic that he suspected that a few of them had actually attempted to cross the desert on foot.

A flock of galahs, noisy parrots with gray and pink plumage, was now collecting in the skeletal branches above him, invading his space with their chatter and distracting him momentarily from his book. He had been reading *The Iliad* for most of the week, concentrating on it for several hours each afternoon before beginning his regimen of exercises. The classic, despite its shopworn imagery and repetitious slayings, was liberating in its conceit: its assumption that fortune did not spring from chance but from the handwork of deities. He did not trust the gods, celestial playboys whose fickleness belied their status as Olympians, but his predicament had rendered him susceptible to the most improbable of saviors. He took hope in their tendency to favor some mortals over others, an intimation that his fate, a matter he could no longer take for granted, might be trusted to whims less dispassionate than his own.

He put down the book, tired of it now, but the lingering blur of the trees reminded him that he that he had been reading it for most of the afternoon. It was a full minute before he could identify the subtle images alongside the road—forms he mistook for gods before his recovering vision identified them as rock wallabies. The animals, evening feeders, were approaching gingerly over the highway, clearly distrustful of the simmering asphalt that separated them from the grove, and he admitted, as he watched them creep nearer, that it would only be moments before the sun set upon his campsite for the seventh time. He still anticipated the sunsets, that sliver of day when the spinifex grass softened and the rocks, as though preparing for the chill of a desert evening, appeared to be lit by an internal glow. He sighed softly, conceding to the pleasant monotony of another day lost, and he pocketed the book.

Moving stiffly, as though shaking off sleep, he began to gather scrubwood for his fire.

On the eighth day of his sojourn he had an adventure. It took place in the early afternoon, several hours after he had broken camp to await a ride; it was then that he noticed what appeared to be a watery figure approaching him alongside the highway. It was coming from the far north and its outline, inconstant in the vapory heat, gave it the quality of a mirage. He was hopeful, as the outline slowly grew bolder, that it would indeed prove to be unworldly—if not a rescuing spirit then at least a dismissible haunt, an entity sufficiently earthbound as to offer no interruption to his routine. That the form might turn out to be a woman—a probability given its enduring fragility— did not dampen his hope that it would prove impalpable. There were several erotic books in his knapsack so he was used to the consolations of fantasy. His taste for erotica, in fact, seemed less of a perversion than an adaptation to his nomadic lifestyle.

Twenty minutes passed and he sat attentively upon his knapsack, watching the figure as it fluctuated in the desert heat. It did not appear to have grown any larger and he suddenly wondered if it had spotted him as well. Perhaps it had taken note of his exceptional circumstances and—deeming him too eccentric a figure to approach—was retreating back into the desert. Abandonment, after all, seemed the legacy he most deserved—a fitting Karma even if administered by an emissary from Olympus. Had he not himself abandoned a country at war, proclaiming it to have been duped by a duller siren—a sprite unworthy of his critical eye? His severance had come with a minimal jolt—he had simply booked a one-way passage aboard a tramp freighter—but the momentum of his journey had persisted years after he had arrived in Sydney Harbor. So compelling was the option to drift—so unobtrusive an addiction—that a country no smaller than his own had acquired for him the status of a playground. Jenny, a prostitute he had shacked up with years ago in Sydney, had said it best. "You're a *swagman*, Tom Hemmings—a bloody desert rummy. Rob you blind, they will, and go walkabout by morning."

The figure, now just half a mile away, appeared to be moving at a trot, and he could tell, at this distance, that it was a female. This was not because of its shape—even at a closer range it remained pencil-thin—but because of the grace with which it moved. Its gait was unusually comely—still fluid although it had outrun the heat waves—while a shock of dark hair was bouncing gently upon its shoulders. For a second, he thought that he recognized her, not as an intimate—the shape was too boyish to suggest a former lover—but perhaps as a dancer attached to a carnival he had traveled with a year ago. He had worked a sideshow at the time, erecting a tent for the Princess Atasha, a skinny stripper who, with the aid of mirrors, was transformed nightly into a mighty ape. His carnival tour, which had taken him through Queensland, New South Wales, and most of South Australia, had been prolonged by an eight-month affair he had had with his foreman's wife, a disheartened woman of forty who had seen him as a soul mate. He suspected he would have tired of her sooner had it not been for the chance that they would be discovered, a fear that had given their affair an unconquerable excitement. He remembered the intensity of their couplings, performed quickly in the back of a truck, and regretted that he had not stayed longer with the carnival.

The figure was now close, about fifty feet away, and its features had sharpened into those of a very young woman. Sadly, she was not a specter: her feet, bony and bare, were stained reddish brown from the roadside dust, and her aggravated squint implied that she had recently lost a pair of spectacles. Her dress, a black sheath, did not cover her coltish legs, yet it all but concealed the slight swell of her breasts. Her eyes, contemptuous of her shortsightedness, were examining him carefully as she approached, but the neutrality of her expression convinced him that he was not a priority to her.

He rose from his knapsack, slowly so as not to alarm her, and slapped some of the dust from his jeans. The gesture was optimistic since he half expected her to trot on by, dismissing him as an unimportant bit of scenery, but a show of manners seemed called for under the circumstances. It was perhaps the airiness of the moment, its similarity to a daydream, that inspired his courtesy and he was therefore disappointed when, after jogging the final few yards that separated them, she halted.

Her manner remained impersonal, as though he were a sentry she had come to relieve, and he suddenly felt conspicuous.

"Would you like to throw the first match?" she said.

The question, though inane, did not surprise him. It struck him instead as an opportunity—a chance to diffuse the encounter with a flash of wit.

He said, "I don't smoke."

She did not answer him at once. Her eyes, which were continuing to examine him, retained their squint, an exertion that suggested her myopia was very severe. He did not pity her her handicap, however, since its overall affect was one of temperance. Her sharp features, particularly her long narrow nose, made her resemble a bird of prey.

"Don't mind *me*," she said at last. "I'm just a snotty little boy."

The remark was also unintelligible, but it seemed to have ended the conversation. He took some comfort in the reward that followed: a forgivable view of her hips, which continued to roll innocently as she trotted once again in the direction of Ti Tree. She was running on her toes with a slow looping stride, and her imprints in the dust were like those of a small animal.

He knew that she was about to disrobe. His anticipation was so strong that he suspected he had willed it when, after a few seconds, she halted once again and began to unfasten the top of her dress. The garment, unimpeded by her boyish hips, fell neatly to the ground, becoming a dark puddle from which she freed herself with a hop. She ran on methodically, traveling a hundred feet or so before stopping once again, as though hobbled by the afterthought of her bra and panties. She bent over, tugging impatiently at the strip beneath her waist, and he saw a whisper of pubic hair as the cloth dropped to the ground. Her bra, which she relinquished with a high toss, sailed a remarkable distance before falling onto the asphalt, a flight that impressed him as something of an overstatement. Her breasts, smaller than plums, did not seem to deserve so dramatic a liberation.

He stood motionlessly, his eyes riveted upon her as she continued to jog along the highway. Since her nakedness seemed

130

more pubescent than sensual, the insistence of his arousal could only be extravagant. It was in fact an irony that his jeans, a drifter's rugged garb, had acquired a large and uncomfortable key. Still, the moment had clearly defined itself as something beyond reason, and the comedy was only enhanced by the jiggle and roll of her buttocks, a rhythm now in keeping with the hammering in his ears. He stood for a half-hour—the time it took her figure, already pale and twiggy, to lose its definition completely. Only then did he glance about him, diverted by a silhouette, a shadow belonging to a wedge-tailed eagle soaring in wide circles above the grove. He looked in the direction from which she had come, not in hope of spotting a clue to the incident but in the manner of a thief hoping to elude discovery. The highway was barren, its stillness broken only by the returning shadow of the eagle.

He did not contemplate the matter for long. Speculation was impossible, scenarios seemed empty plots, and he was more impressed by his vulnerability to the event than whatever had set it in motion. He was therefore startled when a southbound vehicle pulled alongside of him an hour later: he could tell at a glance that it was the same battered Land Rover that had dropped him off a week ago. He did not recognize the driver, a bull-necked man wearing a damp singlet, yet he regarded the man with a sense of fraternity as he leaned out of the cab.

"G'day," the man said.

"Good afternoon," he replied.

"Ya see a nude sheila come runnin' this way?"

Tom pointed in the direction of Ti Tree feeling, at that moment, a pang of utter betrayal. The man's sweaty face was far too enthusiastic to suggest anything other than a superficial regard for his quarry. He seemed loutish, contemptible, a voyeur of an inferior grade, and Tom looked at him with distaste as he ducked his head back into the truck.

"Good on ya, mate."

The statement, too patented for the uniqueness of the event, was chastised by a stern rumble from the heavens as the Land Rover hurtled forward. Within minutes the desert had hidden the van in a fading plume of dust. When the dust had evaporated completely, he tugged at his knapsack, removing his rain jacket from behind the flap. He would have preferred to re-erect his groundsheet, a more sensible protection from the afternoon rain, but he had no desire to abandon his vigil by the highway to return to the cover of the grove. This was not because his chivalry had endured, but because he did not want to be distracted; he did not doubt that the incident, like a stone thrown into a lake, would relinquish a final concentric ripple before sinking into oblivion.

It was another half-hour before the police car appeared, a white sedan belonging to the cop shop in Ti Tree. He did not recognize it as an official vehicle until it had come to a full stop on the opposite side of the road, and he felt his pulse leap when a short stocky man, heralded by another roll of thunder, popped out from behind the wheel and strutted towards him. He was wary of the authorities, having experienced several roadside interrogations during his past travels, but his fear, as the man approached him, seemed attributable to a different script, as though he were observing not a Territorial policeman but an angel from a court of Heaven.

"Hello," the man said in a clipped voice. He was holding a notebook and a small gold pen.

"Can I help you?" he replied. He sensed, as he made the offer, that he was unlikely to incriminate himself. It was evident from the man's attention to his notebook that he was not the object of the query.

"Did a woman pass this way, sir?"

He nodded.

"She say anything about a fire?"

"Not much," he remarked. "She asked about a match."

"I see," the man said. He did not seem to have comprehended the pun and his pen, as he held it over the notebook, wiggled like something autonomous. The aloofness with which he scribbled suggested that no further light was likely to be shed upon the incident.

When the man had finished writing, he closed the notebook with a snap and tucked it into the pocket of his shirt. He seemed satisfied that the incident if not comprehensible, could at least be sanitized by a report. He bore an attitude of official complacency, a bureaucrat's insularity to the irreclaimable.

"Anything you need?" the man asked him. "Some tucker perhaps or maybe a lift into town?"

"Some grub ought to do it," he said.

The man nodded.

"There'll be a mail truck out this way tomorrow. I'll see to it the driver brings you a bit of tucker. Oysters if you want 'em."

"Anything will do," he replied, unwilling to acknowledge the jibe.

The man chuckled hollowly as though embarrassed by the joke. He appeared to be grateful for the thunder, the change of topic it provided him, and his eyes settled briefly upon the cumulus. The rain would be pouring down at its usual hour.

"This bloody monsoon," the man muttered. "Bit of a bore, sir, these afternoon soakings. You'd think we'd be quit of them by April, wouldn't you now?"

A few minutes later, as he watched the police car vanish into the desert, he conceded reluctantly that the matter had come to an end. He still felt no urgency to erect his camp, but the effort was now overdue: the clouds had acquired a dark abundance and the first heavy drops were imprinting the dust. It consoled him that the dress lay forgotten upon the highway—a suggestion, perhaps, of Olympian grace or at least an indication that he might have overrated the incident. A tongue of cold light seemed to set it aflutter, affording it a bright but soundless illumination as he fitted his knapsack to his shoulders. He picked up the dress, folded it neatly, and set it beside a milepost.

•

Hunting Bear

RYAN O'SHAUGHNESSY IS STANDING in front of *The Pink Panther*, a strip club in downtown Sydney. His gaze is narrow, like a cop's, and complements his close-cropped hair and walnut-sized knuckles. The fact that he is a street thug in no way belies his sense of proprietorship. His mission is sacred, after all, for tonight he is hunting bear—not the grizzled variety, but a snitch who badly needs killing, a tall bearded jerk who fingered him to the cops after selling him a bag of meth. The cops had tried to squeeze him as well but Ryan, a man of *real* character, had told them nothing. And so he had been forced to spend another year in the city jail. *And a damn hard year it was.* Even buggering the Nancy boys had not kept the walls from crushing in on him. It seemed as though the jail had swallowed him alive.

But *tonight* he is back to living in Hyde Park. And *tonight* he is hunting for bear.

His gaze remains steady as a cop car rolls past him, its black body shivering in the bright lights of the strip. This time Ryan refuses to flinch. Fuck the cops—he has served his time and now has comeuppance to collect. The informant's name is Stork—if that's what he's still calling himself. Street names are usually changed every month—if not, it's too easy to get snitched out. Ryan has had over fifty different street names and so he has gotten snitched out only *once*. And tonight his name is Hunting Bear, kinda like the Indian brave in that movie he saw last

135

night—the guy who apologized to a deer after killing it. But Ryan is not going to apologize for wasting Stork.

What was the name of that little twitch?—the cute little junkie he's going to marry tomorrow at the Wayside Chapel? Her street name is Miss Muffet, but what's her *real* name? Probably it's Berta or Frieda or something god-awful. She's only marrying him for citizenship papers—so she won't get deported if she's caught shooting heroin—but what the hell: she has promised him fifty bucks and a trick. And money is money—crotch is crotch. That boy who was with her—probably her pimp-to-be—had told him she was a hard lay. Hymen like leather. "If you can bust her, you can have her," he had joked and Ryan had laughed heartily. "I'll bust her," he said. "Busted me a *thousand* cherries."

And so his itinerary is set: First ice that canary. Then bust himself a cherry.

Another squad car rolls by, gliding to a halt when the street light changes to red. The city is thick with cops tonight. Ryan catches his reflection in the side mirror of the squad car: he is a broad-shouldered man with thick horn-rimmed glasses and a rather menacing harelip. And his triceps, swollen from fifty daily pushups on the cell row, threaten to rip through his short-sleeved shirt. *Fifty-five years old* and he can still lick his weight in wildcats. Ryan doesn't even need the pistol—the .44 Auto Mag that is hidden in his crotch. He could strangle that canary with his bare hands.

Ryan studies the street as the cop car speeds off. The hit should be easy—a piece of cake. He has already killed off a hundred snitches—iced them just to keep in shape. His life as an outlaw—his thirty years of breaking into cars, dropping meth, and getting into fights—has turned him into a rock-hard terminator. Even the cops don't intimidate him. Only yesterday, after getting out of jail, he wrote *eat shit* on the back of a squad car. Wrote it in his *own* shit just to press home the point. That's what they get for throwing him into the meat wagon every chance they get. How many cops has he punched?—he's not sure. Maybe he's got Alzheimer's—that's what the jail shrink told him. Or maybe he just forgets things now and then. But he

136

hasn't forgotten that crotch of a jail—the scurrying roaches, the stench of stale socks, and the pulsating racket.

The sidewalks are crowded with tourists and hippies, but Ryan is quick to identify the tall gaunt figure on the opposite side of the street. *Stork—it's got to be Stork.* Only Stork could be so dumb—strutting around in a bright red jacket when he oughta know there's a price on his head. This is going to be even easier than he thought. Ryan takes a deep drag on his cigarette— exhales a silvery stream. With a flick of his finger, he fires the butt at a passing truck. *Bull's eye.*

Slowly, stealthily, Ryan eases himself into the stream of pedestrians. He is forced to walk slowly since a bunch of Hari Krishnas are blocking his way—shoeless kids with tambourines and halfwit expressions. What a way to end up: banging on tambourines, singing like sin. And there's not a real bang in the whole bunch. He had attended one of their feasts only yesterday after getting out of jail. Some feast—raisins and brown apples on a dirty tray. There oughta be a *law* against serving that crap. He had nibbled a piece of apple—politely—and then left. Let them serve him pork chops if they want him back—and maybe some Bristol Cream Sherry. And let them wash their feet.

"*Hunting Bear*" somebody shouts—Ryan tenses. It's one of the fucking Krishnas: a sunken-chested boy with blazing acne. One day out of jail and Ryan has already been recognized. The boy slaps his tambourine. "*Rama*," he bleats. "*Rama Rama.*" The Krishnas are all around him now, laughing and singing— praising him like he's some kind of elephant god. Ryan dances along with them, hoping that by doing so he will avoid greater scrutiny. He is careful not to dislodge the gun. Ryan dances the twist while the Krishnas leap about aimlessly. When the dance is over, he slips back into the crowd.

Stork is still standing on the opposite side of the street. Ryan pats the magnum-powered pistol in his pants. The word is *go.* Sooner or later we all gotta pay—and Stork's gotta pay *tonight.* But the job needs to be done in a vacant alley: *there,* Ryan can take his time about it—*there,* Stork can see the bore of the gun pointed leisurely at his chest. Let him grovel a bit before taking the slug—otherwise, he won't have paid enough. Be a waste of a good hollow-point bullet to dust him on the street.

Ryan crosses the street—hops to the curb. He pauses when Stork looks in his direction, but the boy's wooly face remains calm, benign—kinda like the face of Jesus. Clearly, Stork has not recognized him—probably he doesn't even remember *dropping* the dime. But just wait until he goes into an alley to make a drug deal. Ryan will have a chat with him there—bring him up to speed. Ryan laughs at his joke then ducks into a doorway.

Ten minutes pass and Stork does not budge. Ryan decides to wait him out. Can't make it too obvious though. Ryan glances at a flock of prostitutes, most of them transsexuals, who are also soliciting on the street. He had better pretend that he's one of their johns or Stork may start to get suspicious of him. Ryan winks at one of the prostitutes—an invitation that sets his teeth on edge. It is against his ethics to pay for ass. Hell, woman ought to pay *him*.

The hooker hesitates before approaching. She's a willowy kid with wary eyes and she knows he's not a regular. Ryan pats the bulge created by the gun. "I'm loaded for bear, sister," he says.

She smiles thinly then bites her lower lip. She is young, remarkably young, and her front teeth are smeared with lipstick. She looks like an adolescent who has stolen her mother's makeup kit. "Do you *really* date?" she scoffs.

Ryan nods. "I mean *business*, Sister."

"It's twenty for head."

Ryan opens his wallet and rummages about. Thankfully, he still has his gate money from jail. He makes a show out of handing her the twenty dollars. "Dinner and a movie," he jokes.

Ryan grimaces as she takes the money. What a waste. The only consolation is that she won't bother him *after* the sex. After sex, all women ought to turn into pool tables.

He follows her into an alley and waits patiently while she adjusts her dress. When she kneels at his feet, he can only feign interest: her teeth are so small, her eyes so vacant, that she reminds him of a dead fish. Ryan takes off his shirt and flexes his biceps. Maybe this will get him a discount. He needs to delay matters anyhow—bide his time until Stork comes into the alley. A good Indian brave keeps his mind on the hunt.

The tranny stares up at him. "Don't take all night about it, mister."

Ryan balls up his shirt then stuffs it into his rear pocket. "Twenty minutes of your time—that's all I want, sister. I'm hunting for bear." He opens his wallet and hands her another ten dollars. "Just keep outta sight."

Her eyes flash. "You *ashamed* to be *seen* with me, mister?"

"Gotta be careful. Tomorrow, I'm getting married."

She jumps to her feet and snatches the money from his hand. She then crumples it up—throws it on the ground. "Who'd marry *you*—weirdo?"

Indignant, she sashays back to the street. Ryan lets the money lie. A deal's a deal and maybe she'll come back. He waits twenty minutes, but Stork does not appear. Nor does the tranny so Stork might be suspicious. He might wonder why Ryan did not follow her out of the alley.

Loud voices force Ryan to peek from the alley. The sidewalk is now crowded with demonstrators: a bunch of hippies, longhaired freaks, are yelling at a group of soldiers. The hippies look young—the soldiers even younger; the exchange is tritely familiar. *Baby burner....I'm proud to have fought....You'd fight for any cunt.*

Ryan listens attentively. If a fight should break out, he wants to be part of it. Pop himself a few longhairs—maybe even a soldier or two. He hopes the cops don't show up too quickly.

The judge should have sent him to *Nam* instead of jail. He'd have killed a thousand of those little gooks then chopped off their ears and used them for fish bait. *Hut two three four—dust a foe and look for more.* Plenty of good weed there too.

A cop car arrives. The hippies scatter while the soldiers walk away. Stork is no longer around, but Ryan is not worried. The fucker will soon be back and he can watch for him from the coffee shop across the street. Ryan needs to piss anyhow and only bums piss in alleys.

Ryan crosses the street and struts toward the coffee shop. A street urchin watches him approach—an elfin teenage girl who is panhandling in front of the glass doorway. Her face is so thin that she looks supernatural—like maybe she's a vision of some kind. Ryan doesn't like visions; he's seen too many of the damn things. But that doesn't make him a schizo—or whatever that jail shrink called him. Ryan just *notices* things.

To make sure she's real, Ryan hands her five dollars. She takes the money and pockets it in her jeans. "Thank you, dear sir."

Ryan thumps his naked chest. "I'm hunting bear, Dolly. You'd better get out of here."

She titters. "Then why are your pants still on?"

"Stork I mean. I'm gonna plug Stork."

She giggles again. "Storks deliver *babies.*"

Ryan shakes his head. Maybe she's an angel. He gives her another five dollars then pats her on the head. Never *know* when you're gonna need an angel on your side.

Ryan puts on his shirt and enters the coffee shop. The beak-nosed woman behind the counter watches him as he strides towards the john. Once he has relieved himself, he returns and makes his purchase: a latté and two chocolate donuts. The woman's eyes remain fixed on him—even after he sits at a table and starts to sip his coffee. Ryan watches for Stork through the glass doorway of the shop. The girl is gone.

The shop is dim, the coffee sweet, and Ryan feels good for the first time in months. What more could he wish for than a cool summer evening, a snitch to kill, and sprinkles on his donuts? He does not bother with further reflection: his boyhood in that flea-pit orphanage, those bull dyke nuns that whipped him daily—catching their switches in their holy beads—and his many internments in jails and mental institutions. Had he burned down that orphanage?—fuck it, who knows? His memory is unreliable now—just like those freaks that keep popping up: dog-faced midgets, glowering mimes, hags with painted faces. Only the gun, the hard press of metal in his crotch, can be counted on.

Stork is now back on the other side of the street. He has changed into a denim jacket, probably to confuse the cops. Ryan nibbles a donut—*slowly.* Dry Puss is still watching him from the counter. If he greases Stork now, she's gonna call the cops on him. *Big mistake*—coming into the coffee shop. Ryan is still sitting at the table when Stork, accompanied by one of the trannies, ambles into an alley, probably to make a sale. It's the same damn tranny he paid good money to.

"Ahem." The voice is calm, gentle—like water chuckling in a stream. A gentleman is standing by his table—an elegant man in a gray pinstriped suit. His eyes are soft, his hair silver white, and he is wearing a pink carnation in the lapel of his jacket. He isn't a cop—probably he isn't even a vision. Probably, he's just a tourist visiting the city. Plenty of cruise ships in Sydney Harbor. Plenty of easy pickings on those ships. "Ahem," the man says. "Who might your trainer be, sir?"

Ryan flexes his biceps. "Got 'em hoisting beer bottles."

The man smiles "Perhaps a glass of sherry for a change."

The gentleman sits down. He places two mugs on the table—probably got them from Dry Puss. He removes a slim bottle from inside his jacket and empties it into the mugs.

Ryan sips his sherry then glances towards the counter. Dry Puss, preoccupied with another customer, is no longer watching him. Ryan looks back at the gentleman and winks. He has decided to string him along; that way she'll think he's a hustler—not a hit man. Anyhow, it's against his principles not to roll a faggot.

The gentleman is now boring him with drivel about his family: a dog named Spook, a daughter in college, a wife from whom he's estranged but still loves. Ryan puts down his sherry. "Don't miss the boat, Pops."

The gentleman nods profoundly. His eyes are so soft they are practically misty. "You're very astute."

Ryan laughs heartily. "That's me, Pops. I go *deep*."

Ryan takes the gentleman by the arm—guides him towards the door. The man stumbles as he walks. As they stroll along the street, Ryan keeps his eyes on Stork. He is standing alone on the opposite sidewalk. He is smoking a cigarette—his *last damn cigarette*—but, thanks to this faggot, he will have time to finish it.

Ryan walks in the direction of Hyde Park. His shadow, emboldened by the streetlights, intermingles with the shadow of the gentleman. The gentleman is singing. *"Hoo rah, hoo rah. The Campbells are coming. Hoo rah."*

The punch, when Ryan delivers it, is swift, scientific—the gentleman grabs his stomach. *"Ooof,"* he says—his carnation pops off. Ryan catches him as his knees begin to sag and sits him down in a doorway. He searches the man's pockets, finds his wallet, opens it up. Only forty dollars—hardly worth his time. But principle is principle. Ryan pockets twenty dollars and leaves the rest in the wallet. The coot will need money for a cab. "Let that be a *lesson* to you, Pops." He tosses him the wallet. "What would your *wife* think?"

Leaving the gentleman in the doorway, Ryan marches back towards the coffee house. He knows from experience that the man won't call the cops. And he has bigger matters to worry about. It is late—nearly midnight—and Stork is still alive.

Ryan lurks outside of the coffee shop. While he waits, he swallows a hit of meth—a capsule that he smuggled out of jail. Twenty more minutes pass, but Stork does not appear. Fuck it—there's no sense in hanging around all night just to kill off another snitch. He may as well party instead—have himself a ball. In case the cops get lucky enough to nab him.

Ryan walks two blocks downhill to the classiest nightclub in town. The sign on the Marquee—*Whiskey A-Go-Go*—flashes then fades, flashes then fades. Ryan sucks in his belly as he walks towards the doorway. No sense in advertising the bulge from the gun.

A burly bouncer nods at him and Ryan strolls into the club—*unsearched*. The club, a cavernous place, is filled with Servicemen, cigarette smoke, scantily dressed women serving drinks. The lights from a chandelier force him to squint. His pupils, dilated from the meth, are probably bigger than saucers now.

A hostess approaches him—a pencil-thin woman in her fifties with stiletto heels. Her silvery dress clings like cellophane to her tits and spits back the light from the chandelier. Her cheekbones have the windswept look of a bad facelift. She is looking at him with exaggerated concern. "Are you hungry, my dear?"

Ryan grins. "I could eat."

She points towards an empty booth at a far corner of the club. "Have a seat, poor sir. A waitress will bring you something. It's *entirely* on the house." The woman's eyes are tender, her voice is softer than silk, but there is an unmistakable put down to her offer. *Behave and we will feed you—just like a dog.*

Insulted, Ryan takes a seat at the far end of the nightclub—a corner so dark that his eyes readjust. A half naked waitress brings him his bribe: a hamburger on a paper plate. Ryan orders schnapps with a beer chaser and pays for it with his *own* money.

Ryan takes a bite out of the burger. It is soggy—practically raw. What do they think he is—a vampire? He spits the mouthful out and shoves the plate to one side. He then downs the schnapps quickly to wash away the taste of the burger. He finishes his beer in several gulps.

The room is now glittering like a diamond. A faggot band is beginning to play. A tight-butt woman is singing a Beatles song—something about Mother Mary and letting it be. Ryan gets a hard on listening to the woman. He'd nail her a good one if he wasn't getting married tomorrow—show her what a *real* man can do. And after he had her begging for more, he'd turn her into his squaw. Ryan closes his eyes and listens to the beat of the ballad. There's nothing like a bit of music before icing yourself a snitch. Helps put a man in the mood.

The music fades as Ryan begins to nod off. He wakes up abruptly. The room is now dotted with flashes of light. They mingle with the band, the couples on the dance floor—even with the bouncers standing like sentinels near the doorway.

A towering nun, obscured by the jumping lights, is drifting from table to table. She seems to hover like a bird of prey. What the fuck is she up to—trying to pluck souls? Nuns don't belong here and that's for sure. It's bad enough when they show up in jail.

Ryan slips from the booth and struts towards the dance floor. *Screw* that skinny hostess. Ryan came here to party and he's *going* to party. Time to show the women here his moves. The band is now playing "I Shot The Sheriff"—which has put him in the mood for a war dance.

Standing in the middle of the dance floor, Ryan struts his stuff. He bobs nimbly from side to side while singing. "*Hiii* yah *yah* yah yah." The bouncers are watching him intently while the women are checking him out. When the song is over, the room is spinning: an aggravation since Ryan needs to piss—*badly*. His bladder has swollen to the size of a medicine ball. Slowly, as though navigating a carousel, Ryan makes his way towards the men's room.

The door to the men's room is hard to find. When he finally spots it, it seems as though an hour has passed. Ryan enters the room judiciously as though walking into a church. It is empty— thank God—and a shiny urinal sits before him like a shrine.

Ryan throws back his head as he urinates. The relief is so great that he closes his eyes. He sighs profoundly when he has finished and shakes himself for several seconds. A good strong piss is as good as jacking off.

The door to the bathroom bangs open.

Instantly, Ryan crouches. His shoulder is turned towards the door, his fists are balled and ready to strike. A jailhouse stance.

His muscles relax when he sees the intruder—a beetle-browed man with a pork pie hat. He couldn't be more than five feet tall and he's scuttling into the bathroom like a centipede. The man halts when he sees Ryan. He yelps and then scuttles back out. That cocksucker *better* run. He *deserves* a good ass whipping—just for looking like a bug. *And* he might have *knocked*.

Ryan stumbles to the sink—turns on the faucet. Time to wash up and get the hell out of here. Time to get on with his mission. When he presses the liquid soap dispenser, he pauses. The soap is red and irresistibly glossy. Ryan covers his fingers with the soap and then combs four streaks onto each of his cheeks—*bear claw marks*. It looks like he's wearing war paint now. He admires his reflection in the mirror as he finishes washing up.

Ryan strolls back into the clubroom. The lights are still jumping—popping all around him like flash bulbs—but he can make out faces now. The women are watching him, mouths agape—the men are applauding him loudly. Ryan bounces as he walks and chants, "*Woo woo woo.*" It's about *time* they paid homage to an Indian brave. Even the hostess is looking him over, her eyes growing wider than doorknobs.

The hostess is in front of him now and her tits are heaving with excitement. Let her wait her turn—she's a little too skinny for his taste. He should have brought a rubber hose just to beat off some of the women in here. When she speaks to him, she is still gulping for breath—so much so that it sounds like she's uttering a single word. "*Siryou'reindecent.*"

Irritated, Ryan thumps his chest with his fist. "I'm *Hunting Bear*, woman. Show some *respect.*"

She is wringing her hands as though ridding them of ants, but her voice is now measured and stern. "That's just the *problem*, sir. You're a little *too* bare."

Ryan bows his head and sighs. It's not a good day for meat. Still, she didn't have to call him *indecent.* Twelve inches on the slack is pretty damn decent.

Reluctantly, Ryan shakes his head. She has *forced* him to even the score. Not that he wants to upset her, but *honor* is *honor. No one* talks that way to Hunting Bear. *Especially*, when he's on the warpath.

Ryan grabs the front of the woman's gown—yanks. The fabric tears—her breasts spring free, wobbling about like water balloons. Not a bad rack for so skinny a broad. The woman gasps. "The *cleaners*," she says. "This dress just came back from the *cleaners*, sir."

Ryan takes off his wristwatch and hands it to her. It's gotta be worth thirty dollars to a pawnbroker. "That oughta cover it," he says. "Save me the bill if it costs any more to fix."

She doesn't accept the watch—instead, she clutches her dress to her breasts. Her voice is now shriller than a police siren. "*Get this tramp out of here. We fed him and look how he acts.*"

Ryan shakes his head. Some hostess *she* is—can't handle a little tit for tat. Hell, the bitch is lucky he didn't spank her.

The bouncers are on him now: a hand grabs his collar, yanking him backwards—more hands pin his arms to his sides. "*Zip it,*" a voice cries, but Ryan cannot move. There's got to be four of them, at least—that's how many it takes to handle *Hunting Bear.*

'WE EVEN FED HIM," the hostess cries. "*We even fed him. We even fed that boar of a man....*" Her voice grows fainter as the bouncers frog march him to the back door of the club. Bouncers and cops—they're all the same: too chicken shit to fight him one-on-one. And they always take the woman's side.

Although Ryan struggles mightily, he is thrown into an alley behind the club. His hands—quicker than a serpent's tongue—break his fall as he hits the pavement. The door to the club slams shut behind him.

Remarkably, Ryan can still feel the press of the pistol in his crotch. He could have popped all four of them, but fuck it. The bouncers were just doing their job—even if they *were* gutless about it. It's that Goddamn *Stork* who needs popping.

Ryan rises to his feet, dusts off his knees, and eases his tallywhacker back into his pants. Oughta have a *pulley* to reel in *that* baby. Zipping his pants up, he steps from the alley back onto the sidewalk.

A street clock reminds him that it's two o'clock in the morning. It may as well be noon, *high noon*, like that movie he saw a year ago with Gary Cooper as the sheriff. Now there's a *real* man: he popped off four bad guys who all needed popping. Slaughtered them like hogs. *Do not forsake me, oh my darlin', on this our wedding daaay.* The theme song from the movie runs through his mind as he marches back to the coffee house.

The streetlights are floating like jellyfish; the storefronts sweep by him as though borne upon a current. He has all but forgotten the incident in the nightclub; like a piece of flotsam, it will soon be lost in the swampland of his memory. Ryan is grateful his memory is shot—the streets are no place for a cluttered mind. Stick to the *basics* and the *basics* will take care of you. And so hussies you hump, snitches you kill, faggots you roll, and angels you guard—that is if you can *find* an angel. The streets are practically empty now.

146

A SECOND, LESS CAPABLE, HEAD

That he still has the gun means his mission is sealed. It is in the stars that he rid the world of scumbags. And a man can't be arguing with the *stars*. The sanctity of his mission grows clearer still when he sees Stork standing alone at the top of the hill. With his back pressed against a storefront wall, his eyes staring blandly ahead, he looks like a prisoner awaiting execution. Stork turns his head slowly in Ryan's direction. He slowly looks away.

Ryan slaps the clip into the gun. The clip has four rounds in it, but he will only need one. Ryan, an expert marksman, can hit a dime at fifty yards. Too bad for Stork that he had to go and drop one.

Since his mission cannot fail, there is no point in putting things off. He will lure Stork into the alley himself. He will use the pretense of making a buy. Stork did not recognize him, after all. He does not know that Ryan, Heaven's avenger, will be the last person he sees on earth.

Ryan racks the slide, chambers a round, and puts the gun back into his pants. The time is *now*.

Stork's face softens as Ryan approaches him. His smile is warm, infectious, and utterly disarming, but it is a smile of solicitation—not recognition—much like the smile of a supermarket clerk. *Sample our cheesecake*, the smile seems to say. *The first piece is free.* That asshole would need plugging even if he *wasn't* a snitch. It's too bad he has to look like Jesus.

Stork continues smiling as Ryan plants himself in front of him. The fucker *still* doesn't know who he is. Ryan snaps his thick fingers. "A dime's worth of speed."

Stork's eyes crinkle warmly as he looks Ryan over. He seems amused by the red soap streaks on Ryan's face. Obviously, Ryan is not a narc. "Might I see the money, my friend?"

Ryan dips into his pocket and pulls out a wad—a roll of one-dollar bills wrapped up in a twenty. Stork seems convinced that he is holding a hundred dollars. "Come into my office, my friend."

Ryan follows Stork into the alley. The alley is darker than he remembers and smells of piss. When Stork turns to face him, Ryan is pointing the pistol at his chest.

Stork shows no alarm—only benign interest. His smile seems chiseled upon his face. "Do you do hits?" he asks.

Ryan shakes his head. The cocksucker still thinks *he's* in charge.

"Do you do hits?" Stork repeats. "I could *use* a man with courage. Now you can rob me for chump change or you can earn some *real* money. And I'll give you that dime's worth for free."

Ryan extends his arm. The gun is now six inches from Stork's chest. So the fucker wants him to kill for *drugs and money*? That's not a bad idea, but Ryan has *justice* to perform. And Stork needs to *know* that his hour has come.

"I hittin' *you*, asshole—let's get that straight. You *dropped* a dime."

Stork's smile remains frozen upon his face. "My friend, I don't know you from Adam."

"Get a *clue*, sister. Adam wears a *fig leaf*."

"I see," Stork replies. "That must be him *behind* you."

Ryan looks over his shoulder—no one is there. When he looks back at Stork, the cocksucker is fifty feet away and running. The oldest damn trick in the book.

Ryan wraps both his hands around the pistol grip. Anticipating the kick, he presses one hand against the other—the old push-pull. Can't ice a snitch if the gun isn't steady. He pulls the trigger—*twice*—and the gun starts bucking like a bitch in heat.

Ryan's ears are humming—he should have put plugs in them. He lowers the pistol to finish Stork off, but the fucker is still sprinting like a deer. *Impossible*—he's got to have two slugs in him. Ryan fires again—the sound splits his eardrums. Pavement explodes near Stork's heels.

Ryan kneels down to steady his aim. The damn hollow points are dragging too much. He raises the pistol. "*I'll pay you*," Stork shouts, but his voice is practically buried by the ringing in Ryan's ears.

Stork is zigzagging as he runs, throwing off Ryan's aim. That fucker's been shot at before. Ryan squeezes the trigger—g-r-a-d-u-a-l-l-y. *POW*. Stork stumbles the instant he fires and falls down. Ryan hears the slug ricochet off the alley wall.

Stork is back on his feet—running like a greyhound. His footsteps echo hollowly as he disappears down the alley. He should have taken his punishment like a *man*. Now Ryan is *really* pissed.

Ryan rises to his feet. He does a quick war dance. *No one* gets the better of Hunting Bear—not even when his gun is empty. He will track Stork down and beat him to death with his *tallywhacker*, if necessary. Ryan can track an ant across a desert.

For now, Ryan needs to get out of here. A police siren, wailing like a banshee, challenges the ringing in his ears. Ryan picks up the shell casings, hotter than live coals, and shoves them into his pocket. He plunges the gun back into his pants. He'll have to dump it somewhere else.

Ryan's belt snags the trigger.

The gun bucks and roars.

A blow knocks his leg out from under him.

Ryan tries to run, but can only stagger. *Hunting Bear is hit.* He must have miscounted the bullets.

Pulling a handkerchief from his pocket, Ryan quickly wraps the wound. The handkerchief reddens instantly—no matter. Ryan has survived a dozen wounds.

Dragging his leg behind him, Ryan peeks from the alley. The street is still empty—he can make his escape. If he can make it to Hyde Park, just a half mile away, the police will never find him. Like a true Indian brave, he will vanish among the trees.

Ryan depresses the clip from the gun. Catching the clip, he tosses it into a dumpster. He throws the gun back into the alley since he has to get rid of it quick.

Moving gingerly, Ryan hobbles in the direction of Hyde Park. His leg feels transformed—it is now a dead log—but it is not the *leg* that is slowing him down. A fat clown, juggling water balloons, is blocking the entire sidewalk. The clown's mouth is crimson, like an open wound, and he is calling cadence as he tosses the balloons. "One, two, three, *faw*. One, two, three *faw*." His concentration is so intense that he may as well be throwing up grenades.

Ryan veers sharply to avoid the clown. He falls to the ground—pain shoots through his knee. Another damn rip in his pants. Scrambling to his feet, Ryan continues to stagger toward the park.

That clown needs an ass whipping—hogging the entire sidewalk—but Ryan hasn't got time to do it. Hopefully, the circus will take care of him.

The police siren is growing louder, but the street is still empty. Ryan limps on, his leg dragging with every step. The wound starts to thaw as he approaches an intersection. His thigh is now aching like a bad tooth.

The street light changes. A towering mass, dumped in the center of the cross walk, is bathed in a scarlet glow. The mass takes shape as Ryan draws nearer. It's that fucking nun again.

The nun turns toward him and he can now make out her face. Her lips are pursed, as though she is preparing to kiss him, and her jaw is moving mechanically. She is holding a small pig, stroking it behind the ears. The pig grunts affectionately, unaware that it has been stuck—that one of its intestines is dangling like a dick.

The nun nods as Ryan approaches her. She is looking at him possessively, a dominion not born out of reverence—not even concern for his injury—but from the tacit understanding that he will be her next meal.

Ryan dashes past the nun and finishes crossing the street. Fuck that bitch—she will have to *catch* him first. And *no one* catches Hunting Bear.

The park is now only a block away. The trees, the lamp posts, the bushes emerge—much like soldiers advancing through a fog. Ryan staggers on—only fifty yards to go—but the siren is growing louder.

Distracted by the fog, Ryan practically trips over the elfin girl—the waif he gave money to earlier that night. She is sitting upon the sidewalk, giggling loudly, and polishing an apple. Her feet are bare and her naked toes are wiggling like newborn mice. She is wearing a pink dress.

Ryan stares at the girl. "*Beat* it, Dolly. I *told* you that once already."

She laughs merrily. "Storks deliver *babies*," she says.

Ryan shakes his head. He's seen *geese* with better sense. If she gets herself shot, she can't say he didn't *warn* her. And the police are just about to close in on him.

Ryan staggers on—only thirty yards to go. The park grows fainter with every step he takes, as though he is approaching a mirage. It is not until he feels the grass beneath his shoes that he realizes how far he has come.

The siren is deafening now but Ryan, crouched behind some bushes, knows he has made his escape. His wound is now pounding like a war drum, a tribute to his triumph. Ryan closes his eyes, stretches out on the grass, and allows the fog to deepen.

Ryan awakes to a popping sound. It is morning, he is alive, and a bunch of Nancy boys are playing cricket. Ryan hobbles to his feet, unimpressed by the contest. He has nothing to fear from *Nancy boys*. Dressed in white and scuttling around the green, they look like a bunch of geese. The fuckers don't know what *real sport* is. *Real sport* is dodging cops, rolling drunks, and icing snitches. If it wasn't his wedding day, he'd go and have a talk with them.

Ryan rummages through the bushes, locates his backpack, and pulls out a change of clothing. Kneeling behind the bushes, he peels off his ruined pants. When he inspects the wound, he is pleasantly surprised. Although his thigh is splotched with gray and yellow bruises, the bullet holes are scabbing over. The slug went clean through his leg—didn't even *touch* an artery.

Ryan tears up a tee shirt, re-wraps the wound, and slips on a clean pair of pants. He shaves by running a straight razor over his dry face. Only Nancy boys need soap and water.

Ryan quickly puts on a fresh shirt and a tie. A subtle joy has caught up with him—he is not in jail, his wound is only a scratch, and tonight he will finish off Stork. And this morning he is *getting married.*

Ryan's happiness grows as he limps from the park, rests upon the sidewalk, and then hops on an eastbound bus. His heart remains full when he gets off the bus and hobbles the four remaining blocks to the Wayside Chapel. Even when he spots Miss Muffet, a skanky little broad sitting on the chapel lawn, his chest can only swell. Her greasy hair, her flinty eyes, the needle bruises on her forearms all seem endearing to him.

She looks at him impatiently. "You ready, mister?"

He nods, accepts her hand, and follows her up the chapel steps. He can feel his wound starting to bleed, but fuck it. Get that blood into his pecker and he won't have to *worry* about seepage.

At the chapel door, they are met by a plump minister with a lazy eye—a saint of a man who, after examining the forged blood tests, walks them to the altar and guides them through their vows. Placing a ring on the girl's dirty finger—a ring she had slipped into his pocket—Ryan repeats, "Until death do us part." Not much longevity there, Ryan chuckles. How about *until a better piece of ass comes along?*

When the ceremony is over, Ryan accompanies the girl down the steps of the chapel. A taxicab, paid for by her pimp, is waiting to take them to a suite at the Holiday Inn. The girl hands him a package of rubbers—he smiles. Nothing like a bit of cherry busting to get him into the mood for a hunt.

Following Miss Muffet to the taxicab, Ryan emits a war whoop. The day is young—the cops are nowhere in sight. And his life, for all good purposes, has unfolded like a bouquet of roses. Before him lies sport and connubial bliss. Behind him lie wanton red blots.

•

Cheating the Jail Out of Time

WHEN WE GET OUR FIRST WHIFF of mortality, which typically happens in our sixties, we are inclined to take inventory of our lives. For the self-satisfied, this is an easy matter: one simply declares himself free of baggage and on an express track to heaven. But that is only true for God's favorite children; the rest of us have a harder time of it. The bits of good we might have done fade like yesterday's news. And sins long forgotten assail us like phantoms, leaving us as wary as thieves.

For Johnny Blunt, a wiry con with a sunken chest, there was no such dilemma. His criminal history spanned forty-five years and included eight stints in state prison. Robbery, burglary, theft, and assault were all represented on his expanding rap sheet. Even at the age of sixty, he had managed to catch a three-year grant of probation. The grant was for a domestic battery—he had brained his wife with a frozen chicken. When he sat in my office for his intake interview, he shouldered no blame whatsoever.

"I said, 'Woman, cook me some fries," he groused. "She told me, 'Go fuck yourself.'"

"And that's when you hit her with the chicken?" I said.

"It left a small bump on her head, is all. And it taught her to be *polite.*"

"I'm glad it wasn't Thanksgiving," I joked. "A turkey might have killed her."

He laughed. "You cool, Mr. Hemmings," he said. "I'm gonna *like* having you for my probation officer. Even if you *ain't* a foxy lady." He looked at me with warm muddy eyes and leered like a feral fox. "Didja know I'm a player?" he added.

"Your *wife* good with that?"

"Fuck yeah," he replied. "She don't care who I screw. She just don't like cookin' me fries."

The interview did not take long; there wasn't that much to record. He was drawing a monthly disability pension and living in a subsidized tenement in the Western Addition. A weak heart, caused by decades of cocaine abuse, kept him homebound much of the time.

"Mostly, I watch TV," he said. "Nothin' but Westerns—I get the cowboy channel on Comcast." He cracked his knuckles and chuckled. "Betcha I can name more Westerns 'n you."

A one-time Western addict myself, I could not resist the challenge. "*Bonanza*," I said.

"*Branded*," he replied.

"*Lawman.*"

He patted his crotch. "*The Rifleman.*"

We named over forty Westerns before he began to flounder. "Give up?" I asked him.

"Naw, ya ain't *won* yet. Ya still gotta name one more show."

"*Kung Fu*," I replied. My favorite program of all time.

"Fuck that," he shouted. "That's Chinaman stuff. I ain't lettin' you win on *Kung Fu.*"

"*Death Valley Days*. How about that?"

"Okay," he snapped. "Ya won it fair 'n square. But all that proves is you're sorrier 'n *me.*"

I wrote him a referral to a fifty-two week domestic violence program in the Tenderloin. He had forgotten that he had agreed to counseling as a condition of his probation. "Sheeiiit," he said as I handed him the paper. "I gotta miss *Bonanza* for *this*?"

"Isn't counseling what you agreed to?" I asked.

He folded up the referral and tucked it behind his belt. "Listen here, brother, we gotta talk. Now I got me a mean ol' Cajun woman who needs slappin' down now and then. Why ya gotta fuck that up?"

"I don't have a choice."

"There's always a choice, my brother," he said. "An' you're choosin' to be a hard-ass." He wagged a finger at me while glaring like a ghoul. "You trippin' on power, bro."

As he got up to leave, I handed him my card. "Call me anytime."

"Call you?" he blurted. "Now why would I do that? It ain't like I'm havin' you over for tea."

"Phone if you have any problems." I said.

He chuckled like a parrot and tore up my card. "Mr. Hemmings," he said. "Don't wait up for no calls. My only problem is *you*."

The following week, I dropped by his residence on a home visit. He lived in a single room apartment—an enclave so small that a queen size bed took up half the space. His wife, a soft massive woman, eyed me suspiciously from the kitchenette.

"Where's the tea and cookies?" I said. "I *expect* that when I come to call."

He was sitting in a ratty recliner, watching *Have Gun will Travel* on a flat screen TV. He turned down the volume and scowled. "You ain't gettin' no motherfuckin' cookies. I don't even serve those to my friends."

"Your program called me. You haven't reported."

"Ain't goin' to no motherfuckin' program."

He gazed at the television and shook his head. The Richard Boone character, Paladin, was lecturing a desperado while holding him at gunpoint. "That dude is kinda like you, Mr. Hemmings. All the time preaching to fuckers and sticking his nose where it don't belong."

"Wash your hands of me then."

"How'm I gonna do that?"

"Tell the judge you're rejecting probation. Tell him you'd rather serve a few months in jail than put up with three years of me."

He turned off the television, rose from the recliner, and shuffled into the kitchenette. "How 'bout a beer? I'll give you a beer. Ya just ain't gettin' no tea."

"I'm on duty," I said. "A soda will do."

"Sheeiitt," he said. "Ain't choo a cop? What kinda cop drinks soda?"

"A good one," I answered.

"That's jive talk," he said. "The good cops are all alcoholics."

He squeezed his way into the kitchenette and opened a compact refrigerator. After pouring himself a glass of Budweiser, he shouldered his way past his wife. "Move your fat ass, woman," he said. "Can'tcha see we got company here?"

He sat back down in the recliner and slowly sipped his beer. "How much time I gotta serve if I reject this jive-ass probation?"

"Six months—maybe five," I said. "Talk to your public defender. Ask what she can do for you."

He sipped his beer thoughtfully, belched like a cannon, then turned the TV back on. Paladin, having shot up the bad guy, was riding off into the hills. "Punk-ass motherfucker," he said. "Someone oughta cap his ass."

"Maybe just *four* months. It's only a misdemeanor."

"Sheeiit," he said. He glanced at his wife. "Ya hear that, woman? A *misdemeanor*. It wasn't no big deal."

He nodded profoundly and stroked his chin. "I'll see my lawyer tomorrow. I'll tell her, 'Bitch, make me a deal.' But three goddamn months is all I'll serve—not one hour more."

"I doubt you'll get off that cheap," I said.

"Ya think not," he said. "Hell, time ain't so cheap when your heart is acting the fool."

The theme to *Maverick* was playing and he turned the volume up. "Mr. Hemmings," he said, "I'm done speakin' to you. Haul your preachin' ass outta my home."

"Well, good luck in jail."

He burped. "Jail ain't shit. But at least they got cable in there."

The next morning, I returned to arrest him. His wife had moved into La Casa de Las Madres, a battered women's shelter on Mission Street. According to her social worker, she had duked it out with Johnny after I left the apartment. "They have another *disputa*," the social worker said over the phone. "He smacked her eye, she broke his jaw. She's afraid if she goes back home, she will also wring his neck."

My partner, Ron Rosso, a former bond runner, laughed as I rapped on the door to the flat. "Ya don't gotta worry 'bout Johnny," he said. "I've arrested him six or eight times. He never gives you trouble."

As we entered the flat, Johnny nodded to us. He was slumped in his threadbare recliner and holding an icepack to the side of his face. His jaw had swollen to the size of a cantaloupe. "*Pac-Man*," he cried, using Rosso's street name. "I thought I was rid of your ass."

"Gotta back up my road dog," said Rosso.

Johnny put down the icepack, massaged his jaw, and glared. "Mr. Hemmings," he said. "You happy now? This is what happens when I go easy on the bitch."

"I still have to take you in," I said. "You put your hands on her."

"Well, wait 'til the show is over," he snapped.

He was watching *Kung Fu*, one of my favorite episodes. Kwai Chang Caine, the show's outcast hero, was trapped in a pit of poisonous snakes. I waited until Caine had crawled out of the pit before setting the teeth on my handcuffs.

"That Chinaman don't mess with women," said Johnny as I clipped the cuffs over his wrists. "The dude likes to stay on the run."

A group of youths in loose-fitting garb was hanging about on Turk Street. One of them gave Johnny a gang salute as we marched him out of the building. "How come Pac-Man got you?" he said; the rest of them broke into laughter.

"How come you don't mind your own business?" said Johnny.

"Pops," said another. "It's time you retired."

Their laughter floated like butterflies as I eased Johnny into the squad car. "Young and dumb," he muttered while we crept through city traffic.

He was sweating when we cleared the sally port and parked at the jail entrance. I unhooked him quickly, walked him to the booking counter, and sat him at the nurse's station. His skin was grayer than slate.

The nurse looked startled, as though we had brought in a specter. "You okay, Johnny?" she asked.

He snorted. "Woman, keep your *pants* on. If I felt any better, I'd be X-rated."

He clenched his fists, breathing raggedly. The nurse mopped his forehead with a towel.

"The jail ain't gonna take him," said Rosso.

The nurse felt his pulse, all the time shaking her head. "He needs to be in San Francisco General," she said. "We can't help him here."

"C'mon," Johnny said. "Let's get out of this place."

I called 911 on my cell phone while we ushered him out the back gate. We sat him in a breezeway and waited for the paramedics to arrive. His forehead was beaded with sweat.

"Look at it this way," he muttered. "I'm cheating the jail outta time."

"There's other ways to beat time," I said.

"What choo mean by that?"

"You might just retire instead," I said. "It's not too late for that."

"Sheeiit," he laughed "Just do your damn job. Quit lying to save my soul." He blotted his brow with a handkerchief and drew a shallow breath. "Ya gotta stop readin' my rap sheet, bro."

"I gave *up* after thirty pages," I said. "Hell, I bet you'd steal from a grave."

"I know that," he said. "And don't nothing feel better than cheating the jail outta time."

When the paramedics arrived, he patted me on the wrist. He then scooted himself onto the gurney and watched me with heavy eyes. "Jive-ass motherfucker," he said.

His wife came to see me the following afternoon. She wore a black dress and her hair was disheveled. A dab of rouge covered a paunchy bruise that lay under one of her eyes.

I offered her a chair; she carefully sat down as though easing into a bathtub. She smelled of strong perfume and booze.

"Hon," she said, her voice soft as down, "he asked me to give you a message."

"So when did he die?"

"Last night in the hospital. After they brought his supper." She rubbed her eyes and rouge reddened her fingers. She removed a Kleenex from her purse. "S'pose I oughta be grateful," she murmured. "Now I won't have to break his neck."

"What was the message?"

She wiped her fingers. "He said, 'It don't mean shit.'"

•

The Break

IT WAS CLOUDLESS but cold and a late morning sun lit the skeletal boughs of the sycamore trees. Though the sleet had long ceased and the creek had stopped rising, these bones were still heavy with glittering ice. They tinkled like jewelry with each swell of wind and cast wandering shadows upon the uneven ground.

Two men, wearing the field uniforms of Indiana State Farm custody officers, were traveling southward along the bank of the creek. Their movements—slow and irresolute—were perhaps too conciliatory to the pump-action shotguns cradled beneath their armpits or the shallow current that lapped at their boots. The men did not speak yet they moved as a team. With wary precision they crouched then inched forward, inspecting the pebbles and grass near their feet. Since sunrise, when they had broken off from the search party, they had followed the stream at this loitering pace.

The shotguns winked, casting off sunlight, as the men hopped onto an open stretch of beach. The young man moved first over the pebbly sand. A huge farm boy of twenty with a slack windburned face, he appeared to have been shoveled into his powder blue jacket. The fabric was stretched and seemed likely to tear, but he knelt without incident near the water and signaled the lieutenant with a sweep of his hand.

The sand crunched slowly. The other moved closer. His knees snapped like twigs as he knelt by the gurgle and studied the impressions with limpid eyes. He was angular, lanky, with sensitive features. His forehead was shiny when he pushed back his hat. His skin loosely covered his pinched thoughtful face and his spectacles, steel-rimmed, were fragile and thin.

He studied the footprints for over a minute then he rose to his feet, shook his bald head, and brushed off his knee with matronly care.

"Hunters," he declared in a reedy voice. "The treads are froze stiff. Guess they been here and gone over two days ago."

The younger man nodded. He rose with a grunt as though deigning to perform an unreasonable chore. The butt of his shotgun revealed a fine grainy cast where he had supported his weight in the sand. He cradled the stock as though warming a shoat then addressed the lieutenant in a well-practiced whine.

"Mr. Hill," he carped, "them hounds still chasin' rabbits? It's been over an hour since we heard 'em bark."

The lieutenant shrugged patiently and straightened his collar. "Don't know what they're chasin'. Don't matter much anyhow."

He paused for a long moment, squinting against the sun. His eyes combed the woods with habitual caution. He then checked, for the fifth time that morning, the safety on his shotgun.

"It'll be our fortune to flush 'em," he finally observed. "Them dogs don't know where to look."

He stood stock still at the edge of the stream. Dipping into his jacket, he withdrew a crushed tobacco pouch which he held like a bird in the palm of his hand. He reached into the pouch, removed several remaining strands of tobacco, then dropped it into the stream.

His jaw labored as the current grabbed the pouch. The oyster he spat was slender—brown—and vanished at once in the boil of the water.

The pouch shrank from sight while the younger man watched it. He shivered peevishly, as though personally affronted by the cold, and he slipped his free hand into a pocket of his jacket.

"It's too cold to be wadin'."

The lieutenant sighed and spat once again.

162

"Once they've run off," he replied, "you can bet they'll start wadin'. They think they'll be safe if the hounds lose their scent. But that don't do nothing but shorten the chase. They'll be too frozen to run once we've picked up their trail."

"How far is that dam?"

"It'd be less than a mile now—not countin' the bends. There's a fifteen foot drop from the lip of the dam and I'll bet you a dollar we flush 'em before then."

"This don't make no sense," the other reflected. "Heard one of 'em only had two months left to serve."

"Seen 'em run off with less time."

The lad shook his head. "Hell of a time to be scamperin' like hares. Do you usually catch 'em?"

The lieutenant shrugged. "If they're lucky we do. Course some farmer might first. One night one of them rabbits got hit by a tractor..."

He scratched his jaw, "It was the headlights that froze him. Knocked him clean to the ground. But that cracker turned around an' came barrelin' back. Would have struck him again if we hadn't sung out..."

The lieutenant's voice trailed. He looked towards the woods. He seemed keenly aware of the low winter sun and the smoke-like circling of distant birds.

He spat with contempt. He said, "Rabbits ain't smart."

He shouldered his shotgun and trudged towards the woods.

The cornfield was barren, pocketed with snow, the furrows littered with short broken stalks. The creek bed was steeper, protected by bushes. The men walked single file, their muzzles trained earthward while their eyes searched the bare brambles for movement.

The air rattled sharply.

The youth raised his barrel.

He lowered the shotgun as a covey of bobwhite quail exploded from the furrows then darted over the stubbled field.

"It starts out this way," the lieutenant remarked. "But it generally begins early in the spring. First just one or two of 'em

163

catch the fever—like they done today. But if you don't fetch 'em back quick, you'll soon have 'em stampedin'.""

He breathed on his fingers, now raw from the cold, and he watched the quail land a short distance away.

"I remember one spring when the fever was high. Had to chase down almost two dozen of 'em before it was over. Seemed like we were spendin' almost every other day beatin' 'em out of the woods."

It was now almost noon and the snow seared their eyes. The ice on the trees remained diamond-like, hard, yet it glimmered like flame on the drooping boughs. Narrowing his eyes, the lieutenant glanced towards the creek. The snow was unmarred as it followed the banks. It seemed ominous yet chaste, bearing no hint of prints or the wanton red blots, which earlier that morning had betrayed the scramble of the inmates over the high razor wire of the outer prison fence.

A toneless murmur scratched at his ears. The voice, a disembodied drone, kept repeating his number. He sighed, resigned to the aggravation, then unsnapped the leather sheath on his duty belt.

"Hill here," he said in a clipped voice.

The message was short, a perfunctory garble relaying that a tower officer had detected movement a half mile east of the stream. He acknowledged the message with a coded reply then he returned the hand radio to its case.

"A deer more 'an likely," he scoffed. "Seen some droppings still steamin' just five minutes back. Not everyone knows that the woods are full of 'em."

The boy rolled his eyes. He was restless and stiff and the tingle in his toes was beginning to ache. "Had one in my sights around sunrise," he offered. "Almost cracked off a shot just to open him up—warm my hands in his guts."

The lieutenant stopped walking. The spiraling birds, smoke-like an hour ago, appeared to have solidified in the sky. They looked lifeless even for turkey vultures, but their languor was not reassuring. Somewhere in the distance, like an approaching train, they could hear the dull roar of the falls.

"We'll flush more than deer if we stick to the creek."

"Well I bagged mine last Sunday," the younger man boasted. "Put a slug up his ass when he showed me his tail. Exploded his heart, but he must have run another hundred yards before he fell."

"A man will fall quicker," the lieutenant remarked.

He could see a sliver of path beyond the cornfield. It was thin, undertrod, not much more than a deer trail, and it plunged down a piney slope. The gully below was a vein to the creek, but the water would be still at this time of year and its frozen crust would provide a safe crossing for the men.

The lieutenant spoke softly, "One time I did drop one—a kid even dumber 'an you. That was twenty years back—my first time out."

He did not turn his head as he made this confession. His eyes remained steady, remote, and fixed intuitively on the scavenger birds.

"A hundred yards off, but he fell like a tree. I dropped him because he kept runnin'."

The younger man whistled. "Good distance for buckshot. You let the shot skip off the ground? Like they showed us on the range?"

"I tickled the dirt in front of him as he turned to look back at me. But the shot still tore up his chest. Must have bounced off some rock because it had plenty of sting left."

"You waste him?" the boy asked.

The lieutenant shrugged. "Guess the fool killed himself 'cause he didn't stop runnin'. I combed his hair with the warning shot before he took off. He would have stopped then if he'd had any sense."

"He still cheated the state out of time," said the boy.

"A year or two maybe," the lieutenant replied. "He died quick enough once he went into shock. Course we could have let him run off an' then staked out his mama's house. More likely than not we'd have picked him up at the doorstep."

"No sense coddlin' rabbits," the boy replied.

"Damn waste of good buckshot to tell of it now."

The lieutenant looked towards the pine trees that crowned the ravine. The birds were beginning to circle there, impassive and dark in their frozen intent.

The lieutenant coughed crisply. He lowered his eyes.

"They got 'em a carcass," he said.

They did not watch the birds as they crossed the dead stream and began their ascent towards the pines. A powdery snow shrieked like chalk beneath their soles. The snow had not crusted in the deep shade of the trees and their boots barely gripped the slope.

The cold burned their lungs as they approached the pines. They paused, panting rapidly, seeing white veils that grew paler as they caught their breath. Through the cluster of trees, they could see much of the prison—the tall double fence capped with spirals of razor wire and the industry buildings that lay behind it. The electric fence of the dairy was also within view. Several Holsteins were standing like black and white sculptures within the cramped muddy sanctuary of the yard.

The snow smoked beneath the lieutenant and a lemony stain crept towards his boots. When he had finished urinating, he zipped up his pants with a tidy jerk. Retrieving his shotgun from the snow, he wiped off the barrel with the sleeve of his jacket and sighted it tentatively in the direction of the creek.

"There's been drops in these woods," he announced. "Booze and drugs mostly. People toss 'em out of cars from the highway so the chain gangs can pick 'em up."

The younger man snorted, "Hope they left us a bottle. I could use a hard belt if we're kept out here much longer."

"Don't get that relaxed. There's been guns dropped as well. My snitch told me last week there's a .357 squirreled away somewhere near the water treatment plant."

"Who told you that—Franklin?"

"He swore it was true."

"I can't stand snitches—especially Franklin. He's fed me some lies 'cause he thinks I'm a rube. He's just a silly wino who likes to hear himself talk."

"You gotta trust someone," the lieutenant replied. "We found some guns last week and he helped point 'em out to us."

"We could use one gun more if them rabbits need dustin'. I been told we can pop 'em on sight if they're armed. I got me a throw down—a .22 handgun. Next time we're out trekkin' I'll bring it along."

"It's today you might need it," the other advised. "They don't always halt after coming this far."

"We still combin' their curly locks?"

"Just tell 'em to freeze. Make 'em hold up their hands. If one of 'em won't comply, try and score him dead center. Now he'll hit the ground crappin' or his face may be gone, but don't let that stop you from shootin' again. Send that second shot whinin' just over his head."

The youth shook his head. "You must like wastin' pellets. Can't finish 'em off if we're strokin' their hair."

"You ain't wastin' shells if you spend 'em in pairs. A warnin' shot is still called for. That ain't goin' to change. So if you bring it up barkin' make sure it speaks twice."

The younger man shrugged. "I hear *enough* barkin'."

The lieutenant listened then shook his head. The wind was alive with a dissonant chorus, the sound of excited dogs.

"They just treed 'em a squirrel," the lieutenant said. "Don't make no noise as we go down the hill."

The younger man grunted. He stamped the hard ground, but the cottony sensation remained in his toes. He gripped his shotgun and took calf-like steps as he followed the lieutenant down the slope.

They could hear the creek snarl as it edged into sight. The earth had collapsed on the bank nearest them and a sycamore, partly uprooted, sagged over a mantle of earth. White water writhed beneath the shadow of the tree. The current was shallow but swift and looked powerful enough to trip a man.

The men did not talk as they followed the creek. Though cold fingers caressed them, they ducked the stiff branches and kept their eyes fixed on the snow. The lieutenant led the way slowly, haltingly, as though testing the ice of a pond. He addressed the boy finally, "Your union dues paid?"

167

"Got some bills I ain't settled. Them Teamsters can wait."

The lieutenant crouched, his eyes on a swirl. "You'd best get them paid while the trekkin is on"

The youth nodded noncommittally. He looked at the creek. "How long till they cleared you for wastin' that bojack?"

"The investigation lasted eight months. I faced three different inquiry boards. We didn't have unions then so I faced 'em alone."

"Three boards!" the youth spat. "They sure filled up your dance card."

"He didn't die neatly," the other replied.

"He died by the book."

The lieutenant shrugged. "What book would that be if you don't mind my askin'?"

"You did give him a warnin'."

"Ain't always enough. Rumor had it he surrendered the moment I shot him. And the governor called and chewed everyone out. He wanted me charged with murder." He shook his head slowly. "My name made the papers—the evenin' news too. Unless they're dead sure the shoot was righteous, you're gonna be dancin' alone."

He rose cautiously since the creek bank was dented beneath him. The water was darker than lead and it chuckled as it nipped at the bank.

As they rounded a final bend, they could hear the pitched calling of the falls. The lieutenant led the way slowly, his thin shoulders hunched. His fingers shook as he released the safety on his shotgun.

"Three boards for one bojack," the younger man muttered.

The lieutenant sighed. He removed some shotgun shells from one of his pockets. He cupped the shells in his trembling palm then tucked them behind his belt.

"For all the fuss he caused, the kid died kinda peaceful. His chest was clawed up 'cause he had raked out some grain.... But he rattled real smooth—like a tree stoppin' shot—then his fingers spread open like petals at dawn. Seemed he let go his life as though freein' a bird."

"He still shorted the state," the boy insisted.

168

"Well they won't be collectin'," the other replied.

The falls were in sight. The creek, vastly swollen, had buried the top of the dam. They could not see the drop but the thundering was heavy. The water, though dense and deceptively still, was creeping irresistibly towards the falls.

"They finally cleared me," the lieutenant said. "After that, I went before a board to make sergeant." His voice seemed inaudible. Reverent and hushed, it could scarcely compete with the rumble of the falls.

"I don't want no promotion," the boy sneered. "I don't wanna be a member of the goddamn brass."

The older man laughed. "Well, it went well enough. Didn't take 'em much time. Weren't long after that I was given my stripes."

They were close to the dam when they spotted the marks. These were impossible to overlook since the snowdrift was thick and the bank inclined gradually into the stream. The lieutenant breathed deeply, but made no remark. There were two sets of fresh footprints compressed in the snow.

The prints led them eastward away from the water. Irregular, scuffed, easy to follow, they scarcely suggested an orderly flight. It was only the blood that implied moderation. The droplets, no larger than bittersweet berries, were frugally dotting the ground.

As the shade became scattered, the men pulled down their cap bills. The snow glowed then sparkled. The glare became blinding. The men moved begrudgingly, appraising the trees as they lowered their eyes and walked into the sun.

"It's as white in the Keys," the lieutenant remarked.

"The beach as uncrowded?"

"I'll know in a week."

"Hope we've bagged 'em all by then. If the season ain't done, I'll be trekkin' with Captain Flannigan 'til you get back."

The boy flinched as he spoke; a tree branch was falling. The crackle—similar to a fusillade of pistol shots—was followed by a thundering explosion.

The silence returned; the men did not move. They looked at the spot where the broken branch lay. The branches above them swayed like mourners, marking time with a rhythm too faint to be heard. When the boy spoke again, he seemed deeply insulted. His voice was thick, impatient, the tone of a man who had been cheated at cards.

"Ain't nothin' but squirrels could perch in them maples."

"They're too high for rabbits," the other joked.

"That ice ain't grown no thicker," the boy retorted. "It's late for them branches to drop on their own."

The barb in his voice did not fool the lieutenant. The older man spat and kept on walking. His manner was distant, annoyed, as he measured his stride in the deepening snow.

"You're too useless for Flannigan," he finally conceded. "He's weak for a captain. Too scared of his rank. An' he'll snitch you out quick if it keeps him his bars.... But I told 'em I wouldn't miss no more vacations."

"The Farm will miss you," the lad replied bitterly.

"'Ceptin' the hares. You'll have plenty to chase."

"Oughta drop one today just to shape up for spring. There's just three weeks till spring. You come back to the Farm."

The lieutenant chewed slowly then sighed. "Three weeks will 'bout do me. I'll miss it by then."

The snow groaned beneath their weight; they were climbing once more. A boney pattern appeared on the snow as the sunlight was strained through another bare grove. A breeze stung their cheeks, but the limbs did not stir. No itinerant shadows roamed over the boughs that lay broken on the ground. It seemed almost by chance that the smoke crept towards them. A sinewy tendril, defying the stillness, drew their eyes to a small pile of sticks.

The lieutenant squatted, recovering his breath while examining the heap for deposits of ash. A glance was enough to conclude that the wood was too rotted and wet to burn.

"Hares," scoffed the boy. "They can't even light kindlin'."

"They're lucky they're pea-brained," the lieutenant replied. "They'd have fallen asleep if it had warmed 'em up much."

His gaze drifted northward, pursuing the prints. They were watery, veiled by the membrane of heat that still climbed from the smoldering mound. He deduced that the inmates had spotted the highway—a goal it would take them an hour to reach. The road was obstructed by a dense grove of pines and the easterly bend of the creek.

The boy was dejected. "They seen us for sure."

"Wouldn't swear to that yet," the lieutenant replied. "They've come a long way for rabbits when all's said and done. More 'an likely by now they're done havin' their fun and they're just lookin' for someone to surrender to."

He lifted his hand radio, hit the squelch button. After reporting their coordinates, he listened for a moment then slipped the radio back into its leather case.

"Not much use hurryin' now," he remarked to the boy. "They'll run smack into Flannigan recrossin' the creek. If he hushes up those hounds, they'll fall into his lap."

"He don't have that much sense."

"Ain't our fault if he don't. But as froze as they are, guess the hounds won't upset 'em much. They'll take a few bites to get out of this cold."

They picked up their pace, but the boy still shivered. The snow bit his boots and the ground felt remote to him and he wondered if frostbite was hardening his toes. The pursuit of the inmates seemed foreign to him now, a poor reason to stay in the woods.

They could hear the hounds bark as they shuffled down a knoll. The clamor, soft but erratic, was chastised by a sharp empty bellow. The barking grew faint as they again met the creek and was drowned out finally by the perpetual laughter of the water.

The boy remained glum, "Bet he missed by a cornfield. He'd have took one shot more if he'd bloodied 'em up."

"He ain't got no more comin'," the lieutenant remarked. "Be a shitload of paperwork pepperin' 'em now. Bet they're peein' their pants just to turn themselves in."

Ignoring the tracks, the men trudged on in silence. They set the safety locks on their shotguns and breathed heat onto their fingers. Their shift would probably end with the three o'clock whistle, but no comfort could come from this thought. It could scarcely contend with the grainy wind or the cold, brittle limbs that pawed silently at their cheeks.

The lieutenant was starting to limp from the cold. His boots wore a hard skin of ice. He stamped his frozen feet on the ground and tried to pick up his pace.

A drawl broke the stillness.

He listened resignedly.

He shook his head when he once again heard it. A neutral sound, unencumbered by static, it was almost indistinguishable from the rustle of the trees. He paused as he cleared another ravine and studied a cluster of pines.

When another sound drifted, he felt reassured. He could make out the timber of casual voices. The flutter and ebb of these muffled tones suggested the highway was not far away.

He remained near the slope and waited: the pop of a twig was particularly loud. The voices died as though smothered by breeze, but his eyes remained fixed on the snow-wigged boughs. He was doubting his ears when they came into view—two youths, unescorted, wearing prison blues.

They were pallid, bone-white, as ragged as lepers, but they looked too familiar to merit alarm. He could recognize Hacker, a tall knobby lad with a talent for handling the spoiled dairy cattle. The other, named Pollock, was pimply, thinner—a broom shop assignee afraid of the prison yards and the risks of working a less segregated line. Although dopers and thieves in the eyes of the law, he could think of them only as addle-brained kids—lank adolescents who lived by bad instincts and could not think more than twelve hours ahead.

As his hip braced the shotgun, the creek gurgled faintly. The voices grew fuller. The wind again stirred. The lieutenant swore softly, reluctant to move. He unlocked the safety and tried not to shiver.

He shook his head finally. He once again spat.

"Ain't it just like a hare to come doublin' back."

Snow burst into powder. The thunder rebounded, but his hearing was numbed by a riveted whine. The veil also lingered. Hoary, frail, it was drifting like smoke from a buckled bough.

Ejecting the shell, he lowered the bore but the footfalls had faded. The woods looked empty. The shotgun boomed; a patch of ground scattered. The puff of snow tarried—a lingering shroud.

A plume crept from his bore as the second shot echoed. The scent of burned sulfur emboldened the air. The insular pines seemed asleep beneath sheets, yet the hum, cold and probing, remained in his ears.

The boy looked dazed as he rose to his feet. Confused by the echoes and the suddenness of the shots, he had thrown himself onto his belly. Even now, as he stood there and looked at the woods, he seemed barely convinced that he had not been shot at. His eyes were muddy; his hands scraped and soiled. A fat dirty lump, the size of a sparrow egg, had appeared almost magically in the center of his forehead.

The boy puffed out his chest. "They'll stop lead before it's over." His words came in gulps. Although his voice kept its edge, he was winded and weak from the impact of the hard ground.

"Could have sworn they saw us," the lieutenant remarked. "They kept hurryin' towards me like Christmas had come. Weren't but thirty yards off when they bolted like deer."

The boy rubbed his forehead. "Should've walloped 'em back."

The lieutenant consoled him, "It's harder up close."

He unsnapped his hand radio, killed the static, then lifted the speaker to his mouth. His lips were compressed when he finished his message. He sheathed the radio, picked up the spent shells, then he looked pityingly at the boy.

"If we're quick about it," he said, "you may still get a round off. There'll be too many questions if your bore ain't been dirtied. Since I already gave 'em a warning shot, the brass might think you let 'em escape."

The boy made no reply. He pinched his stiff neck. He cocked his head back, like a bird drinking water, and followed

173

the lieutenant drunkenly towards the pine grove where they had last spotted the inmates.

There were numerous footprints criss-crossed in the snow— a sight somehow at odds with the nimble retreat. The blots, tiny berries, seemed sparingly flung; a map scrawled in pencil lay torn on the ground. The shattered bough still clung to the tree, swaying back and forth like a pendulum.

The lieutenant paused to look for a body. The boy's voice was hopeful.

"You wing 'em?" he asked.

The lieutenant kept chewing. He shook his head slowly.

"Can't tell you for sure. There was already blood."

The cornfield was empty, as still as a canvass—a backdrop for only the wandering shadow of a red-tailed hawk. Roaming over the furrows, the tint stretched and shriveled. It did not hold its shape until it skirted the creek and the scarecrow-like form awaiting the men. The form was sitting, propped up by a crooked oak tree. It seemed to be watching the passage of the hawk.

The men approached warily, shotguns pointed. A ribbon of smoke trailed the youth who had managed to squeeze off a shot. The shower of dirt had kicked short of the target, but he had no enticement to shoot again. The scarecrow sat rigid, hands slightly raised, as they slowly approached over the deep ruts of the field.

"Guess he ruined his pants," the lieutenant observed.

He lowered his bore as they stood by the tree, diverting his gaze to the bushes and creek. He dropped his gaze when a voice from his radio reminded him to deal with the matter at hand.

He lifted the radio, silenced the static, and uttered a couple of codes. He then shut off the radio with a twist of his thumb and returned it to his belt.

"They nabbed 'em the other rabbit. He got to the highway."

The boy clutched his pump-action and wrinkled his nose. The air was ripe with the odor of shit, but the body was not embarrassed. The eyes were wooden, the pants torn and stained, the mouth was obscenely agape. Although spry as a fox several minutes ago, Hacker seemed to have been sitting there for a very long time. "What snuffed him?" he asked.

The lieutenant shrugged.

"He's stiffer 'an a goddamn pecker."

Since no wound was apparent, the form did look sculptured. The porcelain bearing and granular skin gave it the appearance of a statue. It did not seem responsible for the nutty turd that lay in the snow beside it.

"They go that way sometimes," the lieutenant replied. "Ain't always much warnin' when one of 'em drops."

The boy patted his barrel. "Seen him jump when I popped him."

His voice lost its edge as a soft shadow passed. A clamor of hounds could be heard through the trees.

The boy belched like a mortar then spat. He looked at the turd the pants couldn't hold. Again, his stomach kicked.

The lieutenant said sadly, "Weren't nothing we done. It just ain't in the nature of hares to live long."

He removed the magazine from his shotgun, took his bearings one more time. There wasn't much need to wait for the police helicopter. The lone sagging oak and the bend of the creek provided easy coordinates for the pickup of the body.

The whistle in the prison powerhouse sounded as the men trudged towards the highway In a minute or two it would blow once again, confirming their shift had come to an end.

When they reached the highway, there was no one to meet them. The prison patrol vans as well as the dog truck had left the juncture where the remaining inmate had been apprehended. The lieutenant spat but made no remark as he contemplated the half-mile walk to the prison.

The boy muttered, "Hares! They get better service than we do!"

"Well, they do cause more ruckus," the lieutenant replied.

The boy clenched his fist. "Just as well that they panicked. If they were a half step slower, I'd have brought down the pair."

The sun, drifting westward, again stabbed their eyes as they began the uphill climb towards the parking lots and

175

administration buildings. Since trees no longer impeded their view, they could make out the archway and the tall northern watchtower. Their soles remained packed with snow and cracked dully upon the frozen blacktop road.

The boy spoke again, his face flushed from walking. The cold barb of anger remained in his voice. "Ain't no profit in rabbits," he concluded. "Out freezin' our jewels just to stroke us a hare. Hell, I hear once they're caught they get only five years more."

"That ain't much time," the lieutenant agreed.

"Oughta nail 'em to trees if they wanna get frisky—or geld 'em like colts at the first sign of spring."

"Seen 'em put on display. Stops the rest of 'em cold. If the season ain't over before Easter comes, you'll see 'em paraded in chains past the dorms."

Conserving his breath, the boy trudged on in silence. His stride grew lighter as they approached the prison. He seemed to be weighing encouraging news, but his eyes remained heavy.

The last whistle blew.

"They'll be struttin' like lords. You may just as well stroke 'em."

"Don't make me no difference," the older man sighed. "They can put 'em in stocks if it takes that to hold 'em. I'm bettin' by then that I'll be in the Keys."

·

The World Baseball League

THE WORLD BASEBALL LEAGUE was born in the basement of our suburban home in Arlington, Virginia. My kid brother and I invented it on a sweltering Fourth of July. It was a heroic invention—a vehicle by which two avowed nerds might wear the colors of champions. Armed with dice, meticulously drawn charts, and a cardboard baseball diamond, Robbie and I commanded the destinies of twenty baseball teams. We played daily throughout the long hot summer—up to six games a day—and we tweaked team standings and player averages after every game. So absorbed were we in horsehide heroics that we rendered the summer neither long nor hot.

Our rosters consisted of four hundred individual players each represented by a 2" by 2" square of cardboard. Batting averages, fielding percentages, slugging potential, and base running speed were recorded on each of these squares along with the name and number of the player. To avoid the stigma of nepotism, we recruited our players liberally. Politicians, demagogues, movie stars, and literary characters were listed among the players—each with his respective stats. Hitler, for example, was a .224 hitter with a .342 slugging percentage and better than average base running speed. Our rosters also included caricatures we made up to lend comic relief to an otherwise serious pursuit. My favorite was Percy the Balladeer, a switch-hitting fop who recited Elizabethan poetry every time he came to bat. Of course, we knew nothing about Elizabethan poetry so Percy's recitals amounted to the merest of doggerel. An example:

Hi diddle de diddle de di.
What a marvelous player am I.
My swing is as keen
As a ripe tangerine
Hi diddle de diddle de di.

To pad the standings of our stronger teams, we created several doormat teams that we allowed John, our toddler sibling, to manage. The lowliest of them all we named Happy Hill after the little fellow's daycare center. Its players consisted of the hapless Peanuts characters who almost always struck out on three quick pitches. But Happy Hill did have one good player, Snoopy, whom I eventually acquired from John in exchange for a coloring book and a Hershey bar. I inserted Snoopy as shortstop on my strongest squad, The Neutralists, and it immediately rose to the top of its division.

Baseball is arguably our national recreation, but The World Baseball League was hardly a pastime. It was more a vocation, a proclivity, a life obsession to be celebrated in legend and song. And so we composed the most vitriolic of anthems, which one of us sang whenever blessed with victory. Polemics, after all, is the privilege of the winner no matter how dubious the enterprise. "This land is your land!" thundered the Lord, giving the Israelites unimpeachable license to wipe out indigenous people. "Manifest Destiny," our nation cried, allowing our Union Civil War generals, the champions of emancipation, an exemption to enslave aboriginals. "Remember the Alamo," cried swarthy Sam Houston as his crew of assassins slew Mexican soldiers who were taking an ill-timed siesta. It was in this spirit of hubris that we composed our personal anthem: a litany of ninety three verses, which we sang to the tune of "Auld Lang Syne." A sampling:

I win again, I win again,
I win again, I win.

A SECOND, LESS CAPABLE, HEAD

So raise the flags and start the band,
For I have won again.

It was during our first World Series, our ultimate struggle for bragging rights, that our anthem reached fever pitch. After edging Robbie's Potomac Patriots three games to two, with just one game left to play, I sat back in my chair, grinned like a ghoul, and belted out a brand new verse. My voice was so clear, so booming and proud, that it echoed throughout the county.

I am a champion of old.
I never ever lose.
I'll beat your pants off anytime
At anything you choose.

Not to be outdone, Robbie beefed up his lineup by giving contracts to several free agents. Dipping into his cash reserves, he recruited George Wallace, a hard hitting right fielder, Holden Caulfield, a formidable catcher, and Ulysses Grant, a third baseman who specialized in long belts. After winning the penultimate contest, and tying the series at three games apiece, Robbie chanted the mother of all verses.

Ten thousand souls will sing my praise.
Their hearts will pound with glee.
So don't despair if I should win.
It's only destiny.

And so the dye was cast for a seventh and decisive game—a clash that would endow the winner with the peerless ranking of a god. Robbie's pitcher was Richard Nixon, a junk hurler with one of the best changeups in the league, so I countered by saturating my lineup with batters adept at hitting low balls. I also put Che Guevara on the mound, a left-handed knuckle baller fresh from three hours' rest. The contest was an epic pitching duel. Idi Amin, Mao Zedong, and Vlad the Impaler—my most consistent hitters—all failed to reach second base while Barry Goldwater, Aaron Burr, and John Hancock—the meat of

Robbie's order—did not even get a hit. Entering the top of the ninth, the score was knotted at 0-0 with the bottom of my order cheduled to bat. But how could I tip the scales with such feckless hitters as Adolf Hitler, Joan of Arc, and Richard the Third?

To my sweet surprise, Adolf, after taking two strikes, was brushed by a high inside pitch and awarded a trip to first. I immediately signaled Joan to lay down a sacrifice bunt. Obeying my signal, she tapped a dribbler down the third base line and took off for first. Amazingly, she beat out the throw after sprinting like her pants were on fire. As Richard the Third shuffled up to home plate, muttering about his winter of discontent, I had two ducks on the pond and nobody out.

When a dropped ball allowed Hitler to slide into third—scoring position!—my heart began to race. But Richard the Third was my poorest batsman. A compulsive chaser of bad pitches, he had not smacked the ball out of the infield all year. I gambled on a hit and run and signaled for a delayed swing. Robbie's second baseman, somber John Hancock, was notoriously slow on his release so there was a better than average chance that Hitler could make it home.

While Richard was fiddling around at the plate, adjusting his helmet and calling for a horse, Nixon tossed a slider down the middle. Startled by the pitch, Richard swung like a girl. *Crack!* A hopper went bouncing towards second base—a perfect triple play ball. *Whump!* John Hancock sealed the out at first. *Whump!* Lyndon Johnson, a strong armed first baseman, beat Joan's slide at second. *Whump!* Hancock's throw to the plate thundered into Caulfield's glove. As I watched the dust at home plate settle, the roar of the crowd told me what had happened. Hitler had beaten the throw by a whisker. We were ahead 1-0.

In the bottom of the ninth, I substituted flame throwing Adolf Eichmann for a tiring Che Guevara. Three pop ups later, The Neutralists were champions of the world. It was the trashiest of wins; it was the cleverest of triumphs. But my victory would not be complete without a verse to outdo Robbie's. As I watched Robbie sit there, fighting back tears, it came to me in a flash. Heroically, irresistibly, I began to sing.

180

A SECOND, LESS CAPABLE, HEAD

The angels will call out my name.
Their harps will keep in time.
That one like me should walk the earth
A boon to all mankind.

I sang it to Gabriel's trumpet; I sang it to Pan's lilting pipes. So rich was my voice that sirens rejoiced and the garlands of Heaven were mine. Later, mobbed by reporters in the locker room, I waited for the president's call.

•

The Wall

YOU WERE LARGE-BONED, ruddy-faced, blond—blondest of the cadets, perhaps because you brush-cut your hair, squaring it on top so that it barely hid the baby pinkness of your scalp. You were blue-eyed, hawkish, almost striking at a glance, but your nose was too blunt for handsomeness and your jaw, thick and square, afforded your face an exaggerated symmetry. Even your chin was symmetrical—a pussy chin we called it; it was deeply cleft, vaguely suggestive, and somehow a complement to the prominent ridges of your knuckles. Your hands, big and chapped, were a laborer's hands, competent only when polishing brass or performing the ritual manuals of rifle and blade. Your rifle, at these times, would pause in midflight, cracking your palm before whirling like a baton twice windmilled in the gleaming black mirrors of your shoes. And your sword, won only halfway through your second year, would leap with a life independent of your fingers, a slicing streak that hummed like a bullet in flight yet somehow captured fleetingly the shimmer of the sun.

That second and final year, when we roomed together, I was slow to ease the too persistent rumors that you waxed the soles of your shoes, slept at attention, and stuffed the rosary into your bore. We did laugh at you frequently, but not in the manner in which we laughed at witless Wippleman, legs apart on his bed as he farted flame over a lighter, or at fat pimply Hopper who howled like a puppy whenever we pink-bellied him after taps with drumming palms and stinging cans of deodorant. The chuckles were tighter when you were the target and the nicknames were mirthless, waspish—lingering jibes like Super

183

Mick, Burr Head, Mickey Military. Still, I felt little guilt when I failed to defend you; your ears did not seem attuned to our comments. You were your own clown, after all, and not ours.

Were you too estimable for a clown?—for I did admire you occasionally, even when you stayed up until one in the morning making guilty my sleep while you fussed over your sword in preparation for the Saturday parade inspection. You even cleaned my rifle when there was time. You were convinced I could one day pass a Saturday inspection, though I never passed a Saturday inspection in my entire two years at Washburn. You were my platoon sergeant that second year, and it could only have embarrassed you when I accumulated the inevitable company demerits. Even so, you were the first to laugh whenever I lost step with the rest of the platoon or found myself marching alone after a sudden flank movement. Was it your poverty of reserve that was so disaffecting? I was not at all impressed by you the first day we met—when you approached me in the mess hall, asked me if I would be on the wrestling team. Your gaze was too candid, your forehead too bald, and a hint of stutter hung trippingly on your tongue. You were so without mystery I could see there would be no getting to know you. This happened too quickly, in almost an instant—the first bland moment of meeting you and perhaps the only one. Because in the months that followed, even the years, my impression of you changed hardly at all. As it turned out, you were not even much of a wrestler, unsurprising since the sport does require a modicum of guile. And clearly you were no opportunist; you were better inclined towards secondary spoils—the tiresome gratuities of a lackey.

For this I always despised you a little myself.

We had come to Washburn for different reasons, both of which were atypical since the small Virginia prep school— despite an Appalachian nesting and ivy-strewn walls— impressed me as little more than a reform school for middle-class boys. As a general's son, you had taken seriously its brochures of military schooling and manicured parade fields while I was an airier dreamer, indifferent to structure of any sort but destined, by having failed the eleventh grade, to complete my high school education in an institution of last resort.

We were issued M-1s on our day of arrival—World War Two relics inappropriate for the enduring war in Southeast Asia, but not too timeworn to carry about on the parade field or perform the nineteen-count manual, which most of us had perfected by our third month. Though we cleaned these antiques constantly, we were never allowed to fire them. We used .22 rifles for actual target practice—an exercise we performed in a bunker range beneath the school foyer. Since the guns crackled feebly, we shot without earplugs and so I was always surprised when the sandbags tore and the small paper targets, which we reeled in by pulleys, were peppered with clusters of tiny holes. I had too few opportunities to narrow my rather sporadic clusters and suspected the school, depleted of federal grant money during those war years, regarded this outlay of ammunition as an inordinate expense. For the most part, we marched about incessantly, mixed shoe polish with spit, and stood numerous parade inspections, a prerequisite for every meal. Given this emphasis on cosmetic soldiering, I could not always resist the impression that an army's worth lay less in its field effectiveness than in the glitter and pomp with which it presented itself in ranks. Such a fetish, I suppose, had its compensations since I grew complacent with the ceremonies of war and did not consider our jaunty battalion a real tributary to the messier ordeal in Vietnam.

At night, before taps, I would ream a single patch through my rifle bore, blow the lint from my belt buckle, and drape a handkerchief protectively over my dully glazed shoes. I had no serious illusions that these efforts would protect me from the morrow's scrutiny, but I accumulated the demerits cheerfully, considering them a wise alternative to the hassle of endless polishing.

I met you on a Sunday. There was no drill scheduled that afternoon so I invited you to the gym to wrestle. I did not take you seriously as a rival for my weight class, but I wanted your measure as a wrestler as well as an opportunity to practice my takedowns.

We wrestled on a dusty peeling mat spread out on a stage above the basketball court. You opened my nose with an awkward jerk of your elbow before I stacked you with a cradle, holding you on your shoulders for the two-second count. I pinned you twice more in the course of a minute and then deigned to notice the rather severe mat burn developing on your forehead. Blood stains, my own, were drying on your cheeks and browning spots dotted the fatigues you had not bothered to change out of.

You were matter-of-fact in accepting the loss—you had not really expected to beat me—and you did not challenge my dominion when we had wrestle-offs for the varsity lineup. You did make the lineup, but only at the urging of the coach since you had to drop twelve pounds in order to fit into the weight class below mine. I remember you padding around and around the gym during practice, a yellow plastic suit plastered to your body, then groaning in the steam of the showers, patting your stomach—"Nothing in there, T-Tom, nothing at all"—then hopping hopefully upon the scales. You would sit over a trash bucket after tipping the scales, spitting away the excess ounces, even pushing a finger down your throat. When nothing came up, you would pull your sweatsuit over the clinging plastic and return to circling the gym.

You were ashen from weight loss when we had our first meet and you were stacked rather neatly by a drowsy looking farm boy from Culpeper. You even cost us a sportsmanship point when you punched the mat in anger or embarrassment after relinquishing the match so quickly. I don't really know why you had expected to win; wrestling was never your first priority and you spent most of our practice time running off weight. I was irritated for other reasons as well; you had preceded me to the mat and your instant loss had deprived me of my warm-up. Still, I won my match easily enough, a first period pin, and condescended to accepting your handshake when the bout was over.

A SECOND, LESS CAPABLE, HEAD

I won all my matches our junior year—a testament less to my prowess as a grappler than to the struggling athletic programs of the small academies and factory town high schools that made up our opposition. We sucked as a team—two and twelve for the year—but our record did not diminish my small gem of accomplishment nor offer you much consolation in your rather unprecedented string of defeats. At least you lost quickly—usually in the first period of your matches—but you continued to cost us hard won points when, red-faced and muttering, you would fling your headgear upon leaving the mat or kick over your chair instead of sitting on it. Considering the overall point total, we would have been no worse off forfeiting your matches outright than retaining you as a member of the lineup.

You did win once—a total surprise since you looked so pale surrounded by the target-shaped mat, waiting for the whistle to blow. Perhaps you rebelled finally at the hollowness of your sacrifice—you had been starving for three days to make the weight—or maybe you were provoked by a mocking word or glance from your opponent, the same hayseed from Culpeper who had beaten you so easily in our first meet. In any case you dropped him to the mat, using the fireman's carry I had taught you, and somehow you remained on top of him when he attempted a clumsy roll and landed himself flat on his back. I think he simply collapsed before you did because you did not realize you had triumphed, not even afterwards when you were helped to your feet and awarded the match.

You fainted shortly after stepping from the mat and you were taken to the school infirmary where the nurse gave you pills and an extra blanket for your bed. You were chastised of course for losing so much weight, but it was still unconvincing to see you eating again at dinner that night. You poked cautiously at your spaghetti, pinching the handle of your fork, as if trying to corral a plateful of worms. You may just as well have skipped the meal; as it turned out you were too weakened from weight loss and dehydration to hold down any solids. You were confined to your room for a week, bedridden with the flu, and we were forced to finish up our few remaining meets without the benefit of a 154-pound wrestler. Your class remained empty.

What made us such friends? I had no use for your shallow obsessions, your pedestrian mind, your childish tantrums whenever you failed to make the honor roll or even when you missed questions on your military science quizzes. And you did disappoint me.

You have forgotten, I'm sure, a parade Saturday. The usual hurrying and scurrying—shoe-dusting, sling-tightening. More competition to begin for the best company flag. The usual bullshit. Except that we started late that Saturday since the weather report was uncertain and the school Commandant kept changing the dyke on us. At first overcoats and barracks hats were announced as the dress of the day, then it was blouses with white cross belting, and finally it was field jackets with caps. These changes, all of them ordered by the Commandant, were relayed by a cadet captain to the surrounding stoops and punctuated by definitive clangs of the archway bell. The irresolution of our parade orders—a rare waver in an otherwise formidable ostentation—awoke in me finally a compulsion to rebel. But it was you who lent me your white dress belting, giggling as you knelt before me to pin it to the dirty fatigues I had put on. "Cute, Tom, cute," you said.

How many others must have laughed when I slipped from our room and waltzed along the first balcony stoop as though hurrying to the formation. It must have been everyone but our Commandant; I saw him actually leap from the guard shack when he grew aware of our prank. How quickly he hurried across the quadrangle and flew up the stairs, bursting into our room only seconds after I had darted back through the door, a portly faculty sergeant waddling behind him.

Back and forth he strutted, huffing as he glared about him, a leathery old man who smelled often of gin. "From this idiot I would have expected it. Oh, yes indeed I would have, I most certainly would have. But from *you*, Max, *you!*" Turning away from you, he ordered me to brace, his scowl now focused, his pinched nostrils flaring; it was only his eyes, swimming frantically behind thick bifocals, that continued to nurture my seizure of power. I tucked my chin charitably, flattening the skin beneath my jaw, a useless tension—"You think it's still funny, son?"—because I couldn't arrest my smile, not even when he marched me down to the quadrangle and ordered me to do pushups while he barked out the cadence like a seal. I pumped methodically, enjoying the workout, and listened to the clusters of cadets collecting along the stoops above me. By the count of thirty, the hooting began. At fifty my arms gave out so I began on squat jumps, holding high my sweaty rifle while I pranced up and down in the manner of a performing bear.

It was surely the din from the stoops—the expectancy of an encore—that kept us so long on the grass of the quadrangle. I felt buoyed by the jumps, as though riding a horse, yet I knew the performance, spontaneous at first, was evolving into a stale and exhausting pose. My leaps grew lower as the minutes dragged on while the Commandant's voice, thin, cracking, was finally unable to rise convincingly above the hoots and cheers. But I think I would have enjoyed myself still if I could have seen you watching us. Your absence was too conspicuous when I looked for you to appear along the rail. You didn't bother to show—not even later when the performance was over and the Commandant left me in order to attend to the grander rituals of the day.

I remained kneeling on the grass for several minutes more; your belting had come loose from my shoulders and it took me that long to disentangle myself from the drooping bands. I had barely removed the pins when the bell in the archway resounded once more, announcing the final call for the formation. Since I was still slick with perspiration, it surprised me somewhat that the dyke would be overcoats after all. I rose too slowly, my legs beginning to cramp, and did not pretend to hurry as I made my way across the quadrangle. The belting, untangled at last, draped loosely from my shoulder as slowly, wearily, I mounted the stairs to change dress and return it to you.

I have almost forgotten the fire. This lapse is forgivable, I'm sure, since the fire was only one of about two dozen blazes that occurred with depressing regularity during my two-year tenure at Washburn. These fires, set by some of our less ingenious mavericks, struck me as too ill-plotted to pose much danger and I did not take them very seriously once I had accepted them as commonplace events. I grew so accustomed to them, in fact, that I would often continue about my business when the usual outbreak of shouts from distant stoops announced that another room was ablaze.

It was not until my senior year that this chaos drew near enough to merit more than a passing glance. Though my desk was closer to the window, it was you who first noticed the caustic scent leaking from an adjacent two-man room. You sniffed the air eagerly, hound-like, then slammed shut your book. "Jesus!" you blurted—an outburst I at first attributed to your obvious frustration with the language in *Beowulf*, the epic we were studying for a literature and composition course. It was only when you dashed to the door of our room, a blanket in hand, that I realized you were referring to a more imminent turmoil.

I followed you into a burning room, clutching dutifully a blanket of my own, and it was not until I'd been stung by the blistering heat that I realized the arrogance of your lead, that it was simply a coarseness of imagination—that same dearth of intellect that so often frustrated your studies—that illuminated you in the fluttering glare of the room. Standing dimly before the swirl, slapping the blanket against a wall, you seemed incapable of respecting the leap and crackle that had already disintegrated the beds and filled the air with shriveling bits of cloth. Given the impotency of your efforts, you seemed more comical than heroic and I was glad to lose sight of you as I stepped backwards through the thickening haze and eased myself out the door.

There were others answering the call by then so I got out of the way as hands, by now well experienced, directed the nozzles of the fire extinguishers. The bell in the archway leapt and clamored—a timely alarm since the frail whoosh from the extinguishers seemed only to enliven the dark cloud. I called

190

your name twice but the room, now aroar, relinquished only smoke.

When the bucket brigade had formed, I helped pass the dripping waste cans towards the inferno. These efforts seemed inconsequential since more extinguishers were on the way, but my labor ceased only when I noticed you at last, your hand still gripping the steamy blanket as you leaned coughing over the stoop railing. You were sheepish when I scolded you, embarrassed by your belated response to my cries, and you thanked me for my superior foresight.

Can you see what your blindness has made me do to you— even with your eyebrows singed, your hands pimpled with welts, your lungs scorched, retching? But your maladies did not excuse you the formation either—after the fire was out—when the bugle sounded everyone out onto the parade field. Along with the rest of us you came for four hours of rifle manual in the cold night while Leather Face kept popping out of the guard shack to tell us what idiots we all were for protecting the firebug. Suspects were taken to the guard room, one or two at a time, and held for long minutes of questioning before being sent back out. Everyone was to be spoken for.

And meanwhile, under the dim moonlight, our rifles went *Clap! Clap| Clap!* responding to the sharp commands of the cadet captains. "Right shoul-der *harms!*... Left shoul-der *harms!*... Po-o-rt *harms!*" This diminished our shivering but not the slow numbing of our feet. I broke count twice, letting my rifle clatter to the ground, so I would be made to run laps around the field.

Finally, when the cadet officers grew restless, names were picked randomly from the school roster and called out at one-minute intervals; then the same questions, voiced by Childers, our fox-faced cadet commander, would illicit the same stiff replies.

"Gillespie!"

"Yes, Suh!"

"Did you set the fire?"

"No, Suh!"

"Do you know who did?"

"No, Suh!"

"Wippleman!"

"Suh!"

"Did you set the fire?"

"No, Suh!"

"Can you tell us who did?"

"No, Suh!"

And finally my name.

"Hemmings!"

"Participating, Suh!"

"Smart, Hemmings. That'll cost you another lap. Do you know who set the fire?"

"No idea, Suh!"

"Double-time it, Hemmings, if that's all you're good for. And don't step on your pecker again tonight."

Grateful, I circled the field yet again, my rifle held high above my head, but I would have appreciated the jog even more had I known it would be my last concession to Childers. It would only be a matter of weeks, in fact, until he and four other cadets would be indicted and then expelled for gang-banging Theresa Scrud. This shoddy adventure, announced to us at chapel assembly the morning after the indictments were served, impressed me as a rather typical operational overkill since Theresa, a local girl of loose associations, was renowned for giving hand jobs to cadets in the town movie theater. This incident, however, had not yet become news the evening of the fire formation, so we answered to Childers throughout the night, disclaiming ourselves of a stealthier mischief as he put us through our paces.

Half the roster by three a.m. The names, by then, were harder to hear, muffled by the low tones of complaining cadets and the angry thumps with which we walloped the stocks of our rifles. Our ears, unprotected by our slim field caps, grew brittle in the cold and our fingers, though gloved, became tingly and remote. We stood as though shackled, awaiting the dawn, and looked forward to our turn in the guard shack where we knew it would be warm.

A SECOND, LESS CAPABLE, HEAD

We were mustered in together, you and I. It seemed strange at that moment to be walking between guards or to be walking at all since the ground felt foreign beneath my feet. Our rifles were taken from us at the door of the shack. New rules, we were told.

As we stepped inside the shack, the weary brown wrinkles of the Commandant appeared to perk up. The old man even gave me a wolfish lear as he leaned back in his chair—You again!—and the detective sitting beside him turned on a tape recorder. The Commandant did speak gently, however, sensing perhaps some limits to my depravity, and he seemed to be savoring a small charity as he circled our names on the roster.

"Rite of passage, boys, a mere rite of passage. Tell us the truth, simple and pure, and just maybe I'll scratch two more clowns off the suspect list."

Through tobacco stained fingers, the tips forming a steeple, he addressed his next question to me alone. "Now just where were you, son, when all this began?"

I shuffled my feet, prolonging the moment, as I had been saving my answer for a long time. "Rescuing Max," I finally replied.

The leer survived the relaxing wrinkles as the Commandant lowered his chair to the floor.

And you smiled too quickly when I spoke; I'm sure you must have, although I was watching the Commandant and could not see your face. Because afterwards, when the formation finally broke up, he made you share the first fire watch with me. To make sure I didn't fall asleep, he said.

We assumed our vigil on the windy top stoop of the school. We were the only two awake at the time and we had full view of most of the rooms. It was cold on the stoop, but peaceful at least with heated bathrooms for us to duck into every hour or so. A few faint sparrows were beginning to sing, and we waited for the pale ash of daybreak.

We didn't watch for the firebug, though, who must have been snoring snugly. Our attention instead went to a room opposite our watch on the ground floor of the school—a locale where we hoped to spot the spirit of a deceased cadet. The apparition, known throughout the school as Hensley's ghost, was believed to belong to Paul Hensley, a fellow who had died in the room during our junior year. Quiet and unnoticed in life—I had not even known his name before he passed—he was now popping up unannounced and scaring the wits out of people with his soul's shadow. The room, I'm sure, would have been empty had not the Headmaster assured its reluctant occupants that Hensley had been a very nice cadet and would doubtlessly have a very nice spook. You weren't convinced either, but still we looked for it—you shivering and sucking the welts on your knuckles, me just shivering. The moon was now setting, the shadows were thick, and the birds were beginning to riot.

You told me again of your dream—a chimera more faithful than the one for which we watched. The smoke in your dream was ethereal, not dirty; cloud-like and thin, it rolled slowly from the small swampy hollow exposing first your hands, for some reason clutching a tin of ham and beans, and then your face, relaxed in the winking lights. You lay still in the trembling water, as though you'd been carved out of wood, and your form dimmed and woke with dull regularity, a bold recurring fixture in the mutable shadows cast by the signal flares. The scarves, still curling about in the dirty water, were frail, suggesting a shallow wound, and your face wore a sulpher stain like a birthmark as it studied you, noncommittally, through the veil. You were older even as you spoke to me, your voice clear, without stutter, and you spoke as though describing a past event, a matter long over with and no longer disturbing to you. It was clear that the dream, through the monotony of repetition, had attained for you finally the familiarity of an old movie.

I made no reply when your story was done. Your vision seemed brazen, voyeuristic, and we had a less intimate revelation to watch for from our stoop. I dropped my gaze, holding my breath, as a door opened on the stoop below us, but it was only Wippleman, a compulsive masturbator, tucking in his robe as he shuffled eagerly towards a bathroom. I was skeptical of his avowed record—six times in an hour—but I did not doubt the rumor that he displayed his prowess for those interested enough to pay him a dollar. His business, in any case, was instantly consummated and he waved to us triumphantly as he stepped from the bathroom and wandered on back to his room. I acknowledged the feat with a concessive nod and glanced wearily at my watch as he once more disappeared from our sight. I was surprised to discover that the birds were early, that it was only four o'clock and three hours still remained before the reveille would sound. I turned up my collar, resigned to the cold, since I knew we would not be relieved of this watch.

The stoops were still empty an hour later when I noticed that the specter had indeed appeared. It looked shiny but frail, earthbound rather than macabre, a small incidental presence standing alone by the doorway of the darkened room. It did momentarily return my gaze, but its manner was incurious, self-absorbed, and it showed no particular gratitude that I was aware of its isolation. I woke you up—it was you who slept—although not quickly enough as an instant later it was gone, even before your eyes had opened. But there hadn't been very much to catch. Only a pale little shroud, like fine blue flame, for a moment only.

Our rites of passage had not been reserved for the fortress-like walls of Washburn. Yours came after your graduation from Virginia Military Institute—at My Tho, Ben Tre, Soc Trang, where you served first as an airborne ranger and later as a supply officer once a cracked kneecap had disqualified you from jump duty. Mine came during the first descent on Washington D.C., a relatively controlled peace demonstration where I nevertheless succeeded in acquiring a head gash requiring sixteen stitches. This blow was not delivered by any of the marshals or frightened reservists guarding the Pentagon, but by a member of the American Nazi Party, a fellow arrestee whom I encountered at the work house in Occoquan, Virginia, after I was taken into custody for crossing into the roped area. I had made no effort to provoke him and am not really sure what prompted him to blindside me with a chair, but probably he had simply mistaken me for some other subversive who had berated him on the transport bus. The wound, in any case, expedited my processing from the work house and I was turned loose after only an hour in order to receive medical attention.

My rites continued on Birdstone Cattle Station, of all places, a small dust pocket in the vast Northern Territory of Australia. I had not gone there specifically to defy the draft—I was bored enough with college by then to attempt almost any deliverance—but the notice to report seemed especially presumptuous when it reached me in that huge and consoling emptyness; the parched mud flats and paperbark scrubs at least offered me adventures of my own choosing. You wrote me even then from the delta villages and fire bases, your letters scrawled hastily in handwriting too large for the lines. You were sunburned in the photos you sent me at first, not yet accustomed to the heat as you posed barechested in front of grimy ammunition cases or sat in the small folding chair you often took with you on patrol. You looked leaner in later snapshots, weary but detached, no longer sweat-soaked, and as dark in color as the jungle itself.

I remained too long in Australia—almost seven years—but the cattle stations, coastal mines, and opal digging towns allowed me at least the promise of continued space, a dry and beckoning wilderness for which I could discard the vestiges of civilization at any given time. I grew sinewy as well, perhaps more hardened than you when I executed cattle, dying by the hundreds in the black adhesive mud of the billabongs, or shot wild pig for a diverting thrill and the small bounties their noses would fetch. I competed with you still in these harsh but relevant ways, and my gaze, steady and unattached, grew finally as distant as yours.

They did not know what to make of me when I chose to return stateside in 1973. The country, already long depleted by the Tet Offensive, the siege of the Democratic Convention in Chicago, and the still unremitting flow of body bags, clearly had no use for another superfluous martyr. I had spent only a day in the Los Angeles County Jail, in fact, when my court-appointed attorney, himself a draft avoider, assured me that all charges would be dropped if I agreed to accept a peacetime enlistment in the Army. I rebuffed this offer at first—I owed you more than that—and spent several token months in county lockup before conceding that there were other ways, perhaps no less empty, in which I could squander my time. The post-war ravages in Cambodia's killing fields had already begun when, bored and overfed, I followed a federal marshal from the holding tank and rode with him to a recruitment station to begin the swearing-in process. Were these distant fields—more corpse littered than even the plains of the Outback—a sad and final tribute to my rebellion?

After my induction, I was assimilated with discouraging ease into one of the eight-week training cycles at Fort Knox, Kentucky—an ingestion I attribute not to allegiance but to the durability of habit. The lessons of Washburn had remained with me all too well: I was appointed guide of my training platoon, taught hands less sullied than my own how to disassemble and clean a rifle, and succeeded in picking up a sharpshooter's medal when our platoon took its turn qualifying on the pop-up target ranges. I was even nominated by my company sergeant for the American Spirit Medal, a training bauble which thankfully I did not win when interviewed by an officers' board at battalion level. I completed the rest of my two-year stint without attracting further undue notice and accepted an honorable discharge from the medical company to which I had been assigned long after the last of our retreating helicopters had crashed and sunk in the South China Sea.

I had been back in the country for over ten years before I found myself standing at The Wall. My belated visit to the D.C. Memorial, prompted by my stubborn illusion of closure, took place on a day in late November. It was overcast that afternoon, a fine but persistent drizzle was falling, and the three bronze servicemen, ever frozen in their attitude of bewilderment, looked sweaty and alive. The directory book had been vandalized or accidentally torn where your name would have been so I had to search hopefully along the polished black granite of the Memorial's western wing, using only your approximate dates of service as a guide. The droplets, though tiny, clung tenaciously to the slick dark mirror, muddling the dim reflections and distracting my glance when they skidded finally over the multitude of names. It was by accident, I'm sure, that I spotted you finally—John M. McNaughton—an inscription as innocuous as the rest chiseled neatly into one of the outer panels. You were hard to locate.

•

Hunter's Moon

RYAN O'SHAUGHNESSY is standing in a dim, airless courtroom. A glint of light falls through its solitary window. Dust is dancing in the light.

Judge Dryballs, a shriveled old fart too skinny for his black judicial robe, is reading a report from Ryan's caseworker. Meanwhile, the court reporter is eyeing Ryan's crotch. She's just Ryan's type: a supple redhead with tits like musk melons. The bitch looks ready to tear off his pants—and why the hell not? With his broad shoulders, walnut-sized knuckles, and Popeye forearms, Ryan is a damn fine hunk of beefcake. Ryan wishes he had a dollar for every court reporter he's boinked. He could buy himself a mansion in Darling Point.

Ryan winks at the bitch and shrugs apologetically; she's gonna have to wait until he's out of custody. But, judging from the judge's expression, that may not be much longer. Ryan has been in the Paddington Facility for the Insane long enough to know how the game is played. For that matter, he's been in-and-out of loony bins most of his life. Loony bins and jails.

"Hmmmm," the judge says finally. His voice is all throaty like he's smoked too many cigarettes. Or maybe he's jacking off under his robe. "Hmmmm," the judge repeats. "You've come a little way with your therapy, sir. A *long* way for a man with fifty arrests. Most of them for disturbing the peace."

The judge squints like an owl then starts reading out loud. "Paranoid schiz, Napoleonic complex, antisocial personality." He wags his old head. "And yet you have been a model resident."

Prying his eyes off the bitch, Ryan grins. His erection is at full staff and ready to explode. A year without pussy will do that to a man. That's how long he's been at the Paddington Facility for the Insane. Ever since the cops arrested him for discharging a handgun within city limits. Ryan was really trying to cap himself a snitch—a meth head that dropped a dime on him. But the court don't need *that* much information. Thank god the fucker was too whacked out to press charges.

Ryan bows his head. "Thank you for sayin' so, mate," he replies. Ryan knows from long experience that he's gotta act humble in a courtroom. Gotta act like a law book applies to the streets. Like the streets ain't got their own set of rules—such as keeping your rep intact and killing off snitches. Ryan has iced over a hundred snitches. Blew out their brains with a .44 Mag then cut off their heads and used 'em for bowling balls. That makes *him* the enforcer—not that dry balls judge.

"Mr. O'Shaughnessy," the judge says boldly; the fucker acts like his nuts ain't all shrunk. Like maybe he's still got some juice in his spruce. "I trust you've been taking your meds, sir."

Ryan grins like a rattler. "Every day, yer honor," he says. He's fibbing of course; he's been tossing his meds. Sticking them under his tongue then spitting them into a toilet. That's why his hard-on is fourteen inches and rising. That's why jacking off is easy again. Ryan doesn't even need the meds. Those damn hallucinations—evil looking clowns and a hovering stone face nun—haven't bothered him in months. After forty years of fucking his mind up, his spooks have gone away.

"Ummm hmmm," says the judge. "You keep your room tidy. You help the nurses out. You have even read to catatonic patients. And I see you have taken up the ukulele."

Ryan beams. "That's me, yer honor. I'm tiptoeing through the tulips."

The judge chuckles deeply, like he's trying to cough up a hairball. After a five-minute pause, he sets the report aside. "Mr. O'Shaughnessy," he announces. "I'll tell you what I'm going to do. I want you back here in one week with another report and a placement plan. If all is in order, I will release you to a year's probation, which you will spend in transitional housing. It does appear age has caught up with you, sir. It's hard for *anyone* to be a criminal all his life. Even a derelict like *you*."

Ryan's grin is so tight he can feel his face cracking. Is this how it's gonna end?—his forty years as an outlaw. A life of breaking into cars, popping meth, and icing snitches. Is it gonna end in a halfway house where maybe he'll get himself a state disability pension?

Well, the judge is right about one thing. Even misdemeanors are getting harder to commit. Ryan is fifty-six years old now. He's got himself a heart murmur. And his street instincts are shot—otherwise the cops would have never caught him after he dumped that handgun. Only his tallywhacker—a foot and a half of bleating catfish—is still up to snuff. He's spoiled a thousand women with that beauty—ruined 'em for other men. And the court reporter is gonna be next.

The judge is rubbing his hands together, like maybe he's trying to warm them up. "Mr. O'Shaughnessy," he says. "I will see you back here in one short week."

Ryan clicks his heals and salutes the judge. "I won't let you down, yer lordship," he says.

Just one more week in the loony bin. One week more of kissing ass. One more week of reading to stiffs. And Ryan will be a free man.

Handcuffed and chained, with a constable on either side of him, Ryan shuffles out of the courthouse. The leg irons and waist chain seem kinda funny 'cause Ryan ain't really a crook. He's only broken into Bentleys and Rolls Royces—cars whose owners are ripping off the working stiff. He's only robbed porno shops—places where drug money gets washed. And he's only iced the scum of the earth. None of this is crime when you think about it. It's justice. That's something the courts ain't too good at.

At the bottom of the courthouse steps, the meat wagon is waiting to take him back to the loony house. A mob of riff-raff— prostitutes, pimps, junkies—are milling about on the sidewalk.

They gaze at him as he walks down the steps, but their eyes are deader than stones. They look like living garbage.

Slowly, painfully, Ryan eases himself into the back of the meat wagon. His joints are howling, his breathing is ragged. And his heart is pounding like a bill collector at the door. Once the security locks are set and the van is rolling along, Ryan stares wistfully through the screened window.

The van is passing through Kings Cross, the red-light district of town. He can see his favorite hotspots: *The Whiskey A Go Go*, *The Pink Panther*, and *Les Girls*, where he's rolled his share of faggots. Even bashing those poofters don't make him much of a crook. He never beat 'em up bad—just enough to teach 'em a lesson. And, after rummaging through their wallets, he always left 'em money for a cab.

This afternoon, the Cross is as still as a morgue. The strip joints and nightclubs haven't opened up and there ain't no pussy in sight. Not unless you want to count a mob of transsexuals on the corner of Darlinghurst and Roselyn. Fuckers who ain't real women.

Ryan's hard-on relaxes as the van rolls along and the fence of the loony bin comes into sight. Beyond the barred fence, some patients are playing cricket on the lawn. The fuckers are so full of downers that they look like they're in a slow-motion film.

As the van pulls up to the gate, Ryan's pants become flaccid and loose. Like a tent that's folding down. By the time the checkpoint guard unlocks the gate, his Willie is smaller than a grub.

Hours later, Ryan is sitting in his room in the loony house. A room that he don't share with no one. It's a six-by-ten-foot chamber with an iron- back bed and a chest of drawers. The room is his reward for being a model resident. Otherwise, he'd be stuck in one of the dorms with a bunch of crazies.

The window to his room is small and heavily screened, but Ryan can see out of it just fine. He can see the flower beds outside, the acres of manicured lawn, and the eight-foot barred fence with spikes on top. The place looks like a goddamn cemetery.

His caseworker, an old Irish fucker with a bulbous red nose, has already given Ryan his afternoon check-in. His caseworker's name is Patrick O'Leary, but Ryan calls him Abraham. That's 'cause the fucker is older than dirt. But that don't stop the jerk from collecting porno mags. He's got a stack of 'em that's taller than Ryan—gay stuff mostly like *Ploughboy* and *Broads with Rods*. The dude needs more help than Ryan does, the way he keeps raving on like a sot. Ryan's ears are still ringing from his afternoon check-in.

Ryan, me boy, the old fucker muttered. *To let go the past you must first admit it happened. Or those ghosts will never go away. And so you must raise the dead, dear boy—remember what you seem to have forgotten. Admit that you were born in a crack house, that you were raised in a youth lockup, that you were probably abused there. Admit that you suffer from grandiose daydreams—that you have seen too many adventure movies. Admit you've been pond scum all of your life—a drug addict, a jailbird, and a petty thief. Admit these things, lad, in order to let them go. Forty years of crime is enough for any man.*

Gestalt therapy, that's what ol' Abraham calls that crap. Makes him sound like a goddamn Nazi. But that dude wouldn't last a day on the streets. A man can't be thinking too much on the streets or the streets will eat him alive. But there's no way a therapist fucker—a dude who hides in an office all day—can know stuff like that.

Ryan wanted to say he ain't raisin' no dead—that the only thing worth raisin' is a stiffy. But he smiled like a fat cat and didn't say nothing. Gotta play by *Abraham's* rules if he wants to get out of this mausoleum.

Ryan rises from his bed, goes to the window, and looks out over the grounds. It's dusk and the moon is rising—the biggest damn moon Ryan has ever seen. It's larger than a medicine ball and as orange as a jail-issued jump suit. It seems to fill the whole fucking sky.

A Harvest Moon—that's what the Indians call it. Ryan saw such a moon in a movie once—a movie about settlers and redskins. It's also called a Hunter's Moon. That's 'cause when the corn is high the Indians go out hunting. Gotta bag themselves game for the winter.

Ryan's spine starts to tingle as he looks at the moon. It's as smooth as a tit and brighter than a headlight. He ain't never seen it this close to the earth.

The following morning, Ryan is sitting in Abraham's office. And Abraham is picking the wax from his ear. He acts like he's only pinching the lobe, but he's sneaking his pinkie right into the hole. The sight is disgusting, but Ryan don't care. That's the only hole ol' Abraham's gonna penetrate. Not even a goddamn tranny would bend over for a fossil like him. A dude so old he calls *everyone* "Me boy."

"Me boy, me boy," the ol' fucker mumbles. "The judge wants you to make a wee statement. He wants you to admit the error of your ways before he gives you probation. He wants to know your plan for the future."

Ryan shakes his head. So they want him to jump through more damn hoops. Tell a bunch of lies. Admit to the error of his ways. But it *ain't* no error to ice a snitch or bash a poofter or give a woman what she's begging for. What kinda crap is this?

Ryan looks at the floor and pretends to be thinking. "I'm one baaaad dude," he finally bleats. "And that you can take to the bank."

Ol' Abraham arches his eyebrows. "It's *your* plan the judge wants to bank on."

Ryan's whanger expands as he thinks of his plan. Namely, he's going to nail that horny court bitch who's starvin' for his Marvin. "It's the straight and narrow from here on out, pops. That's gonna be my future."

"Mr. O'Shaughnessy," ol' Abraham says—the fucker's getting pissed off. "I'm aware that you suffer from Alzheimer's. I'm aware that your brain is holier than Swiss cheese. But what do you remember from your past? What *significant things*?"

Ryan pretends to be thinking again. His favorite memory pops into his head. "I remember when meat pies cost just a nickel, pops. And a quarter would get you a pitcher of beer." Ryan smacks his lips. "There ain't nothing holier than meat pie and a beer."

Abraham sighs like a tire losing air. Like maybe he was hoping to hear something profound. His gnarly hands shake as he opens Ryan's file. The file is four inches thick. "Mr. O'Shaughnessy, I've decided to read you something. This was prepared by our psychiatrist a month after you were committed here."

Ol' Abraham peels a report from the file. He clutches it carefully, as though it might burn him. Slowly, he begins to read.

"After much testing and interviewing, I believe Mr. O'Shaughnessy to be the purest type of sociopath. He exhibits cunning instead of intellect, libido instead of love, and narcissism instead of introspection. His life, a forty-year continuum of street mischief, is not a life he seems to regret. To the contrary, he sentimentalizes his deeds with bizarre exaggerations and a macho image. If Mr. O'Shaughnessy regrets anything, it is that he has not accomplished greater crimes. Of further concern are Mr. O'Shaughnessy's hallucinations, a byproduct of long term drug abuse and homelessness. As he ages, and the strain of maintaining his street persona increases, so too will his hallucinations.

"All in all, Mr. O'Shaughnessy is utterly lacking in remorse, perspective, or even memory. As such, his capacity for self-renewal is abysmal while his potential for recidivism is high to the point of inevitability. In summation, he is an aging mugger who thrives on his ego the same way a camel might live on its hump."

Ryan folds his arms. He ain't sure what all that language means, but he knows a frame job when he hears one. But that's what shrinks are for—to cut a man down to size. Make him fit where he ain't supposed to fit. That's why they call 'em shrinks.

Ryan cracks his knuckles. "Money used to be *worth* something, pops. Meat pies once cost a nickel. A quarter would buy you a pitcher of beer. Can't beat numbers like *that*, can you pops?"

Ol' Abraham frowns and shakes his head. "There's another kind of inventory, my lad. The kind a man takes when *his* number is up."

Ryan covers his mouth and buries a chuckle. 'Cause deathbed confessions don't worry him none. He heard too many of 'em back when he was collecting for the loan sharks. Back when he was beating up deadbeats. But he always let the fuckers talk before smashing their noses or cracking their skulls. Can't risk killing a man until he's had a chance to bare his soul. Plead his case to Jesus and all. That wouldn't be right.

Ol' Abraham frowns then wags his pinkie—the same hoary pinkie he stuck in his ear. "May I tell you a story, me lad?"

Ryan shrugs. "I've heard enough stories, pops—they bore me."

"I'll try not to bore you," says Abraham coolly. "We lost a patient a few years ago—a street goon just like you. Congestive heart failure, he had. *I* thought his heart was made of stone, but the bloke started blubbering like a baby one day. He said he could see a dark visitor in his dorm. He said he wanted to light a candle to the Virgin."

Ol' Abraham swallows and draws a slow breath. "Well, I said all the right things to him, lad. I told him he still had time. I told him the Virgin would answer his prayer. But I was lying like a sinner. The reaper took him that very night."

Ol' Abraham smiles uneasily. "Mister O'Shaughnessy, you too are running out of time."

Ryan hangs his head and tries to look humble. A chuckle escapes his throat. "A meat pie and a pitcher, pops. That's as close to heaven as a man needs to get."

As he sits in Abraham's office, Ryan feels his chest thumpety-thump. His brow sweats beads; his life flashes before his eyes. And what a life it was: dodging cops, stalking snitches, and bashing fuckers in street brawls. A life only brave hearts can handle—men with iron knuckles, lightning reflexes, and the instincts of a wolf. Men who hunt jungle cats under the moon. Men who bust cherries with only one thrust. Real fucking men— not slackers like Abraham. Dudes who sit in an office all day and jack themselves off to gay porn. Yet fuckers like Abraham are the law.

Ryan scratches his head like he's thinking real hard. Gotta stroke that old fucker if he wants to get out of here. Judging from all that porn on his desk, ol' Abraham can't get *enough* strokes.

"Pops," he says, "I'm a hell bound dude. You've read me like a book."

Ol' Abraham shakes his head. "In your case, sir, it's like reading a pamphlet."

"Waddaya gonna tell the judge?"

Abraham frowns and starts tapping on his desk. The old fucker wants to get back to his porn. "Mr. O'Shaughnessy," he says, "*you* still have time. A wee bit of time if you don't strain your heart. Either you straighten out your life, sir, or you will die. Whichever way it goes, there will be one less thug on the streets."

"You're supposed to be curing me, pops," Ryan jokes. "Makin' me a better man."

Ol' Abraham flushes and bows his grizzled head. He looks like a drunk that's drooling in his grog. "Mr. O'Shaughnessy," he mutters. "I will tell you what you already know. *Here, we cure no one.* We warehouse our clients and keep them doped up. We confiscate their street drugs and dirty magazines, which somehow they keep smuggling in. But we cure *nobody.* I do admit, lad, that we're making them even worse."

Ol' Abraham pauses then heaves a deep sigh. Like he's blowing the foam off a beer. "So I'm telling the judge that it's time to let you go."

The Hunter's Moon is rising as Ryan strolls the grounds—a privilege he has earned by kowtowing and ass kissing. So every evening at sunset, he is allowed to roam the grounds for half-an-hour. Nature therapy is what the nurses call it. Like he's supposed to get a hard-on by sniffing flowers, hugging trees, and tiptoeing on the grass. Fuck that crap. But it's good to get away from the crazies for a while because a full moon stirs them up. And Ryan needs some peace if he's going to see the error of his ways—his despicable life of crime. But the only *real* crime is how much things cost now. That's gotta be inflation, but fuck it—who cares? The only inflation that *matters* is what's rising in his pants.

Ryan's blood starts to pound as he looks at the moon. He can make out the mountains, the craters, the seas. And it's shinier than a stripper's ass.

Ryan should have been thrown on a desert island—like that Robinson Crusoe fucker. The islanders would have taken one look at his schlong and made him a fertility god. They would have built him a shrine and brought him their virgins for deflowering. *Boom ba ba, boom ba ba, boom ba ba*—that's how the drums would sound. And Ryan would shimmy his hips to the drums, his rod throbbing with every beat. Before that whanger even wilted, he'd have busted fifty cherries.

The moon is now bright enough to read by. Not that Ryan reads. Reading is for geeks and Nancy boys. But the moon also darkens his powerful shadow. Ryan can make out his hulking shoulders, his bulging biceps, and the panther-like grace of his stride. What a magnificent savage he is.

"Hunh unh," someone laughs—a familiar voice. Turning his head, he sees her: an elfin teenage girl with dirty bare feet. She is sitting on a bench with a handkerchief in her hands and she's polishing a cucumber. Ryan has known her for forty years and the bitch never ages a day. All she does is giggle, talk bullshit, and piss him off. Still, she is the most harmless of his hallucinations so the sight of her doesn't bother him. Not until she hops off the bench, titters like a sparrow, and throws the cucumber at him.

The cucumber sails towards his head. Ryan ducks.

"Missed you," she laughs.

Ryan waves her away. "Get out of here, Dolly—beat it. They'll lock me back up if they see us talking."

The bitch shakes her head and starts clapping her hands. "What do you want me to beat?" she pipes.

Grinning mischievously, she skips up to Ryan. Ryan strokes her hair. "Hit the road, Dolly," he says. "I ain't going to tell you again."

Brushing away his hand, she laughs—a sound like a babbling brook. "Missed you," she giggles. "Missed you. Missed you." Her voice fades away as she scampers towards the gate.

Ryan shakes his head. She's gotta be dumber than a box of rocks. But at least she obeyed him when he told her to haul ass. Can't be having her kind around if he wants to get out of this place. But the bitch ain't as bad as the rest of those fuckers: jaundiced looking clowns, hump-backed dwarves, and an eight-foot-tall nun who's the scariest of the lot. Not that Ryan can't stare down a spook or two, but he'd just as soon save himself the trouble. Gotta save his swagger for cops and drug dealers.

Scanning the grounds with his eagle eyes, Ryan resumes his walk. The shadows are shrinking; the trees stand alone. The moon continues to climb.

"Tomorrow," says Abraham. He is looking at Ryan from across his cluttered desk. It is five o'clock in the afternoon and tomorrow Ryan goes back to court.

"Mr. O'Shaughnessy," ol' Abraham mumbles—the dude smells of whisky and lint. "Once the judge sets you free, you will have to make a choice. As God is my witness, you will have to make a choice. What goes around comes around—remember that, lad. Our blessed Lord always evens the score."

Ryan squirms in his chair. His nerves are like hot wires and he could use a hit of meth. That's 'cause he's putting in hard time now. "Gonna score me a choice piece of ass," he remarks.

Ol' Abraham wiggles his eyebrows like he's trying to shake 'em loose. The dude needs a weed whacker to keep those fuckers trimmed. "Mr. O'Shaughnessy," he says. "You're a man pushing sixty. The walls of your heart are paper-thin. So be *very aware* of the choice you now face. It is not a choice to break the law. It is not a choice between jail or the streets. It's a choice between life or death."

209

Ryan scrunches his brow like he's thinking real hard. "I'll listen to my heart, pops."

"Listen to your *maker*," snaps Abraham. "Make peace with the *Holy Ghost*." Ol' Abraham wheezes and shakes his head. "Is there anything *more* you would like to say, sir?"

Ryan clenches his fists and tries not to scowl. He's heard enough Bible thumpers in jail. Sallow faced nuns trying to humble real men. Goddamn soul suckers—*that's* what they are. The bitches give him the willies.

"That ain't how it happened," he finally says.

"What are you saying, lad."

"That fucker who got his candle snuffed. Deathbed confession. Angels took him straight to heaven." Ryan grins like a ghoul. It's too easy to mess with fuckers like Abraham—civil service burnouts sucking the taxpayer's tit. You just gotta know what button to press.

"You think that it's really that simple, lad."

Ryan shrugs. "It is to the Bible thumpers. Ain't you a born again Christian, pops?"

Abraham flushes and Ryan grins broadly. He's gotta be careful with that old Irish pervert. Can't be slippin' no confession to him. 'Cause Ryan's gonna go to Valhalla like Kirk Douglas did in *The Vikings*. In Valhalla you get to drink mead all day. And get into sword fights. And meet Odin, the war god. The only way to get there is *big time sin*—killing off villagers, looting their churches, and raping their wives in the bargain. Ryan should have been born a Viking. Ragnar O'Shaughnessy—that's what they'd have called him. He'd have filled up a barrel with looted gold.

Ryan cracks his knuckles and laughs. "Ain't it a bitch to be born too late?"

"Mr. O' Shaughnessy," ol' Abraham croons. The dude has had enough. "I believe our conversation is over."

It's seven p.m. The sun is going down. Ryan strolls the grounds for the final time. The sky is beet red—redder than ol' Abraham's face when Ryan told him a story of his own. About how he already *met* his maker. *Happened last year, pops—*

during an overdose. My heart stopped for a whole damn minute. And that's when I saw him waitin' for me. He was wearin' flip-flops and had a big G on his sweatshirt.

And what did he say to you, Mr. O'Shaughnessy?

He told me to keep my pecker up.

That part was a lie, but the rest was true. Ryan really did leave his body when a huge cap of meth froze his heart. And all he saw was some dude in a sweatshirt. That was a damn site short of Valhalla, which was kind of disappointing. Ryan may have to kill someone for *real* if he's gonna get into Valhalla. Unless there's something to that reincarnation shit. And he can come back as a stripper's pole.

The moon is now high. Although barren and cold, it looks like a huge living face. The face of some fucker who never turns his back on you.

Ryan's skin starts to crawl as he cases the grounds. The shadows are empty; the lawns are smoother than a carpet. Not a single blade of grass is out of place.

Tomorrow, at this very time, Ryan will be nailing that red-haired court reporter. He'll take her to the Zebra Hotel where he'll show her his dagger-straight rod. And after he's busted her cherry, he'll tell her to hit the road.

Ryan's nostrils flare as he strolls along a pathway. He smells something like pussy already—a stench like rotting fish. In front of him, the source of the smell is taking shape. He can see a head with a pair of devilish horns—both of them taller than a hard-on. He can make out an enormous girth, draped with the shadow of a sword. The face, which is slower to assemble, is sporting a bushy red beard. Even for a Norseman, the fucker is hairy.

The dude folds his arms as Ryan approaches him. Although he reeks of dead crabs, he looks like he's made out of stone. He don't even seem concerned that a battle axe is planted deeply in his skull. Nor does he seem alarmed by the porridge of brain matter clinging to his wooly shoulders. The dude grunts as he speaks—his voice thick with mead.

"Traveler," he slurs. "Dip your saber in blood."

The dude unsheathes a long gleaming blade, balances it in his hand, then starts sharpening it with a stone. Ryan's scalp prickles; his heart pounds with excitement. When he gets to Valhalla, he'll have to swordfight that spook. And the fucker looks ready to run him through.

But at least the dude died with his sword in his hands—the credo of all Vikings. So Ryan salutes him and hustles on back to the loony bin. The fucker stinks too much to hang around with any longer.

The loony bin is silent as Ryan returns to his room. The dorm lights are off and the door to the day room is closed. There's no one around but a fat ol' night watchman who's sleeping in a chair in the hallway. The watchman ain't even made his rounds yet. He ain't even locked down the building.

After closing the door to his room, Ryan looks out the window. He sees only the shadows of well trimmed trees; the Viking dude is gone. But the moon now fills the whole damn sky. It looks ready to fall on the earth.

Ryan knows he will not be able to sleep. Thank god, he's getting out of this place tomorrow. Thank god, he can play some music *now*. Ryan, a born musician, has already mastered the battered ukulele he stole last week from the day room closet. He's gonna take it with him when he's discharged—so he can play for change in the coffee houses. And score himself some pussy. There ain't a bitch alive that won't spread her legs for a musician.

Ryan grabs the ukulele from under his bed then peeks through the door of his room. The hallway is quiet except for the ragged snores of the night watchman. Ryan is supposed to check in with that dude, but fuck it. He don't need that fat slug's permission to play himself a tune. Clutching the ukulele in his fist, Ryan walks on down to the day room. The door to the day room is always unlocked. And the acoustics there are to die for.

Ryan slips silently into the day room. The room is empty, but the lights are still on. A tiny stage sits at the far end of the room where lecturers come to bullshit. A damn good place to practice up for the coffee houses. After selecting a chair on the stage, Ryan sits down and starts plucking the ukulele. And then he starts singing in his rich tenor voice.

And if I kiss you in the garden
With a hard-on, would you pardon me?
And tip-toe through the tulips with meee.

Ryan concentrates hard as he plays, keeping his eyes on the strings. And so he does not see the procession of people drifting into the room. Not until he pauses to catch his breath does he notice that he has an audience. A cloud of seedy looking fuckers are standing around the stage—prostitutes, pimps, meth heads. It's the same crowd of losers that watched him last week as he walked down the courthouse steps.

The crowd looks like a cast from *The Living Dead*, a movie he saw before the cops locked him up. And it's clear from the dead fish glaze in their eyes that they ain't come to hear his music. The only thing their faces suggest is that he will soon be walking among them.

Ryan's skin crawls like it's covered with fire ants. His heart starts kicking like a trapped animal. But he feels his jaw clench with a warrior's resolve. *Fuck all this!* It's bad enough that he's gotta live in a mausoleum. It's bad enough that he has to put up with a dude like Abraham—a drunken sot hiding behind the law. *Now* he's being badgered by dead-eyed freaks that ain't come to hear him sing. Stiffs who are acting like maybe he owes them money. Ryan may be a hell-bound dude, but *this* ain't the hell he had in mind.

Ryan's fists clench. His nostrils boom like wind tunnels. *FUCK ALL THIS!* It's time—high time—he broke out of this place. And if those stiffs want to stand in his way, he'll beat 'em to death with his tallywhacker.

Leaping off the stage, Ryan snarls like a wolf. "*HAUL ASS!*" he bellows. He could use that Viking fucker right about now. They could cut down these assholes together.

The freaks let him pass as he bolts towards the door. Their expressions are passive—their heads bowed. They know a *real* man when they see one. Only the night watchman, a wanna-be cop, is standing between Ryan and the doorway.

"I say," the man stammers. "I say, I say."

Ryan don't let him say *nothing*. Realizing his ukulele is still in his hand, he slams it into the fucker's midriff. "Ooof," says the watchman. He falls on his ass, hugging the ukulele like it's a baby. Quick as a cat, Ryan jerks it away from him and brings it back down on his head. The ukulele smashes into a dozen pieces.

"Umph," the dude says then he don't say nothing more.

Ryan moves efficiently. After checking the dude to make sure he ain't dead, he rummages through his pockets. Since the ukulele's busted now, Ryan's gonna need some cash.

When he finds the fucker's wallet, Ryan opens it up. The wallet has a condom in it and a wad of twenty-dollar bills. Ryan leaves the condom in the wallet—his own schlong would burn it up—and pockets just one of the bills. 'Cause Ryan is *used* to traveling light. Meat pies once cost a nickel—no more. And a quarter was good for beer.

Ryan stumbles through the front door of the looney bin. His chest is kicking, his heart is in his mouth. Out on the lawn, the Viking is waiting for him. And the fucker is jacking off— slamming his ham with a beefy fist. Don't they have virgins in Valhalla? Or did the Arabs in Paradise get 'em all?

As Ryan runs past him, the dude calls out. "*Traveler*," he barks. "*Traveler. Traveler. Dip your saber in blood.*"

The Viking's shouts fade as Ryan sprints on. The meat wagon is parked near the front gate. Like it's waiting for Ryan to grab. Ryan has hot-wired a thousand cars so it ain't gonna be no problem.

Ryan can hear a police siren now. It mingles with the shouts of the guard at the checkpoint. The guard is waving a can of pepper spray at him. "*Don't hurt me*," the fucker shouts. "*Don't hurt me.*"

Ignoring the guard, Ryan dashes to the meat wagon. Screw him—he ain't worth Ryan's time. 'Cause Ragnar O'Shaughnessy don't fight chickenshits.

Snatching a stone from the driveway, Ryan aims at the driver's side window. With a mighty hurl, he lets the stone fly. The explosion is louder than a bomb going off. *Bulls-eye.*

Glass litters the seat like a carpet of jewels as Ryan ducks under the dash. Within seconds, he has removed the access cover, located the starter wires, and stripped them with his teeth. A few seconds later, the van gives a roar—a roar like the fires of hell. Clutching the steering wheel, Ryan hits the pedal. The van gathers speed as it hurtles towards the gate. The tires are squealing like banshees.

The gate is almost upon him—a tall row of bars clamped up tighter than a hyman. Ryan hears the guard holler as he holds the van steady. "Code red," the dude shouts. "Code red, code red." He's got a hand radio pressed to his mouth like maybe it's his mama's tit.

The van strikes the gate like a battering ram. Ryan's head hits the windshield. Lights blanket his eyes. As the flashes diminish, Ryan lets out a whoop. The gate has been knocked clear off its hinges. Ryan can make his escape.

The steering wheel is now slippery with blood, but Ryan holds onto it tight. He again hits the pedal; the van gives a roar then fishtails into the street.

Ryan clenches his teeth as the van careens sideways. The tires are shrieking; the air stinks of rubber. The chassis is bucking like a bitch.

The steering wheel steadies. The tires stop smoking. And Ryan is tearing down Oxford Street. The street is full of poofters, but Ryan can't deal with them now. After he's ditched the van, after the heat is off, he'll come back and bash a few. But *first*, he's gotta make it to Kings Cross.

The wail of the siren is louder—the cops will soon be on his tail. But Ryan's more worried about what's in front of him. At the intersection of Oxford and Darlinghurst, a police car is blocking the road. And three goddamn cops are standing beside it. Cast in the cherry sweep of the flasher, they look like they ain't of this world.

"*PULL OVER*." The voice is full of iron—like maybe it came from his maker. "*PULL OVER*," it repeats. "*PULL OVER. PULL OVER!*"

Let the fucker yell—Ryan ain't gonna pull nothing. Except maybe his Willie when he's made his escape. Gunning the engine, burning the tires, he slams the van into the side of the police car.

Lights are popping like fireworks as Ryan hops out of the van. The cop car is crushed—the air reeks of gas. Miraculously, Ryan isn't hurt. And a tire iron has appeared like magic in his hand. Ryan clutches the iron—he's damn well gonna need it. 'Cause the cops are now on him like stink on shit.

The first cop he drops with a punch to the neck. The second one he brains with the tire iron, a blow so hard the dude's helmet goes flying off. The third cop he staggers with a poke to the knee. As the cop hits the pavement, all the time tugging at his holster, Ryan smashes the iron across his wrist. The bones crack like walnuts; the dude howls in pain. A handgun goes spinning into the street.

Ryan lets the gun lie. The cops are all down so there ain't no point in shooting them. But he's gotta get out of here and *quick*. Before he has to beat up a whole lot more.

A flutter of voices assaults Ryan's ears. He clutches the tire iron—puffs out his chest. His eyes dart fearfully about.

When he locates the sound, Ryan drops the tire iron. It's just a flock of whores on the other side of Oxford Street. The bitches are watching him—checking him out. And they all got lust in their eyes.

Ducking into alleys, hiding behind cars, merging into shadows, Ryan stumbles in the direction of Kings Cross. He can hear the sirens long before the squad cars go zooming past him. The cops will never catch him with their stupid sirens on. When he spots the fluttering lights of the Cross, Ryan feels kind of sorry for the cops.

WooooooOOOOOOEEEE. Another damn siren. Ryan silently chuckles then leaps into an alley. Ducking behind a trash

216

bin, he waits for the squad car to whiz by. Big mistake. Someone has spotted him in the alley. Someone who's taller than a house. Someone who's got him cornered. As the creature approaches him, Ryan's heart leaps. It's that goddamn soul-sucking nun. And the bitch is squealing like a slut in heat.

WOOOOOOOEEEEEEEE!! She's approaching him slowly, haltingly, like a cat about to spring. Looks like he'll have to beat her up too. Slap her silly with his two-foot whanger. Don't matter a damn that she looks like shit—that her eyes are watery, her habit soaked with sweat. Don't matter that she's hemorrhaging from the waist down, kinda like a stuck pig. If the bitch don't haul ass and *quick*, he's gonna lay her out.

WHOOOOOOEEEEEEEEE!!!! Her voice is growing shriller— it's like icepicks in his ears. And her skin has morphed into the color of tallow. "ARRRGH!!" Ryan shouts—he can barely hear his voice. His heart is aflutter. His senses are failing. The alley grows dark as a womb.

The nun is gone when Ryan awakes. And he's sporting a thirty-inch hard-on. But his hard-on wilts fast when he hears a familiar giggle. Can't stroke his beauty with *that* bitch around— she's young enough to be his daughter. Wouldn't surprise him if she *is* his daughter. With all the cherries he's busted, Ryan's bound to have sired a brat or two. The bitch is sitting on the trash bin, wiggling her toes. And she's wearing a pair of gold earrings.

Slowly, painfully, Ryan staggers to his feet. His throat is raw, but he manages to speak. "Beat it, Dolly. I'm wanted for mayhem."

She chuckles like a brook. "Missed you," she laughs. Pocketing the earrings, she leaps from the trash bin. Seconds later, her arms are hugging his waist. "Missed you," she pipes. "Missed you. Missed you." Her teeth are shinier than pearls.

Ryan slaps her on the ass then digs into his pocket. He hands her the twenty dollar bill. "Hit the road, Dolly. Buy yourself some fries."

She tears up the money and throws it in his face. "Fries need ketchup," She laughs.

Ryan shakes his head as she skips from the alley. She's gotta be dumber than broccoli. But at least she ain't bugging him no more.

Ryan peaks from the alley. His nerves start to tingle. His heart is now pounding like a war drum.

Once again, he can hear the sirens. Once again, he is on the prowl. Once again, he's gotta fight crazies and cops.

Thank god for the Hunter's Moon.

•

Another Will Take Your Place

IT STARTED WITH THE FLICKERING of the bedroom light—*on off on off on*—slow persistent repetitions that nibbled away her sleep. The voice was soft but measured, as though integrated with the fluttering of the light. "I have a gun, ma'am."

She rolled onto her back, not quite awake, and turned her head. A man was standing at the bedroom door—a tall ephemeral blur that seemed more shadow than substance. She opened the drawer to her night table and groped about for her glasses. The voice stopped her cold. "I have a gun, ma'am. Roll onto your stomach. Please place your hands slowly on top of your head."

She squinted at her husband who was lying beside her in the bed. He was flat on his stomach with his head turned towards her. His hands were bound behind his neck. She could not make out his face, his ugly red face, but she could smell his fear.

"Bridgett, stop fidgeting," he snapped. "Just do as he says." His voice was habitually reproachful, as though she had once again wrecked the car.

Slowly, she rolled onto her stomach and laced her fingers behind her head. She suddenly felt rebellious, not towards the intruder so much as the waspishness in her husband's voice. It consoled her that his hands had already been tied, but she still wanted to punch his eyes. "Whatever you want, take it," she snapped. "Take it and *go*."

Her anger was so empowering that she felt she had willed it when the rope slipped loosely over her wrists. The rope tightened instantly—the knots had been pre-tied—but it bit only slightly into her wrists as the intruder fastened them to the railing of the headboard. That he was obviously experienced calmed her a little; she wanted the nightmare to end quickly.

The intruder spoke gently, as though addressing an invalid. "There's an easy way to do this, ma'am. Put your weight on your knees. Cooperate and I won't take long."

She obeyed quickly, scrunching her knees against her small breasts while the intruder lifted her nightgown. His hands were gentle and warm, as if he were already familiar with her. And so she was startled by the coldness of the jelly that he thrust between her legs. He smelled heavily of tobacco. "Please don't," she whispered. "*Please.*"

When he entered her, she shuddered—the act was so skillful, so clinically swift that he seemed to be sparing her pain. She clenched her teeth when he shuddered also—when she felt his seed challenge the grip of the condom. He withdrew from her slowly, surgically—she could feel his hand holding the condom in place. It had taken him only a minute to rape her.

He rose from the bed and the mattress springs groaned. A droplet stung her thigh. He was fumbling with his pants. "Would you like to share my towel?" he asked.

She nodded, irritated by the messiness of the gel, and sighed when she felt the terry cloth tucked between her legs. Her husband's tone grew shrill. "You've taken what you came for. Now will you please go?" She wanted to scratch her husband's face and felt vindicated when the intruder ignored him. Her marriage, what little remained of it, was collapsing like the Twin Towers.

"Some water, ma'am?"

She shook her head angrily. "Nu-uh," she muttered. "Nu-uh."

She could hear his footfalls as he left the bedroom—a catlike rhythm that was soon inaudible. Her wrists had loosened slightly in the bindings, but she clung to the headboard as though it were a raft. After a minute, he returned.

"Have some water, ma'am." His voice was calm but commanding.

She turned her head; he pressed the glass against her lips. She gulped the water slowly, haltingly, but he waited patiently until she was done. When she had finished drinking, he placed the empty glass upon the night table.

"Don't move for an hour," he murmured. "If you don't wait an hour, I'll know. I'll come back."

He turned off the light as he left the room and she was stunned by the totality of the darkness. She listened carefully for several minutes, convinced that he was still in the house, convinced that he had forgotten something and would return to the bedroom. And then she heard the slamming of the front door.

Two years later, she learned something about him. His name was Curtis Rollins and he was serving five years for another rape. His DNA had also marked her, but the chain of evidence had been broken, rendering the lab results useless. Even so, he had agreed to meet her through a victim program at the Indiana State Reformatory. In exchange for his participation, he hoped to transfer to a prison closer to his mother's home in East Chicago.

She learned this when a social worker phoned her to arrange the meeting. "You'll talk to him in a neutral setting. It might take him out of your nightmares."

She had answered testily, "I would rather he just stayed in my nightmares. There are far worse places he could be."

"Let him know that if you talk to him," the social worker replied. Her voice was smooth and sweet, like syrup. "Remember, this is his therapy too."

She had clutched the phone as though choking a snake. Would meeting him really take him out of her nightmares? She rather doubted it, but her fear was so erratic that it frequently felt like a bat in her hair. Even death seemed better than keeping this turmoil in her life. And so she agreed to meet Curtis Rollins in a visiting room at the prison.

She now sat with her daughter in the prison reception foyer. Her smug self-centered daughter whom she had begged to drive her to the prison. It was a measure of her desperation that even her surly daughter was a comfort. She could not face her assailant alone.

Although it was the Christmas season, they were the only two people in the foyer. She tried to take cheer from the synthetic fir tree in the corner of the room but its colored lights, winking steadily, reminded her of the night she had been assaulted. Colored bulbs had been strung along the walls, but their glow did not compensate for the sterility of the room: the bare wooden floor, the hardback chairs, and the unvarnished table strewn with paintings that inmates had put on sale. She sat as though drugged, her back to the wall, and held tightly to her daughter's hand. Soon, a representative from the program would be meeting with them.

Her daughter grimaced, as though personally insulted by the drabness of the room. "I still don't believe you're going to meet this creep." It was the same selfish whine that had sparked their argument earlier that day—when she had angrily insisted that she would not pay her daughter's cell phone bill. Her daughter, a freshman at Notre Dame, had been glued to her cell phone ever since returning home for the holidays.

"Answer me, mother. How's *this* going to help?"

"It's only to talk to an aging man. That's how it was *put* to me anyhow."

"*Really*, mother. The kind you find lurking in alleys? You know, people get stabbed here."

She snickered. "So what? I'll bite his nose off."

"Just last month, a guard got stabbed to death. Don't you read the *papers*, mother? It's like Iraq in here."

She squeezed her daughter's hand—this wasn't a joking matter—but she found herself giggling uncontrollably.

"Mother, *none* of this is funny."

"Nor is that phone bill, Missy. I'm *not* made of money, you know."

She released her daughter's hand, blotted her eyes with a Kleenex, and noticed her reflection in a mirror across the room:

222

a squat disheveled woman in her fifties with pale skin and jet-black hair. She looked flirty yet banal—like a statue in a wax museum. "You're a closed book, Bridgett," her husband had once said to her. "Except to any peeper who wants to stare at your ass."

Had two years really passed since the incident? Her night sweats, her hyper alertness, her inability to be alone had not subsided over the months. And her panic attacks were daily sieges, springing upon her with the entitlement of a household cat. She could not remember when things had been any other way.

"I'm not made of money," she said, as though repeating herself would strengthen her courage. "Don't think for a minute I'm paying that bill."

Her daughter sighed. "I *promised* I would pay it. Really, mother, don't be such a *brat*. I put you to bed last night, didn't I?"

The door creaked open. A sallow-faced woman tottered into the room. She was moving gingerly, as though trying not to trip on her three-inch heels. She was holding an open file from which she was reading intently.

The woman glanced up from the file. "Bridgett?" She spoke as though startled.

The woman's voice irked her. It was that same haughty social worker she had talked to over the phone. She answered sharply, "*Yes*?"

"I'm Anna. We spoke."

"Yes, Anna. I *do* remember."

Closing the file, the social worker sat down beside her. She arched her eyebrows. "Would you prefer that I called you Mrs. Hollowell?"

"Thank you, yes. Let's stick with Mrs. Hollowell."

Her daughter groaned. "The name no longer suits you, mother."

"Or maybe it suits me a little too well."

The social worker frowned. "When did your husband leave you?" Her voice was so saccharine that it could have been poured over waffles.

"*The worm*, you mean. Six months ago. And I left *him*."

"It's just as well. Marriages rarely survive these things. Not even the good ones—the ones that appear to survive. Is this your daughter?'

"This is Jasmine—yes. You can see I've spoiled her rotten."

Her daughter sighed stoically and once again took her hand.

The social worker cleared her throat. "Well, she can't accompany you on the visit, I'm afraid. But you'll need her when it's over. Do you remember your briefing?"

"No.... Yes. I'm not to use my last name."

The woman nodded. "First names only. We don't give inmates our last names."

"So what do I call him?"

"He goes by Rashad, but I don't believe he's really a Muslim. He probably just does it to fit in." She reopened the file, scratched a note in it, and then closed it once again. "He has many disguises, you know. *And* many visitors."

"Does he really?"

The woman nodded. "Church folk, Muslims, even some plainclothes detectives. I doubt that anyone sees through his masks, but that's probably for the best."

She felt her stomach churning. She wanted to bolt from the room. "I don't want things to be for the best anymore. The *best* is just something we have to wake up from."

"Is that what you want to tell him, Mrs. Hollowell?'

"What I want is to bite off his nose."

The woman sighed and nibbled her pen. "A pane of glass will separate you from him. And you'll speak to him over an intercom phone."

"How convenient," she snapped. "Do I wish him *Merry Christmas* as well?"

"Discuss only small subjects at first—like the weather, your health, and what you had for dinner last night. Only afterwards should you bring up the incident."

"What should I tell him about it? Should I tell him he ruined my marriage?"

"Only if it's true, Mrs. Hollowell."

"It's not. It's a lie. But maybe it's a lie he ought to hear."

"He must have had something to do with it."

She giggled. "For that I should probably thank him."

The woman frowned again. She brushed her skirt, as though ridding it of lint, and rose from the chair. "Keep your guard up, Mrs. Hollowell. He's not what you expect him to be." She again cleared her throat. "Are you ready?"

"*Must* I be ready?"

"It would help, but no. You'll see him for only an hour. Now don't waste that time getting angry with him—I don't think he'd care. And don't try to write him when it's over."

"Why would I ever *write* him? What would I even say?"

"I don't know, but it's happened. His other victim, the one he's serving time for, has been writing him weekly. Shall we go?"

She heard her joints snap as she rose from the chair. Her heart was pounding like a sprinter's at the end of the race and her stomach was growing tighter. She looked frantically at her daughter. "Any bits of advice?"

Her daughter smiled thinly. "Just one, mother. *Try* not to hog the phone."

She accompanied the social worker into the inner prison. The hallway was narrow, freshly mopped, and shiny with fluorescent lighting. The woman's high heels exploded upon the uncarpeted floor, causing her ears to ring. And so she felt relieved when they paused at a checkpoint and waited on the officer in the control module. "It'll be a few minutes," the social worker muttered. "We have a security alert." Ignoring the social worker, she studied her image on a television monitor. Her hair needed brushing.

A Plexiglas gate inched sideways, and she followed the social worker into a cramped compartment. A mechanical drawer crept away from the module, as though reaching out to grab her. A logbook lay open in the drawer. "You need to sign in," the social worker explained.

When she had penned her name in the book, the officer in the control room asked to see the back of her hand. She turned her hand over, while leaving it in the drawer. She felt coldness against her wrist: an ultraviolet identification stamp that

225

reminded her of the weekly singles dances she had been attending. She did not think much of the dances—hot spots for one-night stands—but this had not diminished their novelty. The pick-up lines, the clumsy suitors, even the thank-you-ma'am sex, were worth putting up with for a few fleeting moments of touch.

The gate closed behind her. A second gate parted and she pursued the social worker into another hallway. They walked through a series of long corridors, passageways so slick and convoluted that it seemed as though the building were digesting her. Were it not for a sudden racket—shouts, laughter, the ringing of gates—she would have felt that she had been swallowed alive. The woman took her elbow. "We're approaching the cell ranges. You'll meet him in the anti-chamber the attorneys use."

"I've *already* met him," she replied. She glared at her escort and threw back her head, but her bravado vanished the moment they entered the visiting room: a severely lit chamber containing several booths with chairs and hanging phone receivers. The room was otherwise bare.

"Have a seat," the social worker said. "He'll be here soon."

She first saw his shadow and then she saw him: a thin balding man in prison blues who stooped as he walked through the doorway of an adjacent room. He was taller than she remembered him to be and his face was as expressionless as that of a cigar store Indian. He was nibbling from a box of cookies.

Noticing her, he smiled—a smile both spontaneous and sunless, as though the pregnancy of the moment, the tension in her face, even the Plexiglas that separated them were of little consequence. His face was so still, his eyes so incurious, that he appeared to be in a trance.

He seated himself in the booth across from her and then guided the phone receiver to his ear. His movements were slow, sensuous—so utterly relaxed that she felt as though she were looking into a terrarium. She lifted her receiver slowly, doubting for a moment that he was capable of speech. When he spoke to her finally, her heart began to flutter. "Merry Christmas, Mrs.

Hollowell." His voice was deep, soothing, and totally familiar to her. She was not surprised that he knew her last name.

She studied him critically through the glass. "*First* names only, Dirtbag."

He smiled once again and dropped his gaze, not from embarrassment but to select another cookie from the box. He chewed the cookie slowly, methodically, as though it required profound concentration. He sucked at a tooth before speaking again. "Mrs. Hollowell," he said. "I am a man inside a cage. Do you really want me on a first name basis?"

She felt suddenly angry, but her anger seemed puerile—a throwback to that irretrievable moment when her daughter had started to baby her. The childish tantrums in which she was now permitted to indulge were simply too delicious to resist.

She snapped at him once again. "Kinda *late* for that, isn't it, Dirtbag? You just walk into people's homes and rape them?"

He smiled, shook his head, and dipped into the box. He spoke patiently, as though addressing a child. "It would be better, Mrs. Hollowell, if you thought of me as a stranger."

"I'd *rather* think of you as a creep."

"And not a stranger?"

"No."

Selecting another cookie, he shrugged. "Have it your way, Mrs. Hollowell. I *was* in your home more than once."

He nibbled at the cookie, impervious to the chill his words had conveyed. It was the same loathsome chill she had felt years ago, when she had discovered that her husband had been seeing another woman.

"It's *my* turn, Clyde. And I'll have it my *way*."

He nodded silently and continued chewing.

"So how many times were you in my home?"

"Seven," he replied. He spoke the number softly, reverently, as though it were a standard.

Seven thieves, seven veils, seven deadly sins, she thought. Could anything be immune to so significant a number as seven? He seemed to be quoting from the Bible.

"Seven," he repeated as though she hadn't heard him. "I stood over you seven times while you slept—you and your husband. And each time I chose not to touch you."

"What were you doing instead? Jacking off?"

He shrugged and averted his gaze. As he looked beyond her, his face grew so still that she wondered if someone had entered the room behind her—maybe that snotty social worker she wanted to slap. She discarded the thought when she noticed the empty reflections in the Plexiglas. She was alone with him.

He again looked at her and smiled. "Let's be formal, Mrs. Hollowell—please."

"Why?"

"It will make it easier to speak the truth."

"Why is the *truth* so important?"

"Anna believes it will help set you free."

"Do *you* believe that?"

He shrugged. "I don't really know. But the truth is better delivered by strangers."

"What's the bitch think you are? A *caregiver*?"

He smiled, dropped his eyes, and looked pensively at the cookies. Was he recalling a past life—a life he had surely abandoned? When he spoke again, he seemed amused, "No longer, Mrs. Hollowell. But *once* I was a surgical nurse."

She gripped the receiver and glared at him. This was not information she wanted to hear. "A surgical nurse. Well, *la-di-dah*. You shoulda let 'em castrate you."

Her words were so forceful, her anger so invigorating, that it disappointed her when he simply nodded his head. The suggestion seemed almost appealing to him and his voice was pleasant when he replied.

"Do you really want to be cured, Mrs. Hollowell? Castration would only cure me."

"I don't want you cured," she spat. "Just want 'em to cut off your balls. That's all you *deserve* for raping innocent women."

A smirk touched the corners of his mouth and he sighed. "There are no innocent women, Mrs. Hollowell. But perhaps you come closer than most."

His words, their pious judgment of her, pricked her only slightly—perhaps because she had grown charitable towards her sins: her three abortions, her chronic alcoholism, the stolen hours she had spent posing for her erotic website. Her decadence seemed an endowment now—something this creep was *not* going to take away. She had had that website for five precious years—long before her husband had stopped screwing her. And long before this creep had crept into her bedroom.

She looked at him sharply, narrowing her gaze. "Quit talking to me like you're Joan of Arc."

"Mrs. Hollowell," he said. "I'm a man with a disorder—no more. There was nothing revolutionary about my deed."

"Well, isn't that a pity. *Minuteman* describes you rather well."

He laughed throatily and clapped his hands—an impact she heard through the glass. "You are a piece of work, Mrs. Hollowell. Thank you for coming here today."

"Thank Anna—not me. She *does* want you cured."

He lowered his eyes and again shook his head. Dipping into his shirt pocket, he removed a packet of Camels. "Must you insult her as well, Mrs. Hollowell? Must you insult a well-intentioned woman?"

"You're pretty sure of yourself, aren't you?"

"No, Mrs. Hollowell. I am only sure of you. You are far less a mystery to me than myself."

Her hand tightened on the receiver as though she had siezed a club. "Listen here, Clyde. I'm a *closed book*." She cringed as she spoke, realizing the idleness of her boast. What was she, after all, but an estranged mother, a librarian in a hick town, and a lush? She felt vaguely consoled that he already seemed to know these things.

"Who told you that, Mrs. Hollowell?"

"The *worm*."

"Your husband?"

"Yes."

He smiled politely, as though responding to a bad joke. "Husbands," he muttered.

"What's that supposed to mean?"

"Husbands are better off blind—don't you think? But a predator must know his prey."

"You make it sound like a goddamn sport."

"To me it's more like a parlor game. Like posing for strangers or cruising in bars."

She rolled her eyes. "You're pretty smug for a rapist."

"Maybe so, Mrs. Hollowell. But I know you far better than your husband ever will."

Her skin prickled as he spoke, a sensation produced less by fear than by the disapproval in his voice—the ridiculous implication that she had somehow proved unworthy of him.

"Sorry to have disappointed you," she said. "I wouldn't want to give *rape* a bad name."

He tore at the pack of Camels then pulled away the seal. "You didn't disappoint me, Mrs. Hollowell. But even a predator has standards. I shouldn't have visited you an eighth time."

She gripped the receiver and glared, hoping to break his maddening composure—a coolness he wore like a pinstripe suit. "I'm sorry I didn't meet your highfalutin standards. My husband thinks I'm a tramp, you know."

"Must you keep boasting, Mrs. Hollowell? He left you for a tramp, didn't he?"

"I gave *him* the boot. The slut can have him."

"I remember him—a frightened little man. You'll do better without him and he without you. Be glad he's bullying somebody else."

"You're starting to *sound* like Anna, now."

"I hope so, Mrs. Hollowell. Sometimes even social workers are right."

"If you're so damn smart, how come they caught you?"

He sighed softly, put down his receiver, and shook several cigarettes loose from the pack. When he had selected a cigarette, he returned the receiver to his ear.

"Mrs. Hollowell," he said. "I chose to be caught. Otherwise, I would not be here."

The room behind the glass suddenly reminded her of the animal shelter she had visited as a girl—where she had selected, at her father's insistence, a beagle puppy with a spotted nose. The dog was her just reward for the many evenings she had allowed her father to sneak into her room while her mother was sleeping in bed or nodding in front of the television. At first, she had been content to punish the puppy—whacking its head with a rolled-up newspaper and pouring red pepper into its food—but finally she had loved it, loved it more tenderly than she had ever remembered loving. And so she had remained silent when her father reminded her that the puppy could be taken away. Was this man behind the glass—this smug, superior interloper—an extension of the dark covenant she had made as a girl? Had she instead drowned the puppy in the bathtub or cracked its head with a rock, would this man have had the wherewithal to creep into her bedroom not once but eight times? Looking into his eyes, his soft intelligent eyes, she knew that she had sealed this moment long ago.

He had lit the cigarette and the smoke, like the tendril of a jellyfish, lazily approached the glass.

"They let you smoke in here?" she asked.

He laughed and coughed crisply. "No, Mrs. Hollowell—they don't. But I'm only required to be honest with you."

"Then why did you let the cops catch you?"

He sucked the cigarette slowly, deliberately, as though it were an obligation rather than a pleasure. He smiled. "I must have felt sporting, Mrs. Hollowell. They're not very good at *their* game."

"Or maybe you just couldn't get it up anymore."

He chuckled and dropped his gaze. "That would have been a blessing. When you have done it a hundred times, there is nothing more tiresome than sneaking into houses and taking women by surprise."

"A hundred times?" She was stunned by the apathy of his disclosure: it was not a boast, not even a confession, but the mere recitation of a number. And so she believed him.

"The cops should have caught you sooner," she muttered. "Those poor damn women."

He sighed and rubbed his eyes. "For me it was worse—many times worse."

231

"How could it have been worse for *you*?"

"Mrs. Hollowell, don't you know forbidden fruit is toxic? If lightning had struck me I would have preferred it, but God doesn't share my precision."

"So what made you do it?"

He glanced towards the doorway—hesitated—then looked back at her with hospitable eyes. "What answer would you like?"

"That you did it to get your rocks off. That you're nothing but a fancy talking rapist. And a voyeur to boot."

"All right, Mrs. Hollowell. I did it for the thrill. A thrill that had vanished a long time ago. Sadly, you are not the only one chasing ghosts."

The smoke behind the glass was now thick enough to remind her of the dances she had been attending—dim celebrations where a couple of vodka tonics and an hour's conversation were enough for her to follow a stranger to his car or scrawl her phone number upon a napkin. Although wary of the dances, she also ached for them and frequently counted the hours remaining until the weekend—the hours separating her from the soft muted lights and the all-embracing smoke. She hoped never to tire of this vice—not as this creep had tired of his. Suddenly, she resented him all the more.

"It's not a *crime* to be a slut."

He looked at her tenderly and shook his head. Clearly, her presence was beginning to tire him. "Would you stop if it were?"

"Of course."

"Perhaps it should be a crime."

She winced and lowered her voice. "Who died and made *you* the law?"

He shrugged. The question seemed to bore him—or perhaps it was the redundancy of his reply. "Who if not you, Mrs. Hollowell?" he said. "Didn't you surrender instantly—as though I were a cop or a magistrate? Didn't you ask me to hurry—as though I were taking you by right? Even now, don't you tremble obediently whenever the door shakes or the window rattles? Who if not you?"

She felt the blood draining from her face. His boast, its haunting truthfulness, was like a hard winter freeze. "So I made you the law," she muttered. "My, but you *do* like to brag."

He laughed. "I consider that an insult, Mrs. Hollowell. I'm far less corruptible than the law."

"Then what were you doing on my website?"

"Scouting, Mrs. Hollowell—that is all. You're so very bad at it, you know—the stiff poses, the outdated gowns, the insincere promises of a grand time. You looked like a child playing dress up."

"So you *do* want an innocent woman?"

He chuckled. "Admittedly, I do. But you were the closest thing I could find."

He put down the phone receiver and sucked once more at the cigarette. The smoke seemed to claim him now—as though it were a mist into which he would shortly vanish. Slowly, he returned the receiver to his ear.

"Do you wish to hear my story?"

She glared. "Who am I to argue with the *law*?"

Slowly, serenely, he told her his story—his voice so relaxed that he appeared to be reading from a script. And so she listened to him doubtfully, weighing each word in the manner of a book critic. Soon the warmth of his voice made her feel reprehensible, as though she were colluding in the production of a bad play.

He had grown up in a Chicago slum. He had briefly attended Indiana State University, leaving when a trespass charge had cost him a basketball scholarship. He had been drafted into the Army and had served as a cook in Vietnam. He had been married, a childless union that ended before his military service. After leaving the Army, he had roamed the Middle East where he versed himself in The Koran. Later, he had studied nursing in East Chicago. He had worked ten years at an East Chicago hospital—a career he gave up when he was caught stealing amphetamines from the pharmacy. Weeks later, he had been arrested for peeping—a charge for which he received probation. When his probation ended, he forced himself upon a prostitute who would not consent to bondage.

He had been sentenced to prison for this incident—four years at the Indiana Penal Farm where he had been assigned to the prison infirmary. Paroled two years later, he began to perfect his art—studying his victims for days before committing his assaults. He had raped a hundred women before he had discovered her on her website and he had spent eight days profiling her—watching her drive to work, reading her mail, studying her as she slept. After assaulting her, he had stalked and raped a dozen more women. The bust for which he was now serving time could not be attributed to the skill of the police but to his having left a condom at a crime scene. He had plea-bargained for five years—one of which he had already served. With good time, he would be released in another 18 months.

She looked at him curiously when he was finished. He had told her much and he had told her nothing. "You're supposed to be setting *me* free."

"Free to do what?" he replied. "Free to tease men and numb yourself with booze?"

"That's better than shadowing women," she snapped.

He stretched and rubbed his eyes. "Mrs. Hollowell," he murmured, "isn't it sad that I was your only real adventure?"

She stared at him, disbelievingly. The receiver was now slippery in her hand. "Let me inform you of something," she hissed. "You're not exactly an adventure."

He lowered his gaze as though inspecting his pants for cookie crumbs. "The law would agree with you there, Mrs. Hollowell. Why do you think I received just five years?"

"Because the cops didn't do their jobs. Because the judge was a *real* pussy."

"No, Mrs. Hollowell. Because *I'm* the one who informs."

"Are you telling me you're a snitch? That you're dropping a dime on other crooks?"

His tone grew sharper. "I'm a registered informant, Mrs. Hollowell. Since I live among shadows, there's much that I see. Much that the law finds useful. And so I am serving a nickel—no more. A nickel is all they're requiring of me."

"Who are they letting *you* snitch on?"

He looked at her protectively. "Haven't I shocked you enough, Mrs. Hollowell?"

An ash fell from his cigarette, grazing his receiver. She looked at the streak of ash and the sullen expression on his face. "You're not proud of it, are you?—being a snitch. You think it's *worse* than raping and peeping."

"I'm not proud of it—no. But at least I *deliver* on my promises."

"So does the Devil."

"And it's not always wise to refuse him. But you know that already, don't you?"

"All I know is you'll get what's coming to you."

"I was worse off before I came here."

"Stay longer. Don't they know *half* of what you've done?"

"They don't *want* to know, Mrs. Hollowell. And so I have told only you."

"They should have booked you for all those rapes. You should be here for *at least* a hundred years."

He gently smiled, "The law will take care of me."

"What do you mean by *that*?"

'I've already been booked."

He looked at her calmly, his eyes growing softer.

The cold double meaning of his words began to register in her face. *Was he really a conscripted informant?* she wondered. *Was he really that valuable to the police—the stupid fucking police?* Since he was only serving a nominal term, he had probably told her the truth. She felt her scalp prickle, her palms grow damp. "You're getting out even *sooner*, aren't you?"

He shrugged. "We must all make sacrifices, Mrs. Hollowell."

"*Hogwash. Why are they taking care of you?*"

"Not every devil is courteous—or content to remain in your nightmares."

"That doesn't exactly *console* me," she snapped.

"Read the papers, Mrs. Hollowell, and be consoled. The community is safer because of me. And the prison."

"Well aren't you a hero."

He laughed and shook his head. "In the land of the blind, a voyeur is king. But know there are far greater monsters than me."

Her eyes flashed. "I'd *rather* stay innocent."

"Well and good, Mrs. Hollowell. But know this, at least. Even to the law—the people responsible for your protection—you don't amount to much."

"So how many *more* will you rape?"

He smiled. "Maybe a hundred—if I get what's coming to me."

"*Must* you repeat that number?"

"Yes, Mrs. Hollowell, I must. Haven't I sworn to be honest with you?"

"That's too much information."

He laughed. "I have told you almost nothing. But I have told you all that you need to know."

"And what is that?"

"I will not be back to see you. You barely interested me the first time. But another will take your place."

These words teased her like the smoke, not because she disbelieved them but because she suddenly felt ostentatious. It seemed as though *she* were the one in the cage.

"I'm glad you keep your promises," she spat.

He sighed and spoke sadly. "Be glad for small things, Mrs. Hollowell. And be glad that I have remained a stranger to you."

He pinched the cigarette, killing the smoke, and tucked it into the pocket of his shirt. He then scooted his chair back and casually smiled, a smile that conveyed neither warmth nor concession—only her unimportance. He winked.

"Merry Christmas, Mrs. Hollowell."

She did not remember returning to the visitor's foyer—the monotonous hallways, the sterile lighting, the inspection of her wrist by the checkpoint officer. She did not remember the debriefing from the social worker—probably a reminder that she not write him. And when she arrived at the foyer, she barely recognized her daughter—perhaps because she had set aside her cell phone and was concentrating on *Sports Illustrated*.

As she entered the foyer, her daughter looked up.

"So how was your date?"

She shrugged. "He was late."

"But was he a gentleman?—that's what *I* want to know."

"No. No, he was a monster, all right."

Irritated, she folded her arms and stared at her daughter. The gulf between them suddenly seemed wider—an abyss that even sarcasm could not breach. Given the demeanor of her assailant, his thoughtfulness and reptilian calm, she was especially annoyed at her daughter's lack of empathy.

"What did you *expect*, mother?"

She looked across the room, noticing the fir tree once again—the artificial branches, the searing light bulbs, the cheap plastic angel perched on top of it. It was only its triteness, its sapless fidelity to the season, that prevented her from knocking it over. Who had decorated that monstrosity anyway?

She looked back at her daughter and glared. "I *expec*t you to drive me home."

On Sundays, she worked in her garden—a half-acre plot behind her suburban home. She grew squash, tomatoes, and melons—arranging the plants in orderly rows, which the rabbits ate up by the following week. She did not mind the rabbits in spite of their havoc; they were somehow consistent with a lush's philosophy: *Sow your wild oats Saturday. On Sundays, pray for crop failure.*

Six months had passed since her visit to the prison and he had disappeared from her nightmares. This was not something she had anticipated or fully desired: having lost the dignity of martyrdom, she now felt cheated whenever she went to the dances. Now, when she looked in the barroom mirrors, she saw a tramp and nothing more.

And so, on Sundays, she worked in her garden—planting the seedlings, tilling the rows, and sweating out the booze from the previous evening. She detested the work—a filthy gritty business—but she took solace in the rustling of the trees, the darting of the humming birds, and the orbiting of the turkey vultures overhead. In the distance, they looked like kites.

•

The Body In The Bay

NIETZSCHE'S CUTTING QUOTE, "If you gaze into the abyss, the abyss will gaze into you," is by now a redundancy. And so, when I became a San Francisco probation officer, I prepared myself to keep company with the abyss. But I had not quite realized how extensive the abyss was. I saw it in the eyes of the senior probation officers, so exhausted by massive caseloads that they were counting the months to retirement. I saw it in the faces of deputy jailors, disaffected shift workers who were all but deaf to the human clamor of the cell ranges. And, of course, I saw it in my clientele: hollow-cheeked crack heads, asocial gang bangers, vagrants with thousand mile stares. But at least the abyss could be mellow where probationers were concerned. It was mellow in the case of Joseph Shepherd, a middle-age drug peddler on probation for chocking his girlfriend. Entering my office for his intake interview, he glanced at the tower of case files on my desk and chuckled. "I know you have it rough," he remarked in a voice that could be poured over waffles. "So I plan to make it easy on you, sir." He smiled with the insular charm of a sociopath then shook my hand with a python grip. He seemed to be a man of elemental strength—a brawn with a life of its own—yet his broad open face and puppy dog eyes set me completely at ease.

For a year, he was a model probationer. He was always on time for our weekly meetings, attended his batterer's program regularly, and he so liked to talk about books that I rarely hurried our meetings. After a year, his girlfriend phoned me to say he had choked her again. I quickly called his cell phone and invited him to my office. "You know what I have to do," I confessed. "You must do your job, my friend," he said, and he showed up at my office within the hour. He stood still as a statue as I cuffed him up and he asked me how my day was. He had honed that code of etiquette typical to old style criminals, the kind the gang members called *original gangsters*. And, of course, his girlfriend would probably recant—domestic violence victims usually did. When she appeared in the courtroom the following morning, a small dried-up woman with haunted eyes, she held out her hands like a beggar. "I lied, your honor," she wept to the judge. "Please jail me instead cuz I lied." Sitting at the defense table, Joseph looked at me as the judge threw out the charge. *I apologize,* his gaze seemed to say. *Didn't mean to cause you any inconvenience.*

An hour later, after getting out of jail, he dropped by my office unannounced. He sat for awhile in silence, but clearly he wanted to talk. Eventually, he rested his chin on his thumbs. "She won't cut me loose," he murmured. "I have given her every good reason to leave me. She just won't cut me loose." He shook his head theatrically and smiled his glacial smile. "Why won't she cut me loose?" he said. He spoke as though reciting a mantra—he did not seem to want an answer. "Are you flattered?" I asked him. "You seem flattered." He groaned and showed me a bruise on his arm. "She hits me all the time," he said. "She gets off on the make-up sex." It was classic male-pattern thinking, the type his program was supposed to challenge. Yet his program reports cited progress: he never missed a meeting, he excelled at group role play, and he had become a class leader. He chuckled profoundly, rose to his feet, and pumped my hand before leaving. "I believe I have taken enough of your time. Do give my regards to your wife."

The next morning, when I bought the *San Francisco Chronicle*, I read about the body in the bay. It was the body of a woman, crammed into a suitcase that had floated to shore near North Beach. Her state of decomposition confirmed she had only been dead a few hours. I recognized her name—it was Joseph Shepherd's girlfriend—and I felt a chilling relief. I could not be blamed for letting this happen—my paper trail was in place. I had hooked him up only two days ago; I had walked him down to the jail; and the woman had stupidly sealed her own fate when she came to court and recanted. I felt no empathy for her—only self-righteous contempt. The abyss, its numbing darkness, had settled within my soul.

Had he meant to kill her?—probably not. Probably, he had been choking her for the hundreth time during one of their arguments. But this time his hands had lingered too long; this time he squeezed with a bit too much pressure. And this time she didn't recover when he relaxed his grip on her neck. No, he had not intended to kill her—he had panicked a little too much. According to the homicide report, which I acquired later that day, he had dragged a suitcase through the lobby of his hotel in full view of the security cameras.

I drove to the hotel with a SWAT team, but of course he was not there. So I went to court, picked up a warrant, then faxed his mugshot to several local precincts. Hopefully, a police patrol would nab him and save me the strain of busting him. And when the story about the body made the evening news, I turned the television off. I had no good reason to dwell on the matter—not until our dragnet picked him up.

A week later, I was in our conference room attending some mandatory training. The course was Interpersonal Skills, which struck me as rather untimely. Joseph Shepherd, after all, was a master of interpersonal skills. And so I was already distracted when a front desk clerk burst into the conference room. "He's here!" she whispered into my ear. "Mister Shepherd is here! He is waiting for you in the reception room!"

Had he come to turn himself in? Or had he come to cover his tracks? Since the media had made no mention of him, he may not have known he was in trouble. So I felt I was being uncivil when I asked another officer to help me with the bust. But the officer, Jerry Ferrari, was eager enough for the task. "Right behind ya, Jim," he chirped, and I told him to wait in my office. I reminded him to go fetch his handcuffs, which took him nearly five minutes.

I forgave my hands for shaking as I walked to the reception room. I was about to arrest a murderer, after all. But he was sitting quietly in one of the chairs, much like a commuter at a train station.

He seemed relieved to see me. "Good morning," he said, rising from the chair. "I think we are due for some rain." Did he feel the tremor in my palm as he warmly shook my hand? If so, he was too polite to mention it. Obediently, as though keeping in step, he accompanied me to my office.

Closing the door behind us, I nodded to Jerry Ferrari. He was adjusting the settings on his handcuffs, clicking the bars into place. But he was having trouble aligning the teeth and the bars kept swinging free.

Putting his hands behind his back, Joseph rolled his eyes. "Do you really need backup to bust me?" he goaded. "I thought we were beyond that, sir?" I felt like an ingrate as we double cuffed him then set the safety locks.

"Relax," he said as he sat on a chair. "My friend, whenever you want me in jail you just have to call and tell me."

"So why did you come?" I asked.

He shrugged. "Don't I see you every week?"

He looked at me with welcoming eyes—eyes that carried no blame. But I did not want his friendship so much as I wanted him in jail. So the reticence was mine—not his. Somewhere, in the vast aridity of his soul, something green was growing.

As I waited for the detectives to fetch him, I mentioned his girlfriend's body. I did not read him his rights though he might have been close to confessing. A spontaneous admission, after all, could be legally included in my arrest report. But he quickly clammed up as a pair of detectives burst into the office. One of them was waving his badge like an amulet. "Homicide," he barked. "We got *questions*." The detectives flung him through the door as though he were a sack of laundry.

As the detectives marched him away, Jerry Ferrari looked at me proudly. He was an athletic kid with a collegiate aura—the untempered zeal of a fraternity rush chairman. "Tom," he said to me after awhile. "That was one fine bust."

The following morning, another article appeared in *The San Francisco Chronicle*. The article was about Jerry Ferrari; he was taking credit for the arrest. *Probation Officer Nabs Murder Suspect* the headline boldly declared. The photo featured Jerry Ferrari with a Glock holstered at his hip. He looked like a marshal in a spaghetti western. "I'm like a bloodhound," the quotation read. "When I'm on the scent, I don't quit."

That afternoon, I interviewed Joseph to finish my arrest report. The interview took place in the Glamor Slammer, a state-of-the art jail on Seventh Street where we met in one of the attorney rooms. He had heard about the article in *The Chronicle* and he seemed to be rather amused. "You should have cuffed me up by yourself," he teased. "Have I ever let you down?"

"I had nothing to do with that bullshit," I said.

He laughed. "Let the kid have his fun, my friend. It must be a slow news day."

On advice of his public defender, he did not want to talk about his case. But we chatted for several more minutes before I left his cell pod. "She was a crack head, a thief, and a hooker," he sighed, his voice as heavy as lead. "Even so, I did not do her justice."

"*None* of us did," I said as I slowly shook his hand.

I started scanning *The Chronicle* daily, hoping for more information. A quote from her mother, perhaps, or maybe her personal history. But no more stories appeared about the body in the bay.

•

Acknowledgements

Foremost, I would like to thank my wife, Mary Hanna, for supporting my ambition to become a published writer. To her, I have dedicated this book. And a big thank you to my mother, Catherine B. Hanna, for helping me get myself born.

I am grateful to the following members of my California critique group for their input: Lisa, Chris, Bardi, and Ann. And a big thank you also to my Florida critique group: Robert, Marisa, Howard, Teri, Pam, Shirley, and Elizabeth.

Kudos to the open mic programs where many of these stories were read aloud: Reach and Teach in Redwood City and Wordier than Thou in Sarasota. And a tip of the hat to the many readers who helped bring these stories alive.

Again, special thanks goes to Tory Hartmann, my publisher, friend, and chief editor. Without her, this book would not have been possible.

Thank you for reading *A Second, Less Capable Head*. If you enjoyed it, please consider telling your friends or posting a short customer review on Amazon. Word of mouth is an author's best friend and much appreciated.

About James Hanna

James Hanna wandered Australia for seven years before settling on a career in criminal justice. He spent twenty years as a counselor in the Indiana Department of Corrections and has recently retired from the San Francisco Probation Department, where he was assigned to a domestic violence and stalking unit.

James' familiarity with the criminal element has provided fodder for much of his writing. His debut novel, The Siege, depicts a hostage standoff in a penal facility. Ron Slaven, Top 100 Reviewer, writes: "This is the raw, gritty and complex reality of life in prison and the best of its genre that I have come across."

Call Me Pomeroy, James' second novel, chronicles the madcap tales of a street musician on parole who joins Occupy Oakland and its spinoff movements in England and France. He does not join for political reasons but to get on television, attract an agent, and land a million dollar recording contract. The first chapter, appearing in the inaugural issue of *Empty Sink Publishing*, was deemed Editor's Choice for that issue.

James' short stories are written in many genres, including science fiction. His tales are published in those literary journals that seek stories written in blood. Stories that deal in unvarnished truths over political correctness. *Red Savina Review, The Literary Review,* and *Crack the Spine* have all published James' stories. James has been nominated three times for the Pushcart Prize.

245

About the Cover Art...

Daniel Gale grew up near Farmland, Indiana and discovered his fascination with art in high school. He studied fine art at Ball State University, but went on to a career in technology with General Motors. He returned to his artistic paths in retirement and continues to photograph, paint, and draw in Sarasota, Florida. See a selection of his work at http://daniel-gale.artistwebsites.com/.

If you have enjoyed *A Second, Less Capable, Head*, the author and publisher would appreciate your kind review on Amazon, Goodreads or your favorite place to connect with books and authors.

Other Books by James Hanna

Prison counselor Tom Hemmings is more afraid of the guards than the inmates. When a riot breaks out, sides are chosen.

Available on Amazon, Kindle, and through your favorite bookstore
ISBN: 978-1-937818-00-5
Sand Hill Review Press

Crazy Eddy Beasley thinks all women want him and he is destined to become a rock star. His parole officer knows he's nuts. Or is he? (Adult content)

Available on Amazon, Kindle, and through your favorite bookstore.
ISBN: 978-1-937818-15-9
Sand Hill Review Press

Visit Sand Hill Review Press at www.SHRPress.com